ELVINA

RACHAEL ANNE

D0167171

DEDICATION

Dedicated to those who have been with me and M.T.A.P. from the very beginning.

PROLOGUE

It was a lovely summer morning, boasting the essence of nature in greens and other vivid colors. Floral scents filled the air, and sunlight glistened across the lake's calm surface. Along the shore, three stairs led to a stone gazebo, the elaborate iron topper supported by six pillars. A bench curved out amongst them, except for one portion to allow access.

Eighteen-year-old Elvina Norwood sat facing the lake. Around five foot seven, she was curvy in all the right places. The green dress she wore, with gold embroidery and long, bell sleeves, accentuated those curves, as well as highlighted her hazel eyes and honey brown hair.

She was Princess of Grenester, sole heir to the throne. Her mother, Queen Helaine, died shortly after giving birth to her, leaving her father and multiple nannies to raise her into the young lady she was today.

Elvina was drawn out of her reverie when she heard someone walking along the stone pathway behind her, whistling a cheerful tune. Heart skipping, her lips curved into a small smile. Resisting the urge to look over her shoulder, she greeted, "Good morning, Owen."

"G'mornin' to you, Elvi," he greeted in return.

Second Prince Owen Gravenor of Tiramôr was only one year younger than her and taller by a few inches. His skin was tan compared to her fair complexion, and his dark brown locks reached the nape of his neck, while his bangs hung above his lively brown eyes. Two prominent dots, stacked diagonally on his left cheekbone, looked like a birthmark of some sort. He wore a white cotton shirt underneath a plain, dark blue fitted doublet that laced in the front, as well as gray pants tucked into black leather boots. He might be a royal, but he certainly didn't dress like one.

Grenester was north of Tiramôr. Her father, King Fitzroy, and King Mervin had been friends for ages. The Gravenor family would visit at least a couple of times during the year when possible. Elvina and her father always hosted the four royals.

Owen entered the gazebo and sat directly to his left, choosing to be across from her rather than next to her. "You look tidy this mornin'," he commented.

Being around him for years, she had grown accustomed to his native slang. He meant she looked nice. "Thank you. As do you."

He glanced around curiously. "Not a single guard?" he questioned.

"Whitley's clearly doing her job if you didn't spot her." She arched her eyebrow. "And I can ask you the same thing. Where's Trevor?"

"I ditched him at the castle," he snickered, clearly pleased with himself.

She attempted to mask her mild amusement behind a stern expression. "I'm sure he won't appreciate that. He has to put up with so much because of you."

"Bein' a personal guard to a prince isn't an easy job. He should know that by now."

"What prince is there to guard when you aren't around?"

He shrugged. "There's always Ceron."

"But you aren't your brother."

"Thank goodness for that."

She turned her head to watch a pair of ducks skim across the lake.

"Admirin' nature?" he asked.

Her eyes remained on the ducks when she responded with, "It's quite lovely."

A comfortable silence fell over the duo, until he murmured, "Hey, Elvi?"

"Yes?"

"Have you and Ceron had a goss with each other?"

She didn't know what she and Ceron needed to chat about. "Talk about what?"

He ran his hand through his hair. It was a nervous habit. "Never mind."

All of her attention was on him now. "Do go on. Have Ceron and I talked about what?"

"I'm sure it's nothin'. Just rumors," he replied, avoiding eye contact.

Whenever his family visited, particular rumors always arose amongst the castle staff. They believed their princess and Ceron were a step closer to a wedding.

She didn't resist the urge to roll her eyes. "They're only rumors. They're forgotten just as easily as they come about," she huffed. "If they actually used their eyes, they'd see I spend more time with you than him."

Pleased with her response, his shoulders relaxed. "Right you are."

She thought back to their first meeting twelve years ago. It was a way to introduce her to the brothers, but she and

3

Owen didn't necessarily get off to a great start. "Do you remember when we first met?" she asked, already smiling.

"Bits and pieces, yeah."

"Your first words to me were that I was ugly," she teased, laughing at the memory.

"Oi. I was five then. Clearly, I didn't know what I was sayin' back—" He abruptly cut himself off by clapping a hand over his mouth.

She perked up with interest. "Is that so?"

Pink dusted his cheeks as he lowered his arm. "You aren't ugly."

"That's an odd way to compliment someone," she giggled.

He focused intently on her. "You're beautiful, Elvi."

It was the first time he had told her that. She was stunned. Her ears burned, and words wouldn't come out of her parted lips.

He chuckled. "Cat got your tongue, does it?"

The moment was interrupted when Owen's only personal guard called out, "Oi! Come out, Freckles! I know you're here!"

Owen whipped his head around. "Dammit," he hissed.

"So much for ditching him," Elvina teased.

Jumping to his feet, Owen held out a hand for her. "C'mon, Elvi."

She went with the flow and stood, placing her hand in his. He gripped it tightly and led the way out of the gazebo.

CHAPTER ONE

Not quite a full year later, Elvina walked through the castle she called home. The hem of her deep violet dress barely skimmed the floor covered in long rugs. Torches along the walls weren't lit because sunlight through windows provided light. The hallway was deserted.

Her father had requested her presence, so she made her way to his study without the company of her personal guards. She only hoped he didn't request her presence to meet another suitor.

As she approached, one of the two guards posted outside the room, the one with darker skin, reached over and pulled the door open for her.

"Thank you," she demurred.

The door closed behind her, and she was left to take in the furnished study. The green and gold royal family crest was mounted on the wall to the right, and to the left were two portraits. One was of the king and queen shortly after they married, and the other was of Elvina when she turned eighteen. The wall across from the entrance was made mostly of large windows, with the green curtains pulled back to allow the natural light to illuminate the room. In front of that was a polished wooden desk where her father sat.

At forty-one, Fitzroy's parted brown hair touched the tops of his shoulders. His full beard was trimmed and presentable, both with touches of gray. His dark hazel eyes were intently focused on a letter in his hand.

The other person in the room was Reeves Barrett, the royal adviser to Fitzroy, a man in his early forties. He stood solemnly with his long limbs and impassible expression. He remained off to the right of Fitzroy, in the corner and out of the way. His ash blond hair was brushed back, and his well-trimmed beard was tidy. His sharp green eyes observed every detail as she entered.

Elvina sent a nod in his direction to acknowledge him without saying a word.

Reeves nodded back, a sympathetic look on his face.

Fitzroy looked up as he heard her approach. "Elvina."

"Do I have the pleasure of knowing why you requested my presence?" she inquired, walking toward the desk.

Setting down the letter, Fitzroy stood. With his hands clasped behind his back, he walked around the piece of furniture to stand in front of it before speaking. "I have news."

She felt hopeful. "Do tell."

His lips turn upward in a small smile. "I have received word from Duke Kennard, and he has accepted your hand in marriage."

Her stomach dropped. She stared at her father in stunned silence. "I'm to what?" she whispered in disbelief, looking at Reeves for affirmation.

He gave her an imperceptible nod, confirming her fears.

Elvina looked back at her father when he spoke. "You will marry Duke Kennard Endicott. He's southwest of here. Your betrothment to him is official."

Her mind raced. "I've never even met him."

"I have, and that is what matters. There's plenty of potential. Kennard shall be a fine husband for you, and a worthy ruler of Grenester."

She felt as though the walls were closing in on her. "Do I not have a say in the one I marry?"

"You shall do as I say. That is final."

She opened her mouth to speak but closed it when words didn't form. The reality was still sinking in.

"It's your duty to your people." Fitzroy sighed and looked her over. "When you're the queen of this kingdom, a king will be by your side. Kennard shall help you rule Grenester. You will provide an heir together to continue our line."

She bowed her head in defeat, accepting her already determined fate. She had received this talk from her father multiple times before—more like excessive times. This time was different, though, as there was a name to her future husband.

"Plans have been made for you to visit him," Fitzroy added.

Her head jerked up in surprise. "What?"

"You and your guards shall leave by carriage tomorrow. Kennard is already expecting your arrival days from now."

"T–Tomorrow?" she stuttered. "Tomorrow is so soon. And I just found out about my betrothment today. Right this moment, in fact."

"By now, your lady-in-waiting should nearly be finished with packing your things for you."

She was slightly taken aback. "Millicent knew before me?"

He waved a hand through the air, dismissing the thought. "I only told her that you shall need clothing for a few days of traveling and remaining at a destination for a couple of nights. She needed time to pack, after all."

"Who else knows about the betrothment?" She could account for eight people as of now.

7

Rather than answering her question, Fitzroy replied with, "An official announcement to the kingdom shall happen once you return home."

She could picture it now. The people would rejoice that their princess had finally been paired with a future husband. Of course, most wouldn't care how they ended up together. The people would focus only on the fact that they were together, and they would have a new king to lead them. On the other hand, Elvina would care very much. After all, she didn't choose him for herself.

"I wish to be excused," Elvina blurted out.

"I'm sure that you have to prepare for your journey tomorrow." Fitzroy's face changed slightly as he remembered something. "I'll have Millicent wake you in the morning. She can help you before you leave."

"Is she accompanying me?" Elvina was hopeful she would come along. She would need plenty of support from her close circle of friends.

"No. Just your guards. There's no need for anyone else to join the five of you."

Her heart sank even further. "Oh..."

"Elvina." Fitzroy reached out to place his hands on her shoulders.

She was quick to step back. "I wish to be excused." Rather than waiting for him to respond, she gathered the skirt of her dress and rushed from the study. Without looking back at Fitzroy or Reeves, she slammed the door shut behind her, bolting down the hallway as tears formed, stinging her eyes and blurring her vision.

Navigating through the castle, she made her way to the royal stable. Luckily for her, no one stopped her to question her hurried actions or why she was crying. Once inside, one of her favorite places of wooden and iron stalls, she slowed her pace. Sniffling loudly, she made her way toward the stall in the other aisle. When she rounded the corner, she stopped at what she saw.

A large man waited with two horses that were all tacked up and ready to ride.

Garrick Verity was the leader of the Thunder Squadron, an elite four-member group whose sole purpose was to protect Elvina. The thirty-three-year-old was a skilled, fierce man, with a gentleness few ever saw. His thick, light brown hair was parted to the side. A scar he had gotten while protecting Elvina before he was even a member of the Thunder Squadron ran along his chin. But it was the concern in his blue eyes that caught her attention.

Elvina and Garrick had a special relationship not found between most charges and their personal guards. It involved admiration, not infatuation.

Not caring who saw, she threw her arms around his torso and buried her face into his shirt.

He remained in place, still keeping hold of the two sets of reins. He didn't bother saying a single word, wanting his charge to take as much time as she needed.

She finally pulled away, wiping away her tears. "Where are the others?"

"All at different posts," he stated. "Vallerie's in your bedchamber, Whitley's in the library, and Quenby's in the tower you often visit. None of us were sure where you'd end up when you finished talking with King Fitzroy."

Her heart swelled. She truly did have the best personal guards ever. They all knew her so well. After all, they spent the most time with her.

Garrick held out a set of reins for her. "Shall we?"

Taking them with one hand, Elvina looked at her horse. Luna was a dapple gray mare with black around her muzzle, black socks up to her knees, and dark hooves. Her flowing mane and tail were a deep coal color, while her dark eyes exuded gentleness.

"Hello, girl," Elvina cooed before wrapping her arms around Luna's neck and tightly hugging her. She pressed her face against the mare's soft hair and closed her eyes.

Luna nickered in response to her attention.

Feeling a little better already, Elvina stepped back and looked at Garrick. "We shall," she finally responded.

They turned their horses around and made their way down the aisle, hooves clopping against the stone.

With Luna as Elvina's trusty steed, Garrick followed along with his own. Blaze was a bay gelding, his mane and tail much darker than the rest of his coat. He had a white blaze down the front of his face, white socks at his ankles, and tan hooves.

Grenester was well-known for the horses that were bred and raised there. The three surrounding kingdoms had a tendency to be interested in their stock and what they had to offer. Of course, the royal stable housed the best of the best. Grenester also offered fine oats and hay for its livestock demands.

"We can be out for as long as you'd like," Garrick informed her.

Elvina softly smiled. "I like the sound of that."

"Good."

At least her hair was already done up in braids, so it wouldn't get in her face as she rode.

When the duo made it out under the open sky, Garrick checked the girths of the saddles one more time to ensure they were secure before they mounted and took off.

It was a refreshing spring day to be out riding. Not a single cloud was in sight, and the sun shone brightly. The land of Grenester blossomed with the change of season. Colors became more vivid, and all sorts of life bloomed.

In no time at all, the two horses were cantering through a field of tall grass. Filling her lungs with fresh air, Elvina inhaled deeply before exhaling.

"Better?" Garrick inquired.

"Much."

A comfortable silence fell over them before Elvina asked, "Am I overreacting?"

In this day and age, people took time to get to know each other. After a couple of weeks, if they foresaw a future together, they planned and prepared for their pending nuptials. In less than a year's time, the couple would be married and starting a family.

The timeline was shortened to a degree if a royal was involved. In some cases, love wasn't even a factor since everything was arranged for the couple. Some had been known to see each other for the first time on the day of their wedding. That wasn't uncommon, even if some considered it to be old-fashioned.

"I'm sure I wouldn't like it if my father arranged a marriage for me," Garrick admitted.

"Says the man who has never married," she pointed out.

"Exactly."

She sighed. "He's been discussing arranged marriages to me, but I thought I would have some say in the matter. I had hoped he would've included me when seeking out my husband."

"He's doing what he believes is best for you."

"So he claims. By the way, do you know much about Duke Kennard Endicott? He resides southwest of Arnembury."

He thought for a moment and shrugged. "I can't say I do. Maybe it's a good thing I can't recall anything about him."

"At least there's nothing bad."

"That I can think of," he clarified.

11

"Well, I expect a seal of approval from you and the rest of the Thunder Squadron when you all meet the duke."

"Of course. Oh, and by the way, do you have any plans that this surprise trip will interfere with?"

She shook her head no. "Although, I suppose it will interrupt my normal, everyday life. No princess lessons at least."

"Not if Vallerie can help it."

"Why would you say such a thing?"

"She'll have to make sure you don't become bored out of your mind in the carriage. After all, you will be traveling for days."

"Will it only be the two of us inside? What about the others?"

"Quenby and I will ride on horses since Whitley's already declared that she'll be driving."

"Which leaves Vallerie with me," she reasoned.

He nodded. "Exactly."

"I suppose the situation could be worse, but it could be better if Milli was to accompany us. Actually, it would be best if we didn't have to make the silly trip to start with."

"Your father believes it's best for you to travel there and visit. You wouldn't build up as much anticipation if Kennard were to come to Arnembury. The traveling should distract you."

Something dawned on her. "But why? Does it not make sense for him to visit the castle? Apparently, he's to be my husband and king of this kingdom someday. It only makes sense for him to visit the place he's to call home."

Garrick remained quiet for a moment. "Your father didn't comment on that when he initially spoke to the Thunder Squadron." He sighed. "Nevertheless, it's too late to change things now. The plans are set, and we're to leave tomorrow morning."

Her mind wandered, going from one thought to another.

She thought about Kennard, who she knew nothing about, apart from his name and title, as well as his location. She couldn't even put a face to the man. "My father sure knows how to choose them for me."

"I'm sure if something's amiss with Kennard, then the wedding will be called off."

"If only."

"Hopefully, he won't be so bad." Garrick grimaced, unknowingly tightening his grip on his reins. "I'll personally make sure he's on his best behavior around you."

"Oh, do not fear. I'll make it clear if he causes me any distress. Also, I'll signal if I can't handle the matter."

Feeling better about things, Elvina smiled. "Garrick, thank you. Thank you for talking with me."

He returned her smile with one of his own. "You can always count on me. You know that."

<hr />

When Elvina and Garrick approached the stable after their ride, the remaining members of the Thunder Squadron awaited them.

Twenty-six-year-old Vallerie Woodward was a slender woman with porcelain skin, sky blue eyes, and jet-black, unruly curls that fell to her shoulder blades. Of the four, she was the most composed and had a motherly nature about her when it came to her charge.

She may be petite in size, but Whitley Triggs packed a punch with her actions and words. Even though she looked close to Elvina in age, she was thirty. Her very short, natural hair was full of small and tight curls, but it was her mint green eyes that popped against her brown skin.

The Thunder Squadron had their title all because of

Elvina, in fact. Whitley thought of it because Elvina was striking, and thunder followed after lightning.

Quenby Pemberton stood the tallest, with his lanky, but far from clumsy figure. Along with being the tallest, he was also the youngest at twenty-five. With tan skin, he had floppy, sandy blond locks that seemed to have a mind of their own. He had complete heterochromia iridum. His right eye was green, while his other was blue.

Now that the Thunder Squadron was reunited, it was easy to tell that they belonged together. They all wore matching sets of casual uniforms, each one tailor-fitted to match their body type. Their clothes consisted of a royal green, fitted doublet that laced in the front over a plain white cotton shirt with long sleeves. The trousers and leather boots were black.

"Feeling better, Elvina?" Whitley inquired, hopping down from the fence. Her feet hit the dirt with ease.

Knowing he was the only one allowed to do it, Quenby rested an arm on Whitley's head to help balance himself as he leaned. "She sure looks better."

"Oh, please," Elvina scoffed as she brought Luna to a halt. "You didn't see me before."

"True, but your eyes have a cheerfulness to them now," Vallerie noted.

"The ride did her good," Garrick responded as he dismounted from Blaze.

"That was the point," Quenby teased.

"Right!" Whitley agreed.

With grace, Elvina dismounted from Luna and landed onto the dirt. She looked at each member of the Thunder Squadron that consisted of her dearest friends. "Thank you all so much."

They all smiled at their beloved charge.

CHAPTER TWO

Elvina was ready to blow off some steam. She could get out her frustrations about the surprise betrothal now.

She and most of the Thunder Squadron were in a spacious room inside of the castle. It had originally been used for storage, but now it was Elvina's private training space and special learning center. Here she trained with weapons and learned about drugs and poisons. She considered them to be her special princess lessons. The room was mostly overlooked by others in the castle, and Fitzroy had no idea it even existed.

Wearing a delicate blue dress with the hem to her calves, Elvina sparred against Quenby with Garrick overseeing. He called out mistakes and instructions for both parties. The duo used wooden swords rather than metal.

"Again!" Elvina barked out, wanting to do another set as she wiped the sweat from her brow.

Quenby looked at Garrick for help, hoping to be relieved of his duties for the time being. Sparring with Elvina was great practice for a real-life scenario, but he wanted to sit down and catch his breath. They had been going at it for some time now. "Can't we take a break?" he asked, trying not to whine.

"Elvina, you should take a little break and study with me," Whitley suggested from the rectangular wooden table she stood by. "I've got some things brewed up for you to test."

"I'll do that, then." Elvina smiled at Quenby. "Thank you for sparring with me."

"No problem." His wooden sword clattered to the stone floor and he sat down before lying on his back. "I'm just going to be right here. Don't mind me."

Elvina took her sword over to the nearby bin with more wooden swords and put it away.

"That was a fine job today," Garrick praised.

"I did have a wonderful sparring partner."

Quenby only smiled, not bothering to say a word.

Elvina joined Whitley at the table, which was lined with opened and closed books and pieces of parchment. There were plates with plants on them, and two cups were filled with the same looking liquid in them, one filled more than the other.

Whitley picked up one of the cups and held it out for Elvina. "This here is plain ole normal tea, okay? Smell it."

Elvina took the cup and inhaled the aroma; it smelled like her favorite kind of tea. She set the cup down on the table and asked, "What now?"

Whitley picked up another cup and handed it over. "Here, this one."

There was a distinct difference between the two. The one Elvina currently inhaled had more of a bittersweet smell to it, overpowering what the tea should naturally smell like on its own. "I've never smelled this before," she observed, setting the cup down. "What did you put in it?"

"The juice extracted from a *Nox Mortem* plant. Just enough can knock a person out. Dose does matter when it comes to the size of the target because too much can be lethal enough to kill. Ingestion results in drowsiness first, then unclear thought process and speech. Of course, movements are affected. Then, losing consciousness for a good bit, and the final step is death."

"Is it through consumption only?"

Whitley nodded. "That's the only way it can affect a person. The distinct bittersweet aroma gives it away, but you can't taste it."

"Is there a way to counter it with an antidote of some sort?"

"Juice from a *Vita Mane* plant. The person will still feel drowsy, but they won't black out or die."

Elvina took mental notes of what Whitley told her.

"If you want to try it to fully understand its effects, go for it," Whitley offered. "I only mixed a little bit in that cup. I doubt you'll even pass out."

"Whitley, we can save that for another day," Garrick interjected, not wanting his charge to go through even the minor effects of *Nox Mortem*. She'd been through enough already.

"Fine." Whitley busied herself by grabbing the two plants and held them in front of Elvina to see. "*Nox Mortem* in my right, and *Vita Mane* in my left."

Elvina studied them carefully, memorizing both plants.

The *Nox Mortem* plant had dark green leaves and a thin stem. At the top was a cluster of closed, bell-shaped flowers hanging down. They were purple and had pronounced thick veins of a darker purple running through them.

On the other hand, the *Vita Mane* plant, the only notable difference was the veins. They were barely there, practically slivers through the flowers.

17

"Tell me more about each of them," Elvina said as she continued to observe them, committing them to memory.

"Their colors range from blues and purples, and color doesn't make a lick of difference between the two. Paying attention to the bellflowers is what's key. The flowers never, ever open. They're always shut. *Nox Mortem* has thicker veins, while *Vita Mane* has thinner ones. Even if you see one without the other, you can tell the difference."

"I'll keep that in mind." Elvina looked Whitley in the eye, nodding her appreciation. "Thank you."

Whitley set the plants back on the table. "I figured it wouldn't hurt for you to see them. But now you know what they look like in case you ever need them."

"Hopefully, you'll never need *Vita Mane*," Garrick commented.

"Oh, but I'll need *Nox Mortem?*" Elvina jested.

"No!" all three guards replied in unison.

The single door to the room opened, and Vallerie entered with a familiar face in tow. Being two years older than Elvina, Millicent Downer was her lady-in-waiting and great friend. Far from being a downer, she had a bubbly personality and was simply fun to be around. She and Elvina shared similar heights, but she was far curvier in her bust than Elvina. Her olive skin was highlighted by a beauty mark above the right corner of her upper lip. Blonde locks were held in a single braid, starting at the nape of her neck, the tip reaching the middle of her shoulder blades. Bright blue eyes popped against her complexion.

"El, it's time for…" Millicent's voice trailed off as she tilted her head, looking at Quenby. "What happened to him?"

He weakly raised a hand to show he was alive before it dropped to the floor.

"He's being dramatic," Vallerie said, assuring Millicent that he was fine.

"Milli, what is it time for?" Elvina inquired, bringing up the subject again.

"It's time for you to turn in for the night. Wash up and go to bed."

Elvina gasped in surprise. "I was unaware that it had gotten so late."

"Time flies when you're kicking Quenby's butt," Whitley joked.

Wound up from her comment, Quenby sat up and pointed an accusing finger at her. "Hey, I wasn't going all out on attacking. I was letting her get her frustrations out. I was on the defense!"

"I do feel much better." Elvina smiled. "Thank you, Quenby."

"I volunteer Vallerie to be Elvina's sparring buddy next time!" he shouted.

From her collarbone down, Elvina was submerged under hot water brimming with suds and bubbles. Her personal bathtub was spacious enough for more than one, but she was the only one inside. Millicent was behind her, hands rubbing something into Elvina's scalp that would make her hair extra soft.

"How did Father even expect me to find a husband for myself in the first place?" Elvina grumbled. "I'm not allowed to leave Arnembury. I've never even been to another city in Grenester before. What does that say about the princess of this kingdom?"

"I'm sure King Fitzroy has his reasons," Millicent advised. "Maybe you'll find out when you're older."

"Apparently, I'm old enough to be betrothed to a man I've never met before," she muttered.

Millicent began rubbing Elvina's head to help relax her. She wanted her friend to not be so stressed about things. Although, she did suppose the matter was quite stressful. "Calm down. Close your eyes and take a deep breath. Wiggle your toes an—"

"Wiggle my toes?" Elvina chuckled with amusement, not meaning to interrupt. Of all things Millicent could have said, she wasn't expecting that.

"I guess do whatever it takes to calm down," Millicent responded. "Even something as silly as that."

Unbeknownst to Millicent, Elvina wiggled her toes beneath the sudsy layer. It was a little humorous when she thought about it. "I'm lucky to have you in my life," Elvina told her, growing somber for a moment. "Thank you."

"I'm pretty sure I'm the lucky one. I get to know you in other ways that people don't. That's special."

"Oh, please."

"I bet a lot of people don't know how sassy you can be."

"A princess is never sassy," Elvina jested.

Millicent playfully rolled her eyes. "Sure, never. Right." With one hand, she placed a pitcher under the faucet, turned on the warm water, then turned it off so the pitcher didn't overflow. "Tilt your head back for me and mind your face," she announced before dousing Elvina's head with fresh water.

With her gaze focused on the ceiling, Elvina continued talking. "Do you think things will go over well when I meet Kennard?"

"First of all, he better treasure you," Millicent immediately replied without any hesitation. "The Thunder Squadron better make sure of it."

"I have no doubt they'll see to it that he does." She giggled at the thought.

Setting aside the empty pitcher, Millicent grabbed the

nearby towel. "Okay, it's time to get you dried off, then I'll brush your hair and braid it before you go to bed."

"Thank you," Elvina said as she turned her head to look at Millicent.

"Oh, don't thank me. I'm just doing my job."

Elvina softly smiled. "Still. Thank you, Milli."

Millicent returned the smile. "You're welcome."

❦

Elvina wore a soft cream nightgown fit for a princess. She and Millicent sat on her bed, which had plenty of space for at least three people to comfortably sleep. Millicent set the middle part and brushed through Elvina's still wet hair.

"What do you look for in a man?" Elvina found herself asking.

"Who says I'm looking for a man?" she snorted.

Elvina playfully rolled her eyes.

"But what about you, El?" Millicent asked, turning the tables on her.

"I want..." Her voice trailed off as a face floated through her mind. She hadn't seen Owen or his family for some time. Last fall, Fitzroy received an official document written, signed, and sealed by Mervin. It was a declaration stating that the trading would forever cease between Grenester and Tiramôr as long as Fitzroy ruled. Of course, Fitzroy felt blindsided from what a dear friend had sent to him without much reasoning behind it. After writing to Mervin several times for an explanation, Fitzroy eventually gave up after never receiving a reply.

Ever since then, when battles and wars did happen to break out in Grenester or Tiramôr, neither side came to the other's aid. Likewise, neither aided the enemy they were fighting. It was like neither kingdom acknowledged the existence of the other one. To this day, Fitzroy and all of Grenester still had no reason behind Mervin's sudden decision.

"El?" Millicent urged.

Elvina snapped back to reality. "I want someone nice."

"Just nice?" Millicent snickered, starting a single braid.

"I do expect more than that from him I suppose."

"You suppose?"

"I haven't put much thought into it, all right?"

"What qualities can you name off the top of your head?"

"I want him to be a great husband and a fine king."

"Any specific traits?"

"Specific? Like what?"

Millicent shrugged. "Do you want him to look a certain way? Act a certain way?"

Her heart ached a little. "I love brown eyes."

"That's a start."

Elvina thought more about Owen. "Humor. I want to be able to freely laugh with him. No holding back."

"What if he has a terrible laugh?"

She smiled a little. "Then it's a terrible laugh he shares with me."

"Aw, you're so sappy, El."

A sudden knock on the main door to Elvina's bedchamber interrupted the mood.

"Who is it?" Millicent asked, just as she secured the end of Elvina's braid.

"It's Fitzroy. May I enter?"

Elvina straightened her back. "You may."

The door opened, and Fitzroy walked into the room. He closed the door behind him and stood a few feet away from it, hands behind his back. "Millicent, I wish to speak to my daughter alone."

Bowing her head, Millicent said, "Of course, Your Highness." She stood and headed for the door, leaving the bedchamber. Since Fitzroy had his back to her, Millicent was able to look Elvina in the eye as she closed the door and mouthed, "I'm here for you" before the door shut.

Elvina kept her pose upright until she was told otherwise, remaining seated on her bed. "Hello, Father."

His posture eased, relaxing a fraction. "I see that Millicent took care of you."

She smiled. "She always does."

He glanced at the packed bags on the floor. "Ah, I see that you are all packed."

"Millicent did that for me earlier."

The bedchamber fell into an odd silence.

"I hope things are prosperous when you meet Kennard," he voiced.

She wished to talk about anything else besides Kennard or her upcoming visit, but she did not comment. She knew her words would sound bitter.

"Your impending marriage is prosperous for Grenester—"

"Must it be him?" It was only the two of them, without any form of an audience. She could speak freely to her father.

His expression softened. He walked over to the bed and sat on the edge of it, prompting Elvina to be closer to him. "From my list, Kennard is the most suitable. I see him being the most compatible with you."

"What of Owen?" she asked in a quiet voice. It could be a way to bring back what the two kingdoms once had.

He sighed heavily, looking older than he truly was. "To tell you the truth, I had written to Mervin about the matter. Once, after the snow stopped, and a second time mere weeks ago. I know that would have made you happy."

Her heart tightened. Her father had done what he could for her without marching up to Mervin's castle himself. She placed one hand over his and squeezed.

"I'm doing this to secure a future for my only child," he continued. "My daughter. My Elvina."

"Did you and Mother meet in a similar way?"

His mood lifted. "My parents had presented me with a list of possible brides and their correlations to the kingdom. I selected certain ones and a ball was held so that I was able to meet all of them." A ghost of a smile appeared on his lips. "Your mother was the fourth one I met. After her, well, I had no need to speak with any others."

Elvina recalled a similar situation. Last winter, Fitzroy held a ball at the castle for Elvina to meet suitors in hopes of her finding a husband. Kennard wasn't in attendance due to an illness, so Elvina never met him then. Even without him there, none of the suitors were up to par. Not by her standards, or the Thunder Squadron's.

Before speaking again, Fitzroy took a deep breath. "Elvina, I'm doing this with your best interests in mind."

She understood that now. "I know."

He patted her hand. "I believe it's time for you to sleep. I'll see you off in the morning."

"Good night, Father."

He placed a kiss on her forehead. "Sleep well, Elvina."

CHAPTER THREE

Two days later, Elvina traveled by carriage to meet her betrothed. Her opinion on the matter hadn't changed in the slightest. She sighed as she looked out the window, watching the land pass by. The pinks in the sky were the opening act for the sunset to come. Tomorrow, she would meet Kennard, marking the end of her three-day journey.

"Now, now, Elvina," Vallerie lightly scolded in a teasing manner. "There's no need to be dramatic."

She turned to look at her. "This whole thing is ridiculous," Elvina said yet again, losing track of how many times she had uttered that phrase.

"That's the thirty-third time you've said that since we started this trip," Vallerie pointed out. Apparently, she had kept track for her. "I think you've made your point."

"Do you think so?" Elvina went back to looking out the window to her left.

Garrick nudged Blaze closer to the carriage to be next to the window. "You're more dramatic than yesterday," he teased.

She puffed her cheeks in an unladylike way. "That isn't a nice thing to say."

"But it's true."

"I suppose you're right. I still feel uneasy about all of this."

"You have no need to feel uneasy with us around."

That earned a little smile from her. "That is true."

"Will it help to talk more about it?" Garrick inquired. "Will that make you feel better?"

"But what more is there to talk about? We all have talked so much about the matter." She huffed. "The expectations have been set."

"Your father is doing what he feels is best for you."

"But why is he forcing the issue of me getting married now? He hasn't done anything this drastic in the previous years of my life."

"Maybe he was hoping that you would have—"

A glint of something shiny from the forest across from her caught her attention. "Did you see that?" she asked.

Garrick turned his head to look, keeping quiet while he scanned the area. "Quenby, I need another set of eyes over here."

He came around the rear of the carriage on his horse and joined the Garrick on the other side. "What's going on?" Quenby questioned.

"Check the forest," Garrick instructed. "She believes she saw something." He intentionally skipped using Elvina's name to avoid the risk of exposing her. He didn't want to take that chance.

"I don't see anything from here!" Whitley chimed from above as she drove the carriage.

"It was shiny," Elvina said, so they knew what to be on the lookout for. "Like the sun reflected off—"

A group of men raced out from the coverage of the tree

line. Bandits. They were all on foot, not risking a horse that could have given away their nearby position.

"Whitley, make the horses go faster!" Garrick commanded, readying his weapon. "Vallerie, stay inside! Quenby, with me!" Again, he specifically avoided using Elvina's name. There might be a chance the bandits were unaware of who was inside. After all, the carriage wasn't marked for safety reasons. A flag with the royal crest would be visible when they approached where Kennard was.

The carriage jolted at the increase of speed. Elvina leaned away from the window and steadied herself, her heart racing, the bandits only adding to the stressful situation.

Vallerie prepared her bow and quiver full of arrows. She leaned toward the window to her right, placing an arrow to fire. Once lit, she pulled it back, found a target, and shot.

Elvina knew that if she had a weapon, she could fight as well. It would make her feel more comfortable.

Vallerie readied another arrow. "There's a second group, and some have horses." She only said that so Elvina was aware of what was happening.

Elvina controlled herself to keep from peeking or stealing a glance outside the carriage. She couldn't risk putting herself in danger while the Thunder Squadron was doing their best to protect her. All she could do was listen to the sounds around her: fighting and horses' hooves.

A yelp of surprise slipped from her lips when an arrow flew through the window and lodged itself into the opposite wall. Elvina stared at it before tearing her gaze away to look at Vallerie.

"We'll protect you," she assured her, releasing her arrow. "We've never let you down be—"

The carriage was jostled around, setting it off-kilter, a clear sign that something was wrong. Whitley shouted from above, "Damn bandits took out a wheel with a spear!"

Elvina's heart skipped. To give herself something to do, she moved along the cushioned bench and reached for the arrow, extracting it from the carriage. At least now she had something to protect herself with.

Things only went from bad to worse when the carriage stopped in a rather rough manner, jostling the two inside. Vallerie hit her head and clutched it. Luckily, there wasn't any sign of blood.

"Heads up, you two!" Whitley warned as she prepared to fight. "They're coming!"

As her body pumped with adrenaline, Elvina clutched onto the arrow with both hands. When the door to the right was suddenly thrown open, she whipped her head around. A man poked his head inside. "Knock knock, Pr—"

Elvina delivered a powerful kick right to his face, causing him to lose his balance and fall backward.

"Run!" Vallerie shouted.

Without a word, Elvina opened the other door and quickly stepped out with Vallerie behind her. It was chaos under the open sky. Garrick and Quenby were engaged in combat, easily outnumbered by the twenty or so bandits. Whitley did her best to fend off more, keeping them away from her charge.

An arrow whizzed past Elvina's head and nearly hit Vallerie, who was still behind her. She glanced over her shoulder. "Are you all right?"

"I'll be fine," Vallerie gruffly replied.

Thundering hooves drew Elvina's attention, and she spotted a bandit on a horse heading right for them. "Vallerie!"

Vallerie quickly shot an arrow and it lodged in the rider's right shoulder. She muttered under her breath and readied to fire another. This time, the rider fell, tugging the reins with him. The horse came to a stop.

"You need to get to safety now," Vallerie instructed, steering Elvina toward the jittery horse that paced in place. She took the arrow from her charge, planning on using it herself.

Elvina moved to the horse in a calm manner, not too quick about her movements. "Easy, boy..." She stepped over to the left side and swung herself up, grabbing hold of the reins. She looked down at Vallerie and opened her mouth to speak—

"Go!" Vallerie urged.

Elvina kicked at his sides, and he lurched forward before taking off. She stayed low and guided the horse to the tree line, not wanting to be out in the open. She fought back tears. She wasn't only leaving her personal guards behind, but her friends.

Inside the forest, trees and foliage tore at her pale blue dress, ripping in some places as the horse ran through. She glanced back. Not seeing anyone giving chase, she faced forward and kept going.

She wasn't sure how much time had passed, but her luck eventually ran out due to a fallen tree that was up ahead. Rather than jumping over it with ease, the horse skidded to a stop and reared. Elvina tumbled off and landed onto the forest floor, gasping for air. The horse skittered around before taking off in another direction, leaving her behind.

Elvina slowly sat up, checking herself for injury. Other than being sore, she felt fine. Standing, she looked around, taking in her surroundings. It was quiet, without another person in sight. She was all alone.

"What now?" she quietly asked herself.

❦

Night had since fallen, leaving Elvina with unsettled nerves.

She could hardly see her hands outstretched in front of her. A full moon was high in the sky and full of stars, but the tree-tops cut off most of the light. The scenery was ominous and too quiet, except for the sounds from the fauna that called this place home.

An unlucky string of events had occurred since she had fallen off the horse. Elvina mused that she became cursed the moment she entered the forest. Her dress had snagged and torn so much, she ended up tearing off the remains of it. That was only after she had tripped while crossing a stream and drenched herself. Her white chemise was now stained with mud and tattered, hardly wearable anymore. Low hanging branches she couldn't see tangled in her hair that was styled up, courtesy of Vallerie's handiwork. Her skin was dirtied, and had some scrapes here and there, but nothing too concerning.

Not once did she stop walking. She didn't want to rest for a moment while she was in this forest. She might be tired and sore from head to toe, but she pressed onward.

There were two things she currently was grateful for: one, she was still alive, and two, it was cool in the forest rather than freezing.

The night air was chillier than most spring nights Elvina was accustomed to. Perhaps the weather was different here than it was back home in Arnembury. Although, she wasn't entirely sure where she was now. She could picture a map of Grenester in her mind, but she wasn't positive about her exact location since she left the road.

"Things could be worse I suppose," she said aloud to no one in particular. Even if it was her own, hearing a voice kept her calm.

She had spoken too soon.

After taking another step forward, the ground disappeared from underneath her. Against her control, gravity took Elvina as she tumbled down a ravine, shouting in surprise. As her extremities flailed about, the upper left side of her shoulder hit a tree and scratched against it. Both of her shoes flew off, leaving her with no chance of finding them in the dark.

At the bottom, when she finally came to a stop, her head spun as pain racked her body. Her injured shoulder stung, but she bit back a scream. She tried her best to refrain from touching it, thinking it would only hurt more if she did.

A groan escaped her lips as she moved her head to the side before rolling over to rise to her feet. Something hard nudged her forehead and her body stiffened. She reached out with her left hand and discovered she nearly banged her head on a rock. She'd narrowly escaped dangerous bandits that nearly took her life, only to almost die by tumbling headfirst onto a rock.

Elvina managed to stand, discovering that her left ankle was sprained. She wasn't entirely sure when it had been hurt on her way down. Walking was even more difficult now, especially with bare feet. But she merely added it to her ongoing list of injuries and attempted to focus on something else. She was striving onward for the sake of the Thunder Squadron, wondering if any of them escaped with their lives.

She continued on her way, wary of where she stepped. Remaining mindful of her shoulder, she wrapped her arms around herself and dug her nails into her skin as she hissed in pain. Her sprain wasn't helping in the slightest and was becoming a noticeable nuisance she could certainly do without. Then again, she could do without any of the injuries she had gotten since entering the forest.

As she walked, she noticed the area had become less dense with vegetation. More moonlight peeked through the treetops, so there was more visibility. Perhaps things were looking up for her now.

Something caused Elvina to stop in her tracks. Fire. She smelt fire. Panic flooded her body as she tried to discern if a forest fire had started. Legs moved and eyes darted around, searching for the hazard. She spotted light off in the distance. It appeared to be a campfire.

Fear trickled down her spine as she remained frozen in place. What if she was approaching the bandit's camp? She might as well be walking to her doom!

Faces of the Thunder Squadron flashed through her mind. What if some were captured and being held there now? Elvina knew little of the dangers outside of Arnembury and what to expect being alone in a forest in the dead of night.

As if weights were tied around her ankles, she slowly and quietly limped forward, thinking of the Thunder Squadron's safety. She trudged along until she saw the glow of the fire past a group of bushes and swallowed hard.

Entering a clearing where no trees were, she was able to see better and could make out more as she approached the source of light. She came to a halt when she heard a sound from behind her. Knowing she was no longer alone, her breath hitched, and she resisted the urge to look over her shoulder or simply bolt.

"Don't take another step," a low male voice warned. He had the same accent as Owen and his family. How close to the border was she?

She stayed as still as a statue, even holding her breath.

"Turn around slowly," he ordered. "Hands where I can see 'em."

Keeping her arms wrapped around her, Elvina slowly turned to face the person behind her. Much to her surprise, he didn't look like one of the bandits from earlier. A hood covered his face, but he was different. He was too clean, and his clothes were neat. The drawn sword aimed at her looked pristinely crafted and clean.

She watched it slip from his hand, falling uselessly to the ground with a thud as he quietly murmured something unintelligible. Before she could question him, he spoke in a different tone. No longer was it dark and harsh, but real and unguarded. "This can't be real. You're a fairy havin' a go at me, aren't you?"

"I'm certainly no fairy," she huffed.

"You best not be havin' a go at me," he practically pleaded.

She wasn't sure what to make of their conversation. Was he all right in the head?

Unexpectedly, he strode toward her, not bothering to pick up his sword.

Elvina gasped and stumbled backward, looking for anything she could use to defend herself. "S–Stay away!" Perhaps she would have to use hand-to-hand tactics to keep him at bay.

He stopped as to not further alarm her. "Elvi, it's me."

Her world slowed. Only one individual called her that. "Owen?" she whispered.

He slid back his hood to reveal his face. Time had somewhat changed him. He was taller, his features had matured, and his voice had even dropped.

How could this be real? Perhaps she had bashed her head against the rock and was unconscious, dreaming of being reunited with Owen.

This time, he didn't stop until he reached her and embraced her tightly to him, tucking her head into his neck and chest. She squeezed her eyes shut. This was really happening.

"You're freezin'," he commented, pulling his head back to look at her. "Wait, what's occurrin'? What're you doin' here?"

"I was traveling with the Thunder Squadron when bandits attacked. Vallerie had me escape on my own. I've been in this forest since the sun was still up."

His grip tightened. "You need help. Come with me." His eyes widened. "Wait, this won't do." He looked toward the campsite and called out, "Oi, Walla! C'mere!"

Elvina recognized the nickname. "Trevor's with you?"

"And my other guards, but he knows you."

Sure enough, Trevor Cadwallader emerged in a hurried manner. The twenty-three-year-old was taller than Owen, had more of a muscular build, and was tanner. His dark, sandy brown hair had a naturally disheveled, windblown look, with his bangs pushed up and everything. He had light blue eyes and a little nick that formed a scar on his right eyebrow. Some prominent freckles and little moles were scattered on his clean-shaven face.

He took one look at Elvina and stopped dead in his tracks. He was shocked beyond belief.

"It's really Elvi," Owen assured him. "There were bandits earlier. It's just her. She needs help."

His demeanor shifted. He briefly looked over his shoulder before looking back at the pair. "Do you want 'em to know?"

"They'll hafta know. I won't leave her out here."

"They can't know about me, though," Elvina told them. She needed to be wary. After all, Grenester and Tiramôr weren't on the friendliest of terms anymore.

"We'll leave out who you are," Trevor agreed.

Owen jerked his head. "Grab my sword. I'll take her."

"I'm able to walk on my own just fine," she quipped.

"Not on that foot you're not," he pointed out.

She was surprised. When did he have time to notice her sprained ankle?

Owen readjusted his hands and picked her up with ease. Her arms went around his neck and she snuggled in to the best of her ability.

"We'll talk later," Trevor said as he approached the two. "For now, she's a stranger to us."

CHAPTER FOUR

s the three approached the campsite, the voices from around the fire grew louder, but Elvina couldn't make out what they were saying. "What brings you outside at this hour?" she questioned.

"Just me and some mukkas havin' some fun," Owen replied.

She was familiar with the word. It meant friends. "So you're having some fun by camping out in a forest?" she asked, carrying the conversation.

"It's all nice and open out here. Completely beats home." Owen stepped over the line of bushes where two young men sat around the blazing fire, the light from it bouncing off them. Their packs and horses were off to the side, but still in view.

The one to the right, being the only one with glasses, noticed the trio first. "What?" was all he could utter.

The other one, clearly the biggest of the group, craned his neck around to see. "Whatcha got there, Freckles?"

"She was attacked by bandits and escaped," Owen said as

he approached. "She's been walkin' around for hours and needs care."

"And you brought her here?" the bespectacled one questioned, arching his eyebrow.

"We couldn't just leave her out there," Trevor admonished.

Owen gently set her down on the empty blanket by the fire. The heat covered her skin with warmth, and she welcomed the sensation from the dancing flames as they soon chased her chills away.

Plopping down directly to her right, Owen looked over at Trevor. "Get my cloak."

He walked to their packs and returned with a solid black cloak, tossing it to Owen who placed it around Elvina, bundling her up.

It was meant for this season but still kept her warm. The cloak was made from high-quality material, similar to a couple of cloaks Elvina owned.

Trevor reclaimed his spot to Elvina's left. Now all five were seated around the fire.

Elvina fought away the drowsiness that plagued her body. The odds weren't against her, so she could allow her guard to be down. Though she wanted to remain awake since this moment seemed so surreal.

Owen held out a canteen for her. "Here you go. You're probably thirsty."

She didn't have to worry about being drugged from it. The water was better than she ever imagined, and she drank it down to the last drop.

"Bandits, huh?" the biggest guy grunted once she finished.

After setting the empty canteen down on the blanket, Elvina looked at him and nodded. "I was traveling with others when we were attacked. My friends held them off in hopes that I could escape." Her voice slightly softened. "I have no idea where any of them are. I don't even know where I am exactly."

"This is the Kingdom of Tiramôr," the one wearing glasses across the fire informed her. "The capital city of Helidinas isn't far from here."

She did more walking than she thought.

"Oh, you dunno any of us," Owen suddenly said. "I'm Owen." He started at his left and went around clockwise. "My mukkas are Trevor, Rory, and Urian." He looked at her. "Do you need"—Elvina yawned and slowly blinked—"anythin'?" he lamely finished. "You need sleep from the looks of things. You're zonked."

She couldn't deny she was tired. "I should stay awake."

"You're exhausted from what happened earlier," Trevor pointed out. "You need rest."

Owen draped his arm around her and pulled her close, allowing her to snuggle up against him. In case she did doze off, he didn't want her tipping over. "Just rest your eyes for a bit. We'll keep watch."

His voice practically lulled her to sleep. Her eyes stay closed longer and longer each time she blinked. "I'm fine."

"Sure doesn't sound like it," Urian mused.

Rory looked at him. "Hey, leave her alone."

At one point, Elvina's eyes didn't open again. She attempted to focus on their voices as a way to keep herself awake.

"She's lucky those bandits didn't find her while she was in the forest," Trevor said in a hushed tone, keeping his voice down.

"Or even something like a bear," Rory added. "That could have been nasty."

"She's pretty banged up, though," Urian pointed out.

"That's just from being in the forest," Owen commented,

knowing a little more about the subject. "She sprained her left ankle from what I could tell, and scrammed all over."

"Did anybody catch her name?" Urian asked. Owen and Trevor didn't speak up. "Guess not, then. She kinda looks like some lost forest critter."

"I'd say more like a woodland fairy," Owen mused.

Trevor chuckled. "That sounds like something Flirtsalot would say."

"I must be rubbin' off on him," Rory teased.

"Ugh. We don't need two of 'em," Urian groaned. "Just one's more than enough."

"We should get goin'," Owen suggested to the group.

"Where to?" Trevor asked.

"Home," he replied.

After that, Elvina didn't remember slumber claiming her.

Her eyes fluttered open, and she became aware of her surroundings. The sunlight coming through the parted curtains lit the room. She was lying down on a comfortable bed, tucked under soft sheets with a pleasant scent to them. "It was all a dream..." she mused as she closed her eyes.

Her body stiffened as it flooded with panic. She was incredibly sore. It should be impossible for her to feel that way because of some dream. Besides that, she should be in a moving carriage.

Elvina pushed up on her hands and eased herself into a sitting position, noticing some bandages along her left arm. Securely wrapped, her shoulder was better than before. From the looks of things, she had received proper treatment for her injuries at some point. She removed the blankets covering her and looked at the rest of her body. Bandages were wrapped around her sprained ankle, and all the dirt and mud had been washed away where her skin was visible. She was clothed in a cream-colored chemise that reached her thighs.

She took in her surroundings, beginning with the bed. It was about the same size as her own, with lavish sheets and pillows. The wooden frame was made from a polished dark wood that gleamed, and the white curtains hanging around the bed were pulled back, allowing her to easily see the rest of the room. Large rugs covered the floor, and rich tapestries hung from the walls, one of which had the Gravenor's royal family crest on it. Around the fireplace was a cozy sitting area with two sofas and a table. This place reminded her of one of the many spare bedchambers her castle had.

Without warning, a door opened and an adolescent girl poked her head inside. Standing less than five feet tall, she had rounded features that were perfectly fine the way they were. Her dirty blonde hair was pulled back into a bun, her bangs falling above her eyebrows. When she spotted Elvina with her russet brown eyes, her face lit up with a smile. "You're awake!"

Elvina nodded. "I am."

Slipping inside the bedchamber, the girl closed the door behind her and walked to the bed, carrying a green bundle in her hands. "You look much better compared to the last time I saw you."

Elvina gestured down to herself. "Do I have you to thank for this?"

"Ooh, what a pretty accent!" The girl stood by the bed. "I stripped you down to the last layer of your undergarments to help you. We were the only ones in this room, so please don't be alarmed. I needed to check for any other injuries and treat you."

It was clear to Elvina she knew what she was doing. "Who are you by the way?" she asked.

"Oh, I'm Delyth Prichard. I'm the apprentice to the castle's head medical physician. She's away for now, but I'm here."

Elvina didn't remember arriving at the castle. In fact, she didn't recall leaving the campsite. She frowned due to her lack of memory.

"What's the matter?"

"I don't remember coming here."

"Prince Owen and his guards were having a 'boy's night,' as they called it. No one at the castle expected 'em to return durin' the middle of the night with a girl who survived bandits. Rory woke me up and led me here. I kicked the boys out to treat you, and didn't find anythin' too serious."

Elvina smiled at her. "Thank you. I appreciate your help. I feel much better already."

She beamed at the praise. "I'm happy to hear that, I am!"

Swinging her legs over the side of the bed, Elvina stood and put pressure on both feet. There was still some pain from her sprained ankle, but nothing compared to last night. She was more than sure she would be fine walking.

Delyth glanced down at the wrapped ankle. "I suggest keepin' off of it as much as you can so it doesn't get worse."

"No promises."

"Oh, this is for you." Delyth held out the bundle. "The chemise is temporary, 'cause what you were wearin' before was no good. Prince Owen had a guard fetch this for you."

Elvina took it from her. "Thank you."

"Will you need help dressin'?"

Elvina wouldn't need aid in such a simple task. Being raised a princess had left her quite pampered, but she still wanted the freedom to do things herself. "I believe I can manage on my own, but I appreciate the offer."

Delyth nodded. "I'll wait for you outside, then." After a

quick curtsy, she left the bedchamber and closed the door behind her.

Elvina took a deep breath and looked at the bundle in her hands. Did Owen really have someone fetch this for her? Did he intend to be considerate to her given their kingdoms' circumstances? On top of that, there was much she wanted to ask him. She shook her head, realizing that she couldn't delay for long since Delyth was waiting for her.

Although, she felt rather excited to perform such a simple task. A sense of new freedom washed over her as she dressed without aid for the first time she could remember. In the end, she looked down at what she had accomplished, proud of herself. If only Millicent could see her now!

The dress itself in a rich green was very simple and plain, but still lovely. The light material wasn't expensive, yet it wasn't cheap. Sleeves stopped at her elbows and were held in place with thin gold bands, but the material continued and flared out. The ends reached the tips of her fingers when her hands were down at her sides. Enhancing her figure, another band was under her bust, leaving the dress to drop down to her toes, hiding them.

As she moved to the door, she realized her limp had improved. It wasn't that noticeable unless someone was intentionally looking for it. She stepped out into the hallway and was surprised when she saw a familiar face that she didn't expect to see so soon.

Owen leaned against the wall just to her left, arms crossed over his chest. He wore a fitted royal blue vest that laced up the front. Underneath that, the sleeves of his white cotton shirt were rolled up to his elbows. He also wore a fitted pair of black trousers and black leather boots.

In proper lighting, she was able to make out more of his features. He shaved this morning for a clean look. Had his shoulders always been so broad? It was easy to tell that he kept in shape from his lean figure and toned arm muscles. The activities he did must keep him busy.

"The woodland fairy's awake," Owen mused, taking her in.

"I believe we established I'm no fairy," she teased.

Suddenly, his relaxed position became erect. "Wait, why're you on your feet? You shouldn't be standin'!"

"I'm all right—" She found herself whisked off her feet and in his arms once again. "I'm capable of walking!" she protested, cheeks reddening. "There's much less pain today."

"And I'm sayin' you shouldn't be walkin' around on it. I'm sure Del did, too."

She puffed out her cheeks. "She only recommended that I keep off of it. However, I made no such promises to her that I'd do so."

He rolled his eyes and carried her down the hallway. "You're too stubborn for your own good, you know that?"

"I wouldn't be me if I always listened to others," she huffed, becoming more relaxed. "Where are you taking me?"

"I'm sure you need breakfast."

At the mere mention of the word, her stomach rumbled. Embarrassment washed over her.

"I'll take that as an answer," he chuckled.

Clearing her throat, she confessed, "Breakfast would be lovely."

Along the way, he held her as he descended a set of stairs, ignoring the looks the two of them received from workers and guards of the castle, but he paid them no mind.

She was simply mortified, though, and avoided eye contact. "You don't have to carry me," she repeated.

"Eh, so what?" he said with a shrug. "I'm still doin' it."

He strode into a dining area where others were seated. They were the same three from last night, and she was able to get a better look at the two she didn't know.

Easily the tallest and most muscular of the four was Urian. His skin was a few shades darker compared to Whitley's, and his dark hair was short and puffed out a little in volume. His eyes were a dark shade of brown.

Rory was the slimmest of them all and had the fairest complexion with freckles here and there along his exposed skin. Unruly red locks in thick curls fell above his brown eyes and reached the nape of his neck. His face was clean-shaven, and he wore round glasses.

The trio dressed the exact same way, the royal blue of their fitted tunics matching Tiramôr's flag. The sleeves stopped inches above the wrist, while the bottom portion reached mid-thigh. They all wore a brown leather belt at their waist, and the rest of the look consisted of black trousers and black leather boots. Just like Elvina's Thunder Squadron, it was clear this trio watched over Owen. She briefly wondered why he had two more guards.

Rory flashed her a smile. "How are you farin' this mornin', beautiful maiden of the forest?"

Trevor covered his face with his hand. "Here we go."

Owen gingerly set Elvina down on an empty chair before claiming the empty seat to the right of her. He did that on purpose to block Rory, who was obviously interested in her.

"Decided to join us for lunch, huh?" Urian asked from the other side of the table, his serious demeanor long gone from last night. He seemed easygoing now, much like Owen.

Surprised, Elvina looked over at him. "Lunch? Is it not morning?"

"You slept through the mornin', actually," Owen answered. "We didn't wanna wake you up 'cause we knew you needed sleep."

Rory leaned forward to look past Owen at Elvina. "It would be a great honor if you would bestow upon me the knowledge of your name, O beautiful princess."

44

Her heart skipped. How had she already been found out?

"Easy," Trevor warned. He looked at Elvina, who was directly across from him and said, "He acts like that around pretty faces."

Relieved her secret was still safe, she slyly smiled. "Oh, but I'm more than a pretty face."

Rory grinned. "I do enjoy a mystery."

"You just met her," Urian pointed out.

"True love knows no bounds," he responded.

Owen rolled his eyes and snorted. "Whatever."

"But seriously, what's your name, Chipmunk?" Urian inquired.

Chipmunk? Millicent called her El, but that was close to her name—it was the first two letters of her name. Chipmunk had no correlation to her at all. "Excuse me, but Chipmunk?" she eventually asked.

Urian nodded. "Yeah, Chipmunk."

"We all have codenames," Owen explained with a grin. "Since none of us know your name, we've declared you Chipmunk."

"I'm Pipsqueak," Urian chuckled, clearly amused at the irony.

"It's probably obvious by now that Owen is Freckles," Rory interjected. "I'm Flirtsalot, and Trevor is Walla."

Trevor covered his face with a hand to play along with the farce. "Why're you spillin' all that information to her?"

"Elvina," she offered. "My name is Elvina."

Rory dreamily sighed. "Such a beautiful name. A most lovely name indeed."

"Oi, Flirtsalot, you should see what's takin' the food so long," Owen suggested, hoping to get rid of the nuisance of a personal guard, even if just for a moment.

As if on cue, castle attendants entered the room with plates of food and drinks in their hands.

A smile instantly lit up Owen's face. "Woot! It's grub time."

❦

A ball of fluffy orange fur landed on Elvina's lap. Bright golden feline eyes looked up at her and blinked. The cat meowed, demanding attention.

The whole table stopped eating, some utensils clattering onto plates.

Owen kept his voice under control but sounded worried. "Nye..."

Things clicked into place for Elvina. Owen had talked about his cat before.

"Elvina, don't move," Trevor warned in a low voice as he slowly rose to his feet.

Taking a break from eating, Elvina started to stroke the cat and looked at Trevor. "Why?" She was accustomed to cats. Some roamed her castle and royal stable.

Gulping loudly, Urian's eyes were wide with shock. "Damn," he cursed.

Much to everyone's surprise, Nye nestled down and purred, tail curling around his body.

"I must be dreamin'," Rory uttered with awe. "This must be a dream."

Owen, however, grinned. "He likes her!"

"Is there something significant about him liking me?" she asked, glancing around the table.

"Freckles is the *only* one Nye likes," Urian replied, eyes never straying from the cat. "He'll hurt just 'bout anybody else. Doesn't matter who you are to that damn cat."

"Apparently, you're the exception," Trevor breathed, slowly sitting back down.

Owen appeared to be proud of the entire interaction. "That's 'cause Nye has great taste."

Nye lazily rolled over, exposing his underbelly. He meowed, demanding her hand work its magic touch in a new area.

Smiling down at him, Elvina used her nails for tummy scratches.

"I wouldn't have believed any of you if I didn't see this for myself," Rory said. "Elvina must truly be bangin' for this to happen."

She rolled her eyes. She didn't feel amazing. "I wouldn't go that far."

"It's the truth," Owen said.

She looked at him and found him looking at her intently. "Well, perhaps that's the case if Nye chose a stranger over his master."

That earned a chuckle from all the guys.

"Maybe you're right," Owen teased, poking fun at himself.

Something dawned on Elvina. She was having lunch with Owen and his personal guards. Where were the other three of the royal family? They and their personal guards were nowhere to be seen. In fact, she hadn't seen a trace of them or heard a word about them. "Say, where is your family? I'm surprised they aren't eating lunch with you."

"They're visitin' Ceron's future bride," Owen clarified.

It made Elvina think of herself. She should have been with her betrothed by now. Instead, she was in another kingdom, having lunch with the second prince and his guards. "At least you have the company of your guards to dine with."

"And who do you dine with, Elvina?" Rory inquired.

"My father," she replied, keeping her gaze on Nye.

"Well, you're with us now," Owen noted. "You even have Nye."

Elvina looked at him. "I appreciate the company. Really, I

47

do." Something occurred to her. "I never did properly thank you for saving me last night. I'm not sure what would have become of me if we hadn't crossed paths."

He flashed her a grin. "Don't worry 'bout it."

Trevor looked at Owen. "By the way, you still have to perform your princely duties. Don't even think you're gettin' off the hook just 'cause your guest is awake."

"Oh, by all means, I won't be a hindrance," Elvina said.

Owen folded his arms across his chest, a smug look on his face. "Cari needs her exercise. I want Elvi to come with me."

Elvina and Trevor were the least surprised by his request.

"Do what?" Rory asked.

Owen looked at Trevor. "You can still come, just like you always do."

Elvina agreed with him. It would give the three a chance to be alone and talk.

Trevor nodded. "Fine." He looked at Urian and Rory. "You'll have free time durin' our ride."

Elvina voiced a problem as she wiggled her toes. "What am I to do without shoes?"

"I'm sure we can find you a pair to use until your boots are ready," Owen answered.

She was confused. "What boots?"

"Freckles summoned the city's cobbler to the castle," Urian explained. "The man took the necessary measurements while you were unconscious—er, sleepin'. Sleepin' sounds better."

"A delivery of a pair in your size was promised," Rory added.

Elvina didn't know that had been done. She looked at Owen. "You've thought of everything for my outfit. Thank you."

He merely shrugged. "Eh, I can't have you runnin' around

without shoes anymore. Besides, I don't need you to get hurt any more than you have."

She agreed. "We can go once we finish eating." She picked up her utensil with her right hand while continuing to pet Nye with her other.

CHAPTER FIVE

Not long after they had finished lunch, Elvina's black boots were delivered and were of fine quality and craftsmanship. She tested them out as she made her way to the royal stable with Owen leading the way. He stayed close in case she needed support. Trevor walked at a distance to somewhat give them privacy but kept them in view.

"Wait…so you've never tacked up a horse before?" Owen inquired.

A fine man with a love of horses was her royal stable master, who cared for her beloved horse. Whenever Elvina wished to ride, he prepared Luna for her, so she could focus all of her time on riding. The royal stable master handled everything else.

Elvina shook her head. "Never."

Owen grinned. "Today's your lucky day, then!"

"Is that so?"

"I'm gonna teach you."

"I'm already looking forward to the lesson."

As the three approached the stable, a particular smell

wafted from it. Elvina didn't mind it in the slightest. It was how a stable should smell.

"But before you tack up a horse, you gotta pick one to ride," Owen said.

She felt as if she was betraying Luna. It wasn't possible to take her out riding, though. "Do you have any recommendations?"

"I'll think as we go along." He barely brushed up against her to guide her over to a particular stall. "But I want you to meet Cari first."

On the other side of the wooden door was a beautiful mare. She was jet-black from ears to hooves, the only exception being a white star on her forehead. Her dark eyes were bright with life.

"She's lovely," Elvina breathed.

Cari lowered her head over the door and nudged Owen, nickering her encouragement. With a smile, he used both hands to stroke her neck. "Two years ago, her mam died after she was born. She wasn't s'posed to make it, but I helped raise her."

"The two of you must have a strong bond."

"She's a special girl."

Cari blew out her nose, the particles spraying Owen. He shook out his arms. "Oi, Cari!" he lightly scolded.

She didn't spook at his loud voice. Her tail merely flicked around. Perhaps she was used to Owen's behavior.

"Oi. What have I said 'bout yellin' in my stable, Owen?" a deep voice boomed from behind Elvina.

She turned to see a muscular man with a stubby beard headed in their direction. His slightly graying, dark red, shoulder-length hair was tied back into a short ponytail, revealing his dark eyes. His clothes and boots were rather dirty from his work in the stable.

"Hey, Herne," Owen greeted.

"Afternoon." He gave Elvina his full attention, completely ignoring Owen as though he wasn't there. "And good afternoon to you, m'lady. Are you enjoyin' your day so far?"

She nodded. "Very much so."

He flashed her a grin. "My name's Herne, and I'm the master of this stable."

Owen cleared his throat loudly before clarifying things. "She's only interested in findin' a horse to ride."

"I'd be honored to escort her around." Herne winked at her.

"Prince Owen has already offered his assistance, so I'll have to decline," Elvina said before Owen could counter.

"Okay, then. Holler if you need anythin', m'lady, and I mean anythin'." With that, Herne strolled away, whistling, but glanced back over his shoulder to look at Owen. *"Pob lwc!"*

Owen's lips curved up in a small smile.

Curiosity got the better of her. "What did he say just now?"

"Good luck." He shook his head. "Not hard to tell where Flirtsalot gets it from, huh?"

She was surprised. "Rory is his son?"

"Yeah. Anyway, are you ready?"

      ❦

After meeting a few of the horses in the stable, Elvina ended up choosing a gentle mare named Gwawr. Her coat was golden, while her mane and tail were cream-colored. She had gray around her pink muzzle and a star on her forehead. Her eyes were dark.

With Owen coaching her, Elvina managed to move Gwawr from her stall and put her in the empty one next to Cari where they groomed their horses.

As excitement coursed through her, Elvina brushed

Gwawr's coat. She didn't even mind getting a little bit dirty when the dust came loose. She was enjoying herself too much to care.

"Here, try doin' this," Owen said.

She glanced over her shoulder to watch the movement of his arm and tried mimicking him. "Like this?"

"Nah. You're doin' it a weird way."

She merely puffed out her cheeks in response.

"Here, lemme show you." Owen dropped the brush into the wooden box and used a hand to leap over the wall separating them. He stood directly behind Elvina and placed his right hand over hers, guiding her in the motion he did earlier. His hand made hers look small. "More like this," he told her.

Heat rose to her cheeks and her heart fluttered. "Oh..."

"Yeah, there you go. See? Easy."

"Easy," she agreed.

With that, Owen hopped back over to continue grooming Cari. While tending to his horse, he kept his back to Elvina, so she couldn't see his face.

Meanwhile, Elvina shook her head. She needed a casual conversation to clear her mind. "How do you say horse in your language?" she asked.

"Horse," he snickered.

She stopped brushing Gwawr to narrow her gaze at the back of Owen's head. "You know what I meant..."

He chuckled to himself before answering her question. "*Ceffyl.*"

"Kay-fill?"

Turning his head to look at her, he nodded. "There you go."

"Is there a certain phrase you like?"

He thought for a moment before his lips curved into a smile. "*Rwy'n dy garu di.*"

She liked the way it rolled off his tongue, but she didn't even attempt to try and repeat what he said. "I might need to practice saying that," she chuckled. "I don't want to say it wrong and offend you."

"I doubt you could even if you tried."

Elvina moved to the other side of Gwawr, touching her hindquarters so the mare knew she was there. Now Owen was in her line of sight.

"Typically, royals know the old language of Tiramôr, so they're fluent in it," he explained. "We're taught at a young age, even though nobody speaks it at all times. Traditional reasons, I s'pose."

"If that's the case, then how come Herne knew it?"

"It's still common knowledge if you know where to look. Plus, the old language is still a part of Tiramôr's history. Helps explain where certain things come from. Take Tiramôr for example. It translates to mean 'land and sea,' 'cause the two meet along our borders. Well, excludin' our northern one."

North was where Grenester, her beloved kingdom, was located.

Although, Elvina could honestly say she didn't know that about Tiramôr's origin. "Do your guards know it?" she inquired out of curiosity.

While he spoke, Owen moved around to the other side of Cari and looked across at Elvina. "Walla knows the most. Pipsqueak and Flirtsalot know a lot, too. They all wanted to learn since they're my guards, and thought it would be neat."

She only knew her native tongue. Some written works had an older essence to the words, but those outdated terms only lived in those works. "I think it's neat you can speak two different languages."

"How many do you know?"

"Just the one."

"At least we have that in common."

She nodded in agreement. It finally occurred to her that she didn't ask Owen what the phrase he said earlier meant. She opened her mouth to speak, but he spoke.

"Ready to clean hooves now?"

<hr />

After they finished grooming the horses, Owen vocally guided Elvina as she put on the tack. The blanket was the easiest. She did struggle a bit with lifting the leather saddle and placing it over the blanket, though. She brought the girth under Gwawr's belly and did her best fitting it into the tightest notch she could manage. Finally, it was time for the bridle.

"Okay, just like I showed you with Cari," Owen said as he supervised.

Elvina fit the metal bit into Gwawr's mouth, wary her fingers didn't accidentally get chomped on. She brought the rest of the bridal up and over the ears, leaving the reins on her neck. She turned to look at Owen with a big smile. "I did it!"

He smiled back. "Sure did."

"Are we going now?"

Owen glanced around for Trevor, noticing his horse was all tacked up and ready. He looked back at her and nodded. "You ready for this?"

"Of course."

<hr />

Even though dark storm clouds brewed off in the distance, it was still a great day for riding. They rode through an open field, heading away from the stable. To Elvina, the land in this part of Tiramôr was similar, yet different. There were grass and trees, some hills, and lovely scenery. It was almost like she was back home in Arnembury.

Elvina and Owen were in the lead, side by side. Trevor was right behind them with his horse, Rhys. The large gelding had a skewbald coat—a good mix of brown and white. His white mane and tail flowed freely. From the back of his knees and hocks, solid white feathering ran down his legs. Pink was around his muzzle, while his eyes were a light blue color.

Now was the time for the three to speak freely.

"Those bandits caused you so much trouble," Owen said with disdain.

"Do you think they purposely targeted you?" Trevor asked Elvina.

"There wasn't *anything* on the carriage to indicate I was specifically inside. How could they have known?"

"So it all coulda been random?" Owen thought aloud.

"The ambush was planned," she said. "That much I know."

"There's a chance they targeted anyone who crossed into their territory," Trevor guessed. "A carriage bein' escorted by two men on horses would draw attention." He inhaled sharply. "Could they have recognized Garrick and Quenby?"

"Possibly? If any of them had been in Arnembury for events and saw us together, they probably would have."

"What accent did they have?" Owen questioned. "They got you in Grenester, but they coulda come from Tiramôr."

She thought back to the incident. One bandit had barely uttered two words before she kicked him. "My accent, I believe."

Booming thunder rumbled off in the distance as the sky grew more ominous.

The gears in Owen's mind turned. "What would Tad do now?" he asked himself.

Elvina wasn't sure what his father would do. Truth be told, she wasn't sure why he ended the trade agreement either. It was something she had yet to ask about. When would the right time for it arise? Now?

"At least they'll be back soon," Trevor commented.

"I bet they'd both know what to do," Owen said.

Elvina jerked her head to the left to look at him. "Both?"

He looked at her as well. "Yeah, Tad and Ceron."

"What of Eilir?"

His face fell, and he briefly struggled for words. "She died last winter," he solemnly answered.

The news was a heavy blow. Her stomach dropped, her blood running cold. Eilir had been a wonderful female figure in her life for over a decade. She didn't want to acknowledge the last time she saw Eilir had been the final time.

"I was the target," Owen continued in a gruff voice. "She got in the way to protect me. The dagger was meant for me."

"Owen..." Her jaw tightened as she mentally told herself not to cry in front of him. "I'm truly sorry for your loss."

"I'm sorry you found out this way."

"The news never reached Arnembury." Her composure crumbled. She turned her head forward as silent tears fell.

"I think we should head back," Owen told Trevor. "It's started to rain."

By the time they reached the stable, rain poured from the sky. Needless to say, they had grown damp from the weather.

"Let's run back to the castle," Owen suggested as he dismounted from the left side of Cari.

Elvina shook her head. "I don't want to risk it with my ankle. I'd rather not make it worse now that it's nearly better."

A sly grin crossed his lips. "That won't be a problem." He walked to her left side, offering assistance with arms held out. "Here, I got you."

Just this once, she willingly allowed the help. Rather than ending up on her feet, he held her in his arms once again. "You must stop doing this!" she scolded.

"Not gonna happen." Owen walked away from Cari and Gwawr, leaving them in the care of Herne. "Especially since you're still hurt."

"As I already said, I'm capable of walking," she clarified.

"But not runnin'," he pointed out.

She didn't bother to say anything. She was cornered, and he knew it. She couldn't argue that.

Trevor merely trailed behind the two as they walked along. There was a brief moment of no shelter from the rain. Owen hurried his movements, careful not to jostle Elvina around too much. Even when the three reached the safety of the castle, he continued to hold her in his arms.

"You can put me down, you know," Elvina told him.

"You need to dry off," he lamely countered.

"I'll be all right," she insisted.

He gave in and gently set her down on the ground, keeping a hand on her waist longer than necessary before pulling away.

"Your sparrin' lessons are up next," Trevor reminded Owen of his daily schedule.

Owen ran a hand through his hair, flicking water around. "We can't do it in the activity yard since it's rainin'. We'll hafta find a spot inside."

"The foyer should work. It has in the past, and nothin's happenin' there now."

"While Owen's sparring, will it be possible for someone to lend me a quill and parchment?" Elvina inquired, lowering her voice. "I wish to write a letter to send to Arnembury." Her father needed to know what had happened.

"Consider it done, as long as you do somethin' for me," Owen said.

"What is that?"

"You gotta be there when I spar."

The two royals led the way as Trevor brought up the rear. He remained quiet to observe their interaction.

"Have your skills improved since the last time I saw you spar with Ceron?" Elvina teased.

He lightly bumped her shoulder. "I'm not too shabby, and you know that."

"If I recall correctly, you did lose the last match I witnessed."

"I'll spar Pipsqueak and show you how much I've improved."

Trevor spoke up. "Actually, he won't be sparrin' you."

Owen looked back over his shoulder. "Are you havin' a go with me? He's the one I normally spar with."

"You've got proper lessons with Anwen today."

CHAPTER SIX

Not that Elvina would admit this aloud, but Anwen Hier's skills easily rivaled Garrick's. In her early thirties, she was the castle's head guard and the one who personally trained Owen at times. The tall woman had her reddish brunette hair pulled into a tight, high bun. Her fierce brown eyes matched her strong personality.

"Again!" Anwen demanded when she knocked Owen onto his backside.

"You're cheatin' somehow!" he accused as he sat up.

"Your foot placement is wrong yet again," she scolded, aiming her wooden sword at his feet. "Do as I've shown you."

"He's not doin' a very good job impressin' Elvina," Rory loudly said to the other guards, even though they stood next to each other.

Trevor and Urian snickered in agreement.

Owen shot him a look. "Shut it, Flirtsalot!"

"Focus on the matter at hand!" Anwen snapped, trying to regain his attention.

"He's really doin' badly now, he is," Trevor commented, having a good laugh about it.

"Perhaps Trevor should stand in and spar with Anwen, so Owen can see what he's doing wrong," Elvina suggested, a sly smile on her lips.

He gulped at the thought of trading places. "I mean, this is *his* sparin' session, so *he* should be the one to spar Anwen."

"That's an excellent idea, Elvina." Anwen looked over at Trevor. "Come here with a sword."

He groaned. "Thanks a lot, Elvina," he grumbled bitterly. After grabbing a wooden sword from the bin, he jogged over to Owen and Anwen.

"Glad I'm not him," Urian commented, folding his muscular arms across his chest.

The duo set up to spar. "Owen, watch closely," Anwen said before they began.

Elvina returned to writing her letter to Millicent. At first, she considered addressing it to her father, but she realized that wasn't a wise idea. She planned on telling the messenger who would deliver the letter that Millicent was a friend of hers who just so happened to work at the castle. In the letter, Elvina briefly explained what had happened to her and requested aid to come to Helidinas with an extra horse. That way, they could either ride back to Arnembury together or continue their journey to Kennard.

Wooden swords clashed, but Trevor remained on his feet. "Ha!" He turned around to face Owen. "See? No problem!"

Anwen raised a leg and kicked him in the back, sending him to the ground. She stepped forward and placed a foot on him before looking at Owen. "That was an example to never turn your back to the enemy."

Owen gave her a cheeky grin. "Wait, can you do it again? I wasn't payin' attention."

Trevor grunted and stood when Anwen's boot was removed from his back. "At least I could counter her attack."

"Oi!" Owen barked. "It's no fair 'cause we've sparred before, and she already knows how I move."

"It's not like he's sparred with Chipmunk," Urian teased.

Trevor laughed. "There's no way she can fight."

Now there was a challenge she couldn't back down from. Elvina's ankle was doing much better, and she hadn't been limping in the slightest. A spar would do her some good.

She set the parchment and quill to the side, hoping no eyes saw the words that were still drying. She walked over to Trevor and held out her right hand. "Your sword, please."

He eyed her suspiciously. "Do what now?"

"I need your sword if I'm to spar," she replied matter-of-factly. "I want your sword because you said I cannot fight."

With a dubious expression, he relinquished it to her.

Owen stared at the sword in her hands, finding it to be an odd sight. He grabbed his sword and jumped to his feet. "But I don't wanna spar you."

"Too bad." Elvina took a fighting stance, using her left hand to hold the skirt of her dress so she wouldn't trip over it. "Ready?"

Without a word, he lurched forward two steps, as if he was going to begin the spar.

She didn't even flinch at his phony advance.

He blinked, surprised that she didn't budge.

"I'll allow this spar," Anwen said, having seen her reaction to the feigned attack. Taking her sword with her, she stepped aside with Trevor to watch.

"I'm not gonna go easy on you, Elvi," Owen warned, beginning to move in a circle around her.

She turned, always facing him. "I wouldn't have it any other way."

He quickly moved, and she blocked with ease. He was clearly astonished.

The others were impressed as well, judging by their

silence. That was until a certain one broke it. "Show him how to fight, my love!" Rory cheered.

With an irritated look, Owen glanced over at him, lowering his sword slightly. "Oi, she doesn't even like you—"

Elvina used the broad side of the sword to whack his left side, causing him to gasp for air.

"Don't become distracted in front of the enemy," Elvina instructed, echoing the words of Garrick. "It could be your last mistake."

Anwen silently nodded in agreement.

"Chipmunk knows her stuff," Urian commented.

Four sets of eyes watched as the duo continued their sparring session. Their swords met, but neither gave way. Owen raised his sword above his head with both hands and brought it down. Letting go of her dress, Elvina blocked, keeping both hands on the hilt of hers. She managed to drive him two steps back.

"Where'd you learn to fight like this?" Owen inquired.

"A fine man by the name of Garrick," she replied.

He feigned innocence. "Garrick? Never heard of him."

She laughed at his reaction and advanced another step. "He's known throughout Arnembury for his actions and deeds." After all, he was why Elvina was alive today. If he hadn't intervened years ago when he did, she could be dead.

Excitement sparked in his eyes. "That's bangin'!"

Just as Elvina stepped back, Owen accidentally stepped on the hem of her dress. She fell and dropped the sword, twisting her body around and catching herself with her arms. Now she was on her hands and knees, not facing her sparring partner.

"That was an excellent run, my lovely Elvina!" Rory cheered.

Oh, she wasn't quite finished yet. With a smirk, she grabbed the sword with her left hand and swung around, staying low to the ground. Garrick taught her to fight with both hands just in case she couldn't use the one she favored.

It met the sword in Owen's hand and knocked it away with ease. She found he'd weakened his grip because he thought the match was over. The wooden object merely clattered to the ground.

Owen blinked, glancing down at the hand that no longer held a sword. "Wha…?"

She rose to her feet and extended her left arm to point the weapon at him. "Do you yield?"

"I thought you did 'cause you were down and didn't have a sword."

"I never said I yielded."

With a small smile, he raised both hands in surrender. "I yield, Elvi."

<hr />

By the time sparring was over, Elvina had proven she could shoot a bow rather well. When the session ended, she accompanied Owen with the rest of his princely duties. She finished her letter to Millicent, and the messenger said he would ride out then to deliver it, assuring her that he would take the fastest horse in the royal stable and reach Arnembury as quickly as possible.

Once Owen's duties and dinner were over, they found their way into a lounging room with a cozy feel to it. Warm flames were in the fireplace because of Owen's handiwork. He sprawled out on one of the sofas with Nye curled up with him. Urian sat in the farthest chair from the fire with a book dwarfed by his hands. Unlike the others, Elvina walked around the room, looking at the shelves. A particular item caught her attention.

A wooden lap harp off to the side practically beckoned to

her, begging to be played. Among all of her princess lessons, learning to play the harp was the only type of lesson she ever truly enjoyed. She glanced around at the others.

Owen was occupied with petting Nye, watching the feline's ears flick to and fro. Urian was deep into reading his novel to notice.

Elvina seized the opportunity and stepped over to the instrument before picking it up. She carried it over to a free spot on the sofa across from Owen.

Owen noticed first. "Gonna provide us with some entertainment?" he playfully teased.

"Oh, hush," she huffed as she tuned the harp. When she finished the task, she sat upright and held it correctly, her fingers gracefully moving across the strings. The instrument came to life at her touch, filling the room with music.

It brought back old times for Elvina. Owen and Trevor would listen to her play when she'd practice with Vallerie in her lessons room.

When the song came to an end, the lingering sound eventually faded away. The room was silent, except for the crackling fire.

"Can you play another one?" Owen inquired, his eyes remaining closed.

Urian jumped in surprise at the sound of his voice, having thought he had fallen asleep. Owen normally became so bored while listening to music that he would doze off and start to snore at some point.

"Do you have a request?" Elvina asked.

"Play your favorite," Owen answered.

She instantly knew which song and lined her hands up accordingly. It was a beautifully pleasant tune, one that made her happy just hearing it. The melody was enchanting.

"Is there anything you can't do?" Owen asked when the song ended.

"Cook," she jested.

"I don't have that skill either."

"What skills do you have?"

"He's an artist," Urian replied, still keeping his eyes on the open page of his book.

Owen silently shot him a look for outing him so quickly.

"What do you do?" Elvina inquired with interest. This was a new fact about him.

Owen turned his attention back to her. "I sketch with pencils and quills."

"Do you have any I may see?"

Leaving Nye behind, Owen stood and walked over to a bookshelf. Grabbing a leather-bound book from it, he returned to his seat on the sofa. He untied the wrap tie closure before opening it to the first page.

Setting aside the harp, Elvina walked over to join him.

"I started a new book not too long ago since I filled this one up," he explained, setting the book onto her lap.

She held it carefully as she turned the pages. Familiar faces of people and animals were easy enough to spot. Some were busts, some were full-length, while others were several images on one. She was amazed at his attention to detail. "You have a wonderful skill of capturing people the way they appear," she commented.

He became bashful. "You think so?"

"I know so." She continued to flip through. Along with his family, she noticed that his guards had all been sketched multiple times. Even Nye and Cari. There were some scenery sketches as well.

"Do you have a favorite thing to draw?" she inquired.

"People and animals," Owen replied. "I like the expressions they make."

She laughed when she came across one of Trevor yawning. "I see what you mean." She pointed to it. "Did you have him pose for that or something?"

A grin on his lips, Owen tapped the side of his head. "I go offa memory, I do."

She was surprised. "Just memory alone?"

"It started getting really good when I was, like, ten or so. I'm great at rememberin' details and things that have happened. Names and faces, too."

Elvina turned the page, her eyes going wide. The sketch on the left was of the gazebo by the lake. All the features were correct, with a proportional version of herself seated on the bench. On the other page was a waist up drawing of just her. He had thought of her during their time apart. "And what of her?" she asked softly, looking at him.

There was a tone of endearment in his voice. "She's a lovely person, she is."

Warmth flooded her body all over. She moved her hands, wringing them together before placing them down. Her right one held her left, palm up. "Is that so?"

He nodded. "She's somebody who matters a lot to me." Bashful, he broke eye contact and looked down. "Oi. What happened?"

She scanned over the current pages, thinking something was wrong with them. "What?"

So it was less awkward, he reached over to point at her left hand, gesturing to her scar on the right side of her palm, about as long as one of her thumbs. "How'd you get that?"

She raised her hand to look at it. "It happened last winter. Something was covered in snow and I tripped over it. I couldn't stop myself and gashed my hand open." Quenby had been mortified that he hadn't caught her in time. It was her fault for being ahead of him.

"That musta hurt."

"For a moment," she admitted. She had cried from the

ordeal. A mental image that stuck with her was how the white snow had been stained crimson red.

"When I was younger, do you know what Ceron did for me when I got hurt and cried?"

She shook her head. "No. What did he do?"

Rather than telling her, he showed her. He took her left hand with his right and brought it to his lips, bestowing a gentle kiss directly onto her scar.

Pink invaded her cheeks. "O–Oh..."

Only now did he realize his actions. "Uh, yeah. That's what he did. I thought it was magic."

Urian glanced up again, observing that Owen still held Elvina's hand. Before they noticed he was watching, he went back to reading his book.

"It sounds like Ceron was a great big brother to you growing up," Elvina commented.

Owen nodded. "He still is now." He realized that he still had her hand in his. "Uh, sorry." He set it down, patting the back of it. He twiddled his fingers together, occupying his hands so he didn't do anything else silly.

She smiled a little. "You're fine."

"Anyway," Owen started. "That's my sketchbook."

Elvina completely forgot that it was still on her lap. "It's great." She closed it and handed it to him. "Thank you for sharing it with me."

He smiled, taking it from her. "You're welcome, Elvi."

"I'd love to see more of your work."

"I can show you more."

An idea came to mind. "Can I watch you draw sometime?"

"You certainly can." He held up the sketchbook. "I'd show you now, but it's full."

"We'll have to find one that isn't."

"That can be arranged."

CHAPTER SEVEN

Night had fallen, and Elvina was currently being escorted to where she resided in the castle by a certain second prince. Of course, Rory kept his distance as to not impose on them.

"Today was most interesting," Elvina commented.

"Can't have you bored while you're stayin' here," Owen teased, lightly bumping into her shoulder with his body.

She bumped him back. "You've done well."

"We'll see what tomorrow brings."

"Less rain?" she jested.

"I'd love to take you ridin' again."

"I'd like that."

"Or take you into the city. You haven't seen Helidinas before."

"I'm sure it's wonderful."

He smiled, proud of his capital city. "It is."

They stopped in front of the door that led to her temporary bedchamber.

"I'll have Del check on you in the mornin'," Owen informed her. "Just to make sure you're healin' properly."

"Thank you."

"No problem." He dramatically bowed. "Sleep tight, Elvi."

She curtsied to him. "And you do the same." She opened the door and stepped inside the room lit by candles, turning around to face him. She waved using her fingers before she closed the door and backed away, and then walked over to the bed and collapsed onto it.

Her heart fluttered as she held in a squeal, not wanting anyone to hear her. Especially Owen, since he was just outside the door. Her feelings for him had developed further. He was charming and caring, unlike other royals she had met who didn't even have the status of being a prince. His wonderful sense of humor had never failed to make her laugh.

She curled up on her side, wary of her still wrapped shoulder. Of course, in the back of her mind, she thought of Kennard. Her father had said the two of them were officially betrothed to each other. She dreaded telling Owen the news. How would he react? She sighed. "What am I to do?"

Trevor had told her in private that he and Owen would stop by later. They could converse about touchy subjects without the worry of someone eavesdropping.

Sitting up, she unlaced her boots, leaving them where they fell on the floor before tossing her socks onto them. She didn't care that she wasn't being neat about things. She didn't want neat for once. For now, her dress would remain on. Until the two arrived, she was left alone with her thoughts.

She wondered how the messenger fared riding in the rain. He knew the letter was important because of Owen and hadn't wanted to delay his start. She hoped the way was clear for him.

She worried about the Thunder Squadron. There hadn't been a single sign of them today. Yesterday felt like a lifetime ago, and her heart ached. Was worrying the most she could do? There had to be something else within her power she could consider. An idea struck her. Perhaps she could try to search for them tomorrow. Maybe Owen would let her borrow a horse.

Time trickled by as she fretted over things that were out of her control. She could imagine Garrick scolding her, saying her energy should be channeled into something less negative. That didn't seem like a possibility since her friends' lives were on the line.

Finally, there came a moment when the door to the bedchamber slowly opened.

Elvina sat up, preparing to get out of bed, but froze when she saw who had come into view. Still dressed in his uniform, Urian held a candle. There was no hiding her surprise. "Urian?"

He slipped inside the room and closed the door behind him, before walking to her without a word.

"What are you doing?" she inquired, allowing her legs to hang over the side of the bed.

Catching her completely off-guard, he unsheathed his sword and raised it to her throat, nearly touching her skin. "Who are you?" he demanded.

She was flabbergasted. "What?"

"Who are you?" He eyed her carefully. "A spy? Some assassin?"

She scoffed at the idea, wishing he knew how ridiculous he sounded. "I'm Elvina."

"Who are you really?" The grip on the hilt of his sword tightened, making a subtle sound. "I've been observin' you since we first met. For starters, you speak properly. You're skilled with a sword, not to mention, a bow. You're able to ride a horse and can even play the harp. Those aren't traits of a typical commoner."

He had noticed her abilities.

"For whatever reason, Freckles trusts you, even though he doesn't know you," he continued. "Actually, nobody here knows you. You've said you hail from Grenester and your name's Elvina. You could be lyin' 'bout who you are."

With her head held high, she didn't break eye contact. "I have no reason to lie. What good would it do me?"

"You know, there's somethin' else that's been botherin' me. Can't put my finger on it. Why does he already call you Elvi? Nicknames happen after he befriends people." His gaze hardened. "I'll ask one more time—who are you?"

The bedchamber's door opened, causing Elvina and Urian to look.

"Oi, knock next time—" Trevor began to scold from the hallway.

Owen took in the scene and immediately rushed inside. "Elvi!" Glaring, he stormed up to Urian, who had lowered his sword. "Oi, you wanna start a war?"

Trevor was quick to enter and close the door behind him.

"I wasn't gonna kill her," Urian said to defend himself as he stepped away from the bed.

"You threatened her," Trevor pointed out as he approached the three.

Urian arched his eyebrow. "You're on his side?"

His back to Urian, Owen held Elvina in his arms, her body flush against his. "Are you okay?"

She nodded. "He did me no harm." Relief washed over his face. "Owen, he's observed much about me. He essentially knows."

"What's occurin'?" Urian asked, knowing he was out of the loop.

Turning himself and Elvina in place, Owen looked at Urian. "Swear to me you won't tell a soul, Urian." He used his real name to show how serious he was about the matter.

His voice was firm. "I swear it."

Owen looked at Elvina as a way to prompt her. In turn, she looked at Urian. "I am Princess Elvina Norwood of Grenester," she stated.

He stared at her with wide eyes. His mouth opened, but nothing came out.

"She's been tellin' the truth 'bout the bandits," Owen said. "They attacked her and her guards."

"The letter she wrote was to her lady-in-waitin'," Trevor added.

Urian finally found words. "Grenester's princess?"

"Yes," Elvina confirmed.

Sheathing his sword, one knee bent to the floor, he bowed his head. "Forgive me for my actions, Princess Elvina."

"There's no need for that," she said. "Please, stand."

"Don't treat her like royalty," Trevor admonished.

"Why didn't somebody say somethin' from the start?" Urian asked, back on both feet.

"Owen and Trevor both knew," Elvina reasoned.

"Who all knows?" Urian inquired.

"Everybody in this room," Trevor answered. "And that's the way we're gonna keep it."

Urian seemed surprised. "What 'bout Flirtsalot?"

"No," Owen replied. "I don't think he'd flirt if he knew the truth."

"You don't like it when he does that," Elvina teased, looking up at him.

An irritated look crossed his face as he turned his attention to her. "No," he gruffly admitted.

"I'm sure it's all in good fun."

"Not if I can help it," he grumbled.

"Freckles," Trevor said.

Owen looked at him. "Yeah?"

"I think you can let go now. She's fine."

Elvina became hyperaware of the fact that Owen still held her. She wanted to crawl under something and hide.

"So what?" Owen questioned, attempting to keep his strong composure.

She buried her face into his chest to hide her red cheeks.

"Are they secretly together?" Urian asked Trevor in all seriousness.

Elvina really couldn't show her face now. Her ears felt like they were on fire.

"No," Trevor answered.

Owen rested his chin on the top of Elvina's head. "Not yet," he murmured.

She stilled. Surely she hadn't misheard him. Slowly, her head moved back to look up at him. Her lips parted as she thought of how to word her question.

"Yeah?" he asked.

"Y–You," she stuttered.

"Me what?"

"What do you mean, *not yet*?" she blurted.

He looked confused, but pink tinted his cheeks. "What?"

"You had said 'not yet' to Urian's question."

"No," he denied. "I never said anythin'."

"Yes, you did. I heard you."

"You heard my thoughts?" he gasped.

"You spoke aloud."

His expression shifted as he registered what he had done. Or rather, that he hadn't kept his thought to himself.

Catching on to their embarrassed state of being, Trevor jerked his head toward the seating area. "Should we have a goss?"

Owen immediately looked at him, taking the opportunity of reprieve. "Yeah, we should."

Elvina and Owen sat on the same sofa, while Trevor and

Urian sat opposite of them, a table separating the pairs. Urian had since left his candle on it.

"How come Chipmunk hasn't been brought up before?" Urian looked at Elvina with a slightly panicked expression. "Is Chipmunk okay, or should I call you Elvina?"

"Chipmunk will do just fine," she answered.

His shoulders relaxed.

"Everything happened before you became his personal guard," Trevor said, answering his original question.

"After Mam died, Tad appointed two more guards to me," Owen informed Elvina.

She could picture the timeline. It had almost been a year since the Gravenor family's last visit. The letter ending the trade agreement came in the fall. In the winter, Eilir had passed away. And now, Elvina was in Tiramôr's capital city with Owen.

Urian looked at Owen. "I remember your family bein' away for visits, but I've never heard you talk 'bout Chipmunk before."

"He has with me," Trevor stated.

"Because you've known Elvi," Owen pointed out, "I've kept quiet for the most part, I have."

"Yet you've drawn me before," Elvina quipped in a playful tone.

Trevor shook his head. "Why am I not surprised?"

"I draw what's on my mind," Owen mumbled.

"Just so happens to be a certain princess," Urian commented, looking at her. "What's the plan for you now?"

"I wait. The messenger delivers my letter to Millicent, and she learns of the situation. I know she'll tell Father. I had asked for a small company and a spare horse for me to ride. From there, I'll either go home or continue onward to—" She cut herself off. She hadn't revealed where she and the

Thunder Squadron were going. Or rather, who they were seeing.

"You can tell us, Elvi," Owen encouraged her.

"It's a rather sensitive topic." Her insides squirmed. She wasn't ready to tell him just yet.

Urian circled back. "Wait. So after your company arrives, you'll leave?"

"Yes."

"Why?"

"There's no reason for me to intrude longer than I have. This wasn't even a planned visit to begin with." Besides, she had her kingdom awaiting her.

Urian spared a glance at Owen before looking back at her. "But you—" he closed his lips when Trevor kicked his foot.

"It's no trouble havin' you here, Elvi," Owen assured her. "Truly."

She looked at him. By a twist of fate, they had been reunited. She wished the circumstances were different. Perhaps fate was teasing her, showing her a future she couldn't have. Why did Mervin end the agreement? Things would be different if he hadn't done it to drive the two families apart.

"What's wrong?" Owen asked, noticing how her face fell.

She didn't want to ask her questions in front of Trevor and Urian. Owen was the only one who needed to be in her audience. "I'm tired," she fibbed.

"We'll let you sleep now. You did have a busy day."

"It certainly was busy. Although, I typically don't have my life threatened before bed."

Owen and Trevor looked at Urian. "Oi, I had to make sure she wasn't a threat to Freckles."

"You could have asked me 'bout her," Trevor pointed out.

He parted his lips and froze, processing his words. "Oh."

"At least now you know for next time," Elvina teased.

"Oh, no," Urian immediately denied. "No more night visits from me."

Owen snorted. "At least Walla and I coordinated our visit."

Trevor stood. "And now it's over."

Elvina was the last to stand. To be courteous, she walked with the guys over to the door.

"Del will be around in the mornin'," Owen reminded her.

"She'll see that I've improved," Elvina advised.

"Your limp's gone. How are your scrams?"

"My *scratches* are better."

"Scrams," he said with a smirk. "And that's good."

Urian left the bedchamber before Trevor. They walked away and didn't look back. Owen stood just outside in the hallway as Elvina leaned against the doorjamb.

"I'll see you tomorrow," he said.

"Is there anything planned for you?"

"Not at all. It'll be like today."

"I'm sure that will be pleasant."

He nodded in agreement. "G'night, Elvi."

"Good night, Owen."

He took a step to walk away.

Her mouth worked faster than her thoughts. "Owen," she blurted.

He stopped in place. "Yeah?"

"Can we talk in private tomorrow? Only the two of us?"

He spared a glance at his guards. The distance grew. "Do you wanna talk now?"

Now was much too soon. She wasn't ready. "It's late, and I'm not sure how long it could take."

"Tomorrow it is."

She mentally told herself not to back down from the talk. "Thank you. Good night, Owen."

His lips curved into a small smile. "Sleep tight, Elvi."

She slowly closed the door as he walked away. Her heart squeezed. They'd talk tomorrow. She'd ask about Mervin's choice that ended the trade agreement, and she'd mention she was betrothed.

Her movements were a tad sluggish. She left her dress over a chair and changed into the chemise from this morning. She went around the room to blow out the candles before finally crawling into bed, only to stare up at the ceiling.

Thoughts about tomorrow plagued her mind. What time should they talk? How would he react to each topic? Which one should she bring up first?

Rolling onto her good shoulder, she thought back to happier times. All moments had been enjoyable when the Gravenor family had visited. With no one else in the room, she and Eilir would chat and drink tea. Mervin would tell jokes, and she would share laughs with him. She and Ceron would speak of how they could better their kingdoms when leadership fell on them. As for Owen, there were too many to list. The most prominent ones were their moments at the gazebo. They could be out there for hours at a time, undisturbed by their watchful guards.

A longing ache settled in her heart. She and Owen certainly had a history together. Would it be enough to make their future stronger?

CHAPTER EIGHT

The following morning, Delyth got to work on removing the last of the bandages. From the looks of things, Elvina didn't need anything wrapped or covered again. Although, the bruises were still there, and more prominent than yesterday.

"You look better," Delyth commented.

"I feel much better," Elvina said. She wasn't nearly as sore, and there was no more pain from her ankle.

"That's great to hear." Delyth knelt to touch Elvina's left foot. Her fingers grazed over the skin and pressed here and there. "The swellin' is all gone. You didn't react to pain when I touched it."

Elvina shook her head. "I was walking around without limping yesterday at some point."

Knowing that, Delyth rose to her feet and stood aside. "Let me see."

Elvina slid off the edge of the bed and stood. She took a few steps forward before she spun around to face Delyth. "See? Much better."

"I'm happy you're doin' well. Now, there's still some

RACHAEL ANNE

bruisin' on your shoulder, but that'll go away eventually. That's a process I can't speed up."

"I still appreciate all you've done for me. I know I couldn't have recovered like this without you."

Delyth lit up with a smile. "You're welcome!" She quickly nodded. "I'll be leavin' now so you can get changed."

"Thank you again," she said.

Alone in the bedchamber, Elvina dressed and left. As she closed the door behind her, a meow caught her attention. "Hello, Nye."

He lazily padded his way over to receive attention.

Elvina bent down to stroke his soft fur with a single hand. "Good morning to you as well."

He flopped over onto his back to reveal his stomach and meowed again.

"Does Owen not give you enough attention?" she playfully teased, scratching his belly.

He simply purred in delight.

She stood upright and took a single step before he meowed in protest. "What do you expect me to do? I'm going to look for Owen. I can't stay here all day just to pet you."

His only reply was to slowly blink at her and meow.

"Oh, come here." She bent down to pick him up, holding him against her chest. While she adjusted both arms so she could still pet him, he snuggled up and continued his purring. He was quite warm. "Will we go look for him together, then?"

With eyes closed, he only continued to purr with contentment.

She walked, hoping to come across any familiar faces. She only had part of the castle somewhat memorized from yesterday, so she stuck with what she knew. She didn't want to raise any suspicion by being caught in an area she shouldn't be in. She planned to avoid having another sword at her throat if possible. Her secret had been exposed to only one person, and she wanted to keep it that way.

She rounded the corner, spotting Owen and Trevor heading in her direction. She smiled. "Good morning."

Owen lit up at the sound of her voice. "G'mornin', Elvi!" His eyes narrowed in on his cat.

"We were just comin' to get you," Trevor told Elvina.

"Is that so?"

The three stopped in front of each other, and Owen looked at Nye. "You're such a traitor," he said in a disapproving tone.

He didn't bother to open his eyes for a peek, his purring remaining steady.

"He clearly needs more love," Elvina teased.

"I've never seen him do that with anyone other than Freckles," Trevor admitted.

"What does Del think of you, Elvi?" Owen asked, changing the subject.

"She's happy with my progress. The bruises are out of her control, but they'll go away with time."

"Bruises?" he questioned, clearly taken aback.

"I fell down a ravine and hit my left shoulder against a tree."

Trevor grimaced. "That must have been gompin'."

She knew that word meant something along the lines of not really pleasant, or nasty. "The forest clearly disagreed with my presence there."

"But you're here now," Owen pointed out. "Safe."

"And in good company."

"Oh, speakin' of company, I've got family comin' over!"

Family? Did he mean his father and brother were almost home?

"A cousin of mine and his wife are on their way to visit her family, and they'll be passin' by the castle on their way there. They'll only be here for a couple of hours or so, but it'll be fun to have 'em here, even if it ain't for that long."

She doubted that any extended family of his would recognize her. Her identity would remain safe. "If you are having guests, I'll make sure to stay out of the way. If you like, I can stay in my bedchamber for the duration of their visit."

Much to her surprise, he started laughing. "You're so weird for sayin' that."

"Weird?" she scoffed, momentarily forgetting to pet Nye. "I am most certainly not weird. If anyone here is weird, it's most definitely you!"

He merely chuckled. "Sure."

"Why would you even think to call me weird? What I said wasn't weird at all."

"I don't wantcha stayin' in your room. I wantcha to meet 'em."

She did her best to keep her jaw from dropping. "Meet them?" she squeaked.

☙ ❧

It was easy to see the family resemblance between Owen and Kynan Gravenor. There was no denying they were related. Possibly in his mid-twenties, he had a lean build. Parted down the middle, his extremely dark brown hair was pulled back in a short, low ponytail. Rounded glasses were in front of his brown eyes, and a little scar was along his left cheekbone.

His wife, Siriol, was quite lovely. Half of her curly, golden blonde hair was up and braided in back. Her eyes were a shade of pale blue. Some of her features were rounded due to her gaining a healthy weight, as there was no way of hiding the exaggerated swell of her stomach due to the growing life inside of her.

Everyone gathered in the same lounging room from yesterday evening, and now that introductions were over, the personal guards were off to the side. Rory failed at flirting with Siriol's lady-in-waiting. Trevor and Urian casually talked amongst themselves. All of the royals were seated, the married couple on one sofa, and the other two across from them.

"Okay, I have to ask," Kynan said, looking down at the cat on Elvina's lap. "How are you so friendly with Nye? He's never let me near him before, and he's seen me a bunch."

Siriol looked somewhat impressed as well. "I've seen Nye go to Owen and only Owen. Ever."

"He likes her," was Owen's simple explanation.

"What did you do?" Kynan asked. "Bribe him with fish or somethin'?"

Elvina laughed. "I think he likes me more than Owen is all."

At her statement, Owen gasped. "No way. I've raised Nye since he was a kitten."

"Perhaps there's somethin' special about Elvina that only he knows," Siriol mused with a laugh.

Owen grinned. "She's definitely special." He looked at Siriol. "How much longer do you have to go?"

"Late spring, early summer," she answered.

"That's excitin'!"

Kynan swelled with pride. "I'm goin' to do my best to be a great tad. I can't wait to meet 'em. I just hope the little one takes after Siriol," he chuckled. "They'll be doomed if they take after me."

Elvina was slightly surprised at his words. She had never known a royal to talk of something like that. He thought of his unborn child as something more than an heir, or one to carry on his bloodline. She studied the married couple, who seemed happy and in love with one another.

83

Owen cracked up. "Your kid'll be ugly if it looks like you."

"And your kid would be damn hideous if they looked like you," Urian jested.

Others laughed at the comment.

"What was that, Pipsqueak?" Owen demanded, whipping his head around to look at him.

Before any damage could be done, castle workers brought in drinks. Careful not to spill any of her hot tea onto Nye, Elvina slowly sipped at it. "Have you thought of any names for the baby?" she inquired.

Siriol shook her head. "We're still discussin' because we haven't been able to settle on a single one."

"We've still got some time to think of the perfect name," Kynan added.

"It'll be here before you know it," Owen said.

Siriol ecstatically nodded.

"Where are Uncle Mervin and Ceron?" Kynan inquired.

"Visitin' Ceron's future bride," he answered, and drank from his mug. "They're gonna get married this fall, so that's somethin' else to look forward to."

Siriol lit up. "That's news to me. Tell us about her."

"I've only met her a couple of times. Her name's Gwendolyn, and she's from a city that's on the southeast coast." Owen smiled. "I didn't think it was possible for Ceron, but he cares 'bout her."

"I bet Uncle Mervin's happy about that," Kynan commented. "Remember how disappointed he was when Ceron didn't take that princess from Grenester as a bride?"

Elvina casually sipped her tea.

"Those two are nothin' more than friends," Owen said. "Besides, Ceron never wanted to marry her."

Siriol looked at Elvina. "Did she ever marry?"

"Who?" she asked.

"Your princess. You sound like you're from Grenester."

She was the only one in the room with a different accent. "No, the princess isn't married."

"She's, what, a year younger than Ceron?" Kynan thought aloud. "She's probably due to take up a husband—"

Books from the shelf crashed onto the floor, causing Nye to jump at the sudden noise and quickly scamper out of the room.

"Oops," Trevor said rather lamely. "I wasn't lookin' where my hand was."

He caused a diversion for her sake. She would have to thank him later.

Owen set down his drink and walked over. "Those better not have been Ceron's books."

"They're just books," Trevor huffed, ensuring attention didn't return to Elvina.

"My brother really likes his books." Owen bent down to inspect them, checking their condition. "Try not to be an idiot, Walla!"

"Oi, remember this mornin' when you fell outta bed?" he pointed out.

The two got lost in their banter.

Elvina merely rolled her eyes and drank her tea. She was accustomed to their behavior, even though they didn't act like a head personal guard and charge. Their relationship was much different than what she had with Garrick.

"How long have you and Owen been betrothed?" Siriol suddenly inquired.

Elvina choked on her tea and became a sputtering mess. She managed to place her drink on the nearby table before any liquid could spill from the cup.

Owen immediately turned to look at her. "Elvi!" Forgetting all about his argument with Trevor, he raced over to her. He knelt next to her so he could see her face and gently rub her back. "Are you okay?"

She nodded, but her red face wasn't so reassuring.

Owen looked at Kynan and Siriol. "What's occurrin'?"

"I only asked her a question before she started havin' a fit," she replied.

With Owen at her side, Elvina was more embarrassed than ever. She could only hope he didn't catch on to what the question was. "I'm f–fine," she said rather hoarsely.

"You don't sound fine," Owen said, pointing out the obvious.

She merely dismissed his words with the wave of her hand.

Siriol giggled. "Owen, I think this is the most carin' I've seen you."

He casually shrugged. "Eh, I'm not seein' what you're seein'."

"You didn't waste a second to come over here and check on her," Kynan pointed out.

"'Cause she's Elvi," was his simple explanation.

Siriol smiled. "Oh, I'm just so happy for the both of you!"

Owen looked at her, tilting his head to one side. "Huh?"

"Tell me, how long have you been betrothed?" she inquired.

Only now did Owen stop rubbing circles on Elvina's back. He rose to his feet, his entire body rigid. His face and ears were both bright red. "I, uh, think it's time I took Nye out for a ride." He strode to the door to leave.

"Nye's your cat," Rory corrected with an amused grin. "You can't ride him."

"He needs exercise, after all," Owen said, as though Rory never spoke. Looking back over his shoulder to steal a peek at Elvina, he smacked into the wall, just missing the doorway. He quickly shuffled around the corner and disappeared from view.

"You...you broke him," Urian stammered, breaking the

silence over everyone who just witnessed what had happened.

Siriol teared up and her lower lip quivered. "I didn't mean to break him."

Kynan was the first to react to her distress. "It's okay, *cariad aur*," he cooed. "Owen was broken to begin with. You didn't do anythin' wrong. I promise."

"I'm goin' to go check on him," Trevor announced before jogging after his charge.

"Why did you think the two of 'em are betrothed to each other?" Urian inquired, looking at Siriol.

"I thought so too from the way he was actin'," Kynan responded, as though it was the most obvious thing in the world. "He's a lot happier than usual. Did anybody else notice how excited he was when he introduced her to us?"

"And when Elvina sat down on the sofa first, Owen sat rather close to her," Siriol chimed in. "Not to mention, the way he checked on her to see if she was all right before he left." She smiled and looked at Elvina. "It's easy to see he cares about you."

"I don't—" Elvina began.

"He's just a lovestruck idiot," Urian commented.

She fought back embarrassment to the best of her ability, hoping she appeared calm and collected on the outside.

"But in the end, the lovely Elvina will choose to be with me," Rory dreamily said.

Elvina playfully rolled her eyes. "I doubt that will happen."

"He'll probably fight for her hand if another challenges him," Urian huffed.

Elvina wasn't entirely sure how Owen would react upon learning she was already betrothed.

"I've got a question for you, Elvina," Kynan said.

"Yes?"

"Why are you here in Tiramôr if you're from Grenester and not with Owen?"

"Look who I found!" Trevor called out from the doorway.

Everyone looked to see the two had returned. "Sorry, I got really hot and dizzy all of a sudden," Owen apologized. "Needed some air."

Trevor clapped his charge on the shoulder. "Go get 'em." He walked over to where the other guards stood.

Owen shuffled over to the sofa and sat down beside Elvina, grabbed his mug, and chugged the remaining contents.

"Are you all right?" Elvina inquired.

He loudly exhaled and set down the empty mug before looking over at her. "Yeah."

"If you say so." She returned her attention to his relatives. "When did the two of you meet for the first time?"

"The day we got married," Kynan replied.

At least Elvina had the opportunity to meet her betrothed beforehand. Although, at this rate, she wasn't quite sure that would happen.

"Kynan was more nervous than I was," Siriol giggled.

"I can't deny that." He took his wife's hand in his. "Siriol and I had an arranged marriage. In the beginning, she couldn't stand me. Apparently, I was too much for her to handle."

"As time passed, we grew to love each other deeply," she added, rubbing her stomach with her free hand. "Now we're expecting our first child."

Elvina smiled, hoping that she truly could have a relationship like theirs with her husband someday.

CHAPTER NINE

I t was now time for Kynan and Siriol to leave. After all, they still needed to visit her family.

Siriol took Elvina aside to speak with her. "I wish you the best, and I hope that you have much happiness," she said.

Elvina smiled. "Thank you. And to you, I hope your baby brings you much joy."

Siriol absentmindedly rubbed her stomach. "I can't wait to meet this little one."

"I'm sure Kynan feels the same way." Elvina was still rather stunned because her husband never once mentioned he would have an heir once the baby was born. Nannies taught her she was to be a good wife to her husband and provide at least one heir to him. Of course, she was to do her royal duties as queen, but being compliant to her husband would always come first.

With what Elvina had observed from the Kynan and Siriol and their interactions with each other, she was starting to question what she had been taught.

The two briefly hugged before walking over to the others.

"Are you ready to go now?" Kynan asked.

Siriol nodded. "I believe so."

Kynan looked at his cousin. "Next time, you should visit us."

"You might have a baby by then," he said with a grin. "And hopefully, I'll bring Tad and Ceron for a proper visit. Maybe Gwendolyn if they're married by then."

"That would be wonderful," Siriol happily said, and looked at Elvina. "I wouldn't mind seeing you, too."

"Perhaps we'll meet again," she responded with optimism.

After goodbyes and hugs, Owen's relatives departed.

"They were pleasant," Elvina commented. "I enjoyed their company."

"I think they liked you, too," Owen confessed.

A castle attendant rushed up to them, appearing slightly disheveled. The short man carried some loose pieces of parchment with him, tucked under his arms. "Prince Owen, your sense of direction is required for us to prepare for the upcomin' ball!"

"Wait, why me? Ceron's better at it than I am."

"But Prince Ceron isn't here. Neither's King Mervin. *Your* guidance is needed."

"C'mon, there's gotta be somebody better—"

The attendant pleaded with his eyes. "Please! I didn't want to bother you while family was visitin', and now they're gone. Things may not be ready by the time your father or brother returns."

Owen sighed in defeat. "Fine."

"Excellent!" The short man took his hand and pulled him away. "There's so much to do, and so little time before the ball."

Not sure of what else to do, Elvina followed. While Trevor kept pace with her, the other two guards walked ahead of them.

"Trevor?" she asked, keeping her voice down.

He looked over at her. "Yeah?"

"I have a favor to ask..."

Elvina found herself back on Gwawr with Trevor and Rhys. She had asked if she could go out riding in hopes of finding the Thunder Squadron, or at least some sign of them. Trevor did consider having Urian go with her for a moment since he was aware of her status, but he changed his mind. He believed Owen would feel more at ease upon learning Trevor had accompanied her.

The duo made it to where the guys had been camping the night they all met. With the mid-afternoon sun high in the sky, the place looked different than Elvina remembered. It was an excellent spot for camping and still provided cover. The group of guys probably would have had a great night for sleeping under the stars if she hadn't stumbled upon them and interrupted.

"Do you think they could be in this forest?" Trevor asked.

"I'm not sure," Elvina replied, looking around at the terrain. "I'm not sure what they did after I left them behind. I only hope the four of them are alive..." She stopped herself from thinking the worst.

"I'm sure they are. They're the Thunder Squadron, the best Grenester has for their one and only princess."

She softly smiled. "Indeed."

"Which way did you come from?" he asked, moving Rhys closer to her.

She pointed. "There was a ravine I fell down over yonder. Apart from it, there was nothing like a marker I could use to identify where I was. At least, nothing that I noticed."

"You probably couldn't see anythin' after it got dark."

She nodded. "There was a stream at some point. I came across that not long after I was in the forest. It was still light out at that point."

"I think I can roughly picture where it happened, but I don't know your direct path. I'm sure the Thunder Squadron doesn't know it either. It's unfamiliar territory, after all."

"That might be true, but Quenby is an excellent tracker. I'm more than sure he would have been leading the Thunder Squadron should they have followed after me."

"Which means they could be around here if they tried."

"Or they could have returned to Arnembury to inform my father of what happened. Or they could have ventured onward to the duke I'm betrothed to and sought aid from him."

He did a double take. *"What?"*

She realized her mistake. It had casually slipped out. "Don't tell Owen!"

"You're *betrothed?*"

She couldn't lie at this point. "A few days ago, my father announced to me that I was betrothed. We were to meet for the first time, but the bandits interfered."

"You're betrothed…"

"Yes," she sadly confirmed.

"Why doesn't Owen know?"

"We're to talk today in private about things. It's one of the subjects I wish to discuss."

He solemnly nodded. "I'll keep the others away."

"Thank you." Her mind drifted back to the Thunder Squadron. "What would you do?"

He didn't hesitate in answering. "Break off the betrothment."

"I meant in regards to Owen," she clarified.

"If things were reversed and he was in your shoes…" He was

quiet as he gathered his thoughts. He scratched his chin, the gears turning in his mind. "I woulda stayed behind to look for him with Urian. Rory woulda ridden back to Helidinas to inform people what had happened. That way, Urian and I could still look for Owen while Rory could return with help. If Urian and I were still searchin' for him by the time Rory and reinforcements arrived, all of us would be able to find him faster."

"And once Owen was found, what would you do next?" she inquired.

He seemed confused. "Whaddya mean?"

"Would you continue on your way to your destination or return to Helidinas?"

"Probably return home, even if Owen was well."

"Why?"

He shrugged. "It's what I'd do for my charge."

She believed the Thunder Squadron would have done the same for her. "Can we venture farther?"

"If that's what you wanna do."

She lightly kicked Gwawr's sides, urging her forward at a cantering pace.

Rhys easily kept up with the mare.

Because of Trevor's words, Elvina thought about the Thunder Squadron. She believed that Garrick would have remained with Quenby and ordered the other two to ride back to Arnembury. Although, she couldn't be sure of that because she didn't know how they fared after the surprise attack. Her grip on the leather reins tightened. She could only hope all was well for her friends, and that they were unharmed.

"Hey, Elvina?" Trevor suddenly asked.

"Yes?"

"For some reason, you like Owen. And for obvious reasons, he likes you."

She might be slightly embarrassed at his words, but she wasn't sure where he was going with this.

"Why dontcha break off the promised weddin' with the duke and marry Owen instead?"

"It would be a great insult to different parties," she replied, having already put thought into breaking off her betrothment. "First of all, it would be an insult to the duke and my father. I would be going against what he set forth. Not to mention, it would reflect poorly upon all of Grenester."

"Maybe that'll be the case, but when are you gonna do somethin' that makes you happy?"

She thought before she spoke. "I'm not sure."

"I'm only sayin', it'll be better for you to marry a prince from another kingdom rather than a duke from yours."

"There were rumors of a wedding between Ceron and I. That never came to pass, though."

He smirked. "It seems like they got the wrong prince of Tiramôr."

They came across a small stream and the horses stopped for a drink.

"And perhaps now I'm betrothed to the wrong man," Elvina mused, leaning to pat Gwawr on her shoulder. "If only Kennard could see that as well."

"Wait, who's Kennard?" he asked with confusion. "You haven't mentioned that name before."

"He's the duke."

He eyed her suspiciously. "Duke Kennard? As in, Endicott?"

"Why, do you know about him?"

His eyes grew wide. "Oh, no. No. You're not gonna wanna marry him. Trust me."

She was taken aback. Her father had met the man and had already approved of him. "Why do you say that?"

"He's a ladies' man. A massive ladies' man. Worse than Rory if you can believe it."

"Ah, so he's Rory and Herne combined together?"

He laughed at the very thought of that possibility. "I'm sure Kennard's on a whole other level." His expression changed when he recalled something. "The ball."

"What about it?"

"He'll probably be there."

Elvina was surprised. "Kennard is on friendly terms with the royal family? Even with the situation between the two kingdoms?"

"Basically. I won't be surprised if he's there." His face lit up. "If you stick around long enough, I'm sure you could meet him. Then you can judge Kennard for yourself."

She pondered the idea. "There were intentions of meeting him from the start...It could be good for me."

"Oh, it'll be good for you," he corrected. "You'll see what kind of person Kennard is."

"What do you have to say about him?" After all, she trusted his judgment.

He thought for a moment. "From what I've seen, he's good at speakin' with people. He has valid points and reasons for certain things. He's not a bad ruler from what I've heard." He made a face. "But his downfall is womanizin'. He gets distracted by all of 'em too easily. I'm surprised he's not a tad by now..."

"Really?" she squeaked.

"He's dated a few women at the same time without any of 'em knowin' he was bein' disloyal to 'em. I've heard him brag 'bout it to Owen before."

She was vexed. "That's quite scandalous." Of course, she didn't want her husband being unfaithful to her. She could never be unfaithful to him.

"And who would want that in their ruler?" he scoffed.

"You make an excellent point. Perhaps I will have to speak with Kennard at the ball."

"Good." Suddenly, he laughed.

"What's so funny?"

"Imagine if Owen found out who you're supposed to marry!"

She laughed as well. "Things would probably not end well for Kennard."

"Exactly," he chuckled.

"Perhaps it's best not to inform anyone of who I'm betrothed to." She clucked, urging Gwawr to continue through the forest. "It will probably be a clue that I have a noble status if I'm to marry a duke."

"I can keep it a secret."

With no actual progress made in their search, Elvina and Trevor were back at the stable. Dismounting from their horses, they made their way back to the castle.

"Thank you," she said.

He looked over at her. "Thank me later, after we find 'em."

She half-smiled. "Until then, I suppose."

The duo walked the halls, searching for the others. The castle seemed barren, with no one in sight.

"I'm surprised we haven't run into 'em yet," Trevor admitted. "Maybe they're still in the ballroom."

"Even with how long we were gone?" Elvina questioned.

He shrugged with uncertainty. "No idea." He looked at her. "Hey, what do you—"

"There you are!" Rory called from down the hallway they were passing in front of.

Elvina and Trevor stopped to face him.

"Where'd you two disappear to?" Rory asked as he walked

up to them. "You were with us, and then gone the next second."

"I wanted to search for my friends on horseback," Elvina responded. "I asked Trevor to accompany me."

"Any luck?"

Trevor shook his head. "Not this time."

Rory smiled, trying to be optimistic. "Better luck next time, for sure."

Elvina nodded in agreement.

"Now that you're back, you can have some fun with the ball preparations," Rory informed them. "We're 'bout to get into taste testin' desserts."

Elvina perked up. She loved sweets. "Really?"

"I don't think you need to say anymore to her," Trevor chuckled.

"Come on, then."

"Has Owen accomplished much?" Elvina asked as they walked along.

"He's done a great job, he has," Rory answered. "He's tackled nearly everything that's been thrown at him."

"That's good to hear," Trevor commented.

"Although, he was worried when he noticed Elvina was missin'," he added. "He seemed better when Urian told him Trevor was probably with her."

"That's exactly what happened," Trevor confirmed.

"But he still worried."

"Of course, he would," Elvina said.

The three entered the dining area, where Owen and Urian were already seated at the table.

"Guess who!" Rory proclaimed.

Owen looked over his shoulder and his eyes landed on Elvina. He scooted his chair back and stood, stepping around it to face her. Urian stood as well to follow suit.

Elvina walked faster than Trevor and Rory. "I didn't mean to worry you earlier."

"It was like you disappeared into thin air," Owen told her.

"I wanted to take some time to look for my friends, so we took the horses. Trevor was with me, so I wasn't alone."

"How'd the ride go?"

"No luck."

He frowned. "I'm sorry to hear that."

"We'll keep tryin'." Trevor walked over to the other side of the table.

"Tomorrow's another day," Rory agreed.

Everyone sat down. Rory, Owen, and Elvina were on one side, while Urian and Trevor were on the other. Castle attendants brought out trays of desserts. Everything looked delectable.

From Elvina's right side, an attendant approached to set down a tray. Nye crossed his path at the wrong moment and tripped him up. "Oi!"

Before Elvina could look, something made contact with the side of her head. As big as a pie, the custard-type tart splattered in her hair. She sat rigid in place.

"Elvi!" Owen gasped.

The dessert went down with gravity and smeared along her shoulder, then proceeded to fall to the floor. She slowly stood, too embarrassed to speak.

The attendant was absolutely mortified. "I–I'm terribly s– sorry, m'lady," he stammered. "The cat—"

Owen took control of the situation by grabbing a cloth napkin and cleaning the side of her face. "Have somebody draw a bath in her bedchamber," he ordered.

Trevor left his seat. "On it."

Owen tried to make light of the situation. "I guess you're now the sweetest thing here."

It got a laugh out of Elvina.

CHAPTER TEN

The hot soak did wonders. Elvina sank a little deeper under the water, sighing with contentment. Her body may still be bruised, but this was the best she had felt since she first received her injuries. She looked at the worst of it on her left shoulder. The bruise was varying shades of blues, purples, and some reds. The scrapes were still scabbing over, and some of her other minor bruises looked better than before in her opinion.

Holding her breath, she submerged herself completely underneath the hot water yet again. She remained like this for a moment, allowing her head to clear of all thoughts. She felt at ease.

Owen's grinning face popped up in her mind.

Rather quickly, she surfaced and inhaled, wiping water away from her eyes. Her heart beat a little faster from before. She quickly glanced over at the door, knowing she was all alone, but he was somewhere in the castle waiting for her.

She lightly slapped both of her cheeks, ridding her mind of certain images. She couldn't allow herself to think like that.

Finally, she busied herself by cleaning her body off with soap, filling the tub with suds. This was the first time she had done something like this on her own before. Normally, her lady-in-waiting was the one to assist her with the bathing process. Millicent had never minded because it gave the girls time to chat without anyone else around.

When she finished, she truly did feel much better. She rose from the tub and grabbed the nearby clean towel as she stepped out. Drying herself off, she wrapped it around her body, attempting to cover herself the best she could. Needless to say, she was perplexed when she couldn't find her undergarments where she had left them.

Reality struck. The castle attendant had taken everything away! Panic settled over her. Maybe fresh clothes awaited her on the bed. She left the bathroom and discovered nothing.

"What am I to do?" she asked herself.

She looked around the room. There was a wardrobe she had yet to investigate since she arrived. Sadly, it was empty upon inspection.

Her head swiveled around when the door opened. Much to her surprise, Owen entered with a tray of sampling desserts in hand. His demeanor changed in an instant when he saw Elvina in nothing but a towel. Frozen in place, he openly stared.

Her grip on her towel tightened as her breath hitched. "G–Get out!" she sputtered.

He clamped his eyes shut. "Sorry!" He was quick to retreat and shut the door.

Thanks to quick her thinking, she realized she could use his help. "Owen?" she called out.

"Yeah?"

"I need clothes."

"Uh, clothes. Right. Lemme go grab somethin' for you."

Waiting felt like an eternity. She tried not to think about the awkward interaction they had. She could never live the moment down.

Eventually, the door cracked open and a hand slipped through, tossing a bundle of black cloths inside. Once the hand disappeared, the door shut. "Take your time!" Owen shouted from the other side.

Walking over, Elvina bent to pick up the article of clothing with one hand and allowed it to unfold. It was a plain black tunic with three grommets for string below the collar and long sleeves. It was something she had never worn before. "Huh."

She held it up to her nose and inhaled deeply, finding it smelled like Owen. She held it back and looked at it again. It looked like something he would wear, and she blushed at the thought of wearing a man's shirt, especially if that man was a certain one with dark locks and brown eyes.

She would feel so indecent only wearing a tunic without the support and coverage of her undergarments. Cringing at reality, she let the towel fall to the floor and slipped into the tunic. The sleeves easily went past her fingertips, while the hem fell just past her knees. She felt rather tiny, even though she wore chemises to bed. Perhaps she could borrow a bodice or something if someone had a spare one that fit her.

She grabbed the towel and dried her long hair. Stepping over to the door, she opened it with one hand.

Owen sat on the floor with the tray on his lap, back against the wall. Pink tinted his cheeks as he stood. "I only meant to bring you these. You know, since you missed out earlier. I was gonna leave it on the bed for you."

She smiled at his thoughtfulness. "Thank you."

"Don't tell Garrick. He'll kill me. Or Whitley. Or anybody."

"It'll stay between us, then," she promised, opening the door wider for him.

He followed her into the bedchamber, with the door remaining open. "What should I do with this?" she asked, holding the towel away from her head.

"Leave it on the floor by the door."

She half-turned and tossed it away. After moving her hair to the front, she crossed her arms under her chest for support. Her mind went blank after she looked at Owen. There was no one in the room to chaperone. "Shouldn't Trevor be with us?" she blurted. "Or even Urian?"

"Eh, so what?" Just like a mythical dragon hoarding a princess, he wanted her all to himself. "Besides, it shouldn't be too bad with just the two of us."

She noticed he wasn't walking toward the seating area. "Where are you going?" she questioned.

"The bed."

She gasped. "We can't eat on the bed!"

He stopped and faced her. "Why not? I've done it before."

"I will eat in here with you alone if we eat"—she pointed with a finger at the seating area off to the side—"over there."

He groaned dramatically. "Fiiine."

"By the way, is there a way I can possibly get my hands on a bodice?" she inquired.

"A bod...What?"

Now it was her turn to groan as she sat down on a sofa. "I can't wear just this tunic."

"You look fine in it." He sat down on her left side, their legs touching one another. Of course, she looked more than fine in it. It was his tunic, after all.

"That's beside the point."

"I s'pose you could use more clothes..." He perked up with an idea. "I'll take you to where your dress came from.

You can get whatcha need there. Uh, that is, if you're up for it after eatin'."

She smiled. "I would appreciate that."

Elvina now wore a borrowed, sleeveless brown bodice that was laced up in the front for the time being. She waited with Urian and Rory for two certain individuals. "I still can't believe you three are making Owen wear a disguise just so he can go out into the city."

"It's for his own good," Urian replied.

Rory pushed his glasses up the bridge of his nose. "Besides, it makes walkin' around much easier. We're still alert when we're with him, but we can relax a little bit because he's less recognizable."

"And when dealing with Owen, I can imagine that it's always nice to catch a break," Elvina playfully jested.

"Oi, I heard that!" a familiar voice called out.

She turned, eyes skipping over Trevor to find Owen in something she wasn't expecting. He wore the uniform of a castle guard, complete with a black hat that had a floppy brim. She laughed. "That's an excellent look for you."

"It's not uncommon for guards to patrol the city," Trevor explained. "Some are stationed in certain places."

"We'll be fine," Owen assured her.

"If you say so."

As they ventured away from the castle, Elvina took everything in as she and the others walked toward their destination. The castle sat higher than the metropolis city below, with stone streets winding through the districts. Tiramôr used to supply Grenester with salt, dyes, and sea life goods.

Upon closer inspection, it was clear the city was preparing for something. Shops looked most festive, while some owners set up tables outside. People were busy tending to tasks as they rushed about.

"What are they readying for?" Elvina inquired.

"It's just a festival the capital city holds every spring," Rory explained from the front, looking back over his shoulder when he spoke to her. "People of Tiramôr come from all over."

Something clicked in place for her. "Is that why there will be a ball as well?"

From her left side, Owen nodded. "It's also an excuse for my tad to see mukkas of his. He likes havin' guests in the castle."

"And it's a way for Freckles' tad to try and set him up with a bride," Urian added as he led the group.

Trevor chuckled. "Obviously hasn't happened yet."

"What was that, Walla?" Owen demanded, peering past Elvina since she was between them.

"He'll find her someday," Elvina said in his defense.

"Yeah, what she said," he agreed.

Trevor, ever so slyly, nudged her with an elbow, unbeknownst to the others. She merely nudged back without being caught by anyone.

"There it is," Urian announced.

It was easy to spot due to the dresses displayed in the windows. The wooden sign had flowing black script writing that simply read "Donnelly" hanging on the front of the structure.

"The Donnelly sisters own the place," Owen explained, having noticed that she had spotted the sign. "They're both pretty friendly and great people to know. I'd go with Mam when she wanted company while shoppin'."

Rory opened the doors and a little bell chimed, letting their presence be known. "Guess who!" he called out.

The rest of the group made their way inside, Trevor bringing up the rear.

Two new faces stepped into view, and Elvina looked them over.

The taller of the two maidens had strawberry blonde hair that parted down the middle of her head and reached her waist, with half the wavy locks done up in braids. Her dark blue eyes were simply full of life and joy. From what skin was visible, she was practically covered in freckles from head to toe. She wore a cream chemise and a green overdress.

The other one had much shorter locks in the same color that came just past her shoulders. Bangs helped frame her eyes that were a lighter shade of blue compared to her sister's. Much like her sibling, she was covered in freckles, and her white chemise was paired with a detailed blue overdress.

Unless someone corrected Elvina, she believed they were twins.

"Oh, what brings you here, Prince Owen?" the one with longer hair inquired.

He merely grabbed Elvina's hand and gently pulled her forward. "Elvi, meet"—he pointed at the taller one—"Melva, and"—he pointed at the other one—"Nola."

"If you don't mind me askin', what are you wearin'?" Nola asked.

"This is exactly why we are here," Elvina sheepishly admitted.

"Ooh, I like your accent!" Nola commented.

"It's quite pretty," Melva agreed.

"Thank you." Elvina was unsure of what else to say since she had never been complimented but for once about her accent before.

Melva looked at the guards. "Since you guys are by the

door, can one of you turn the sign to read closed, please? We have some work to do."

"I'm trustin' you to take care of her," Owen told them. "She needs some more things to wear since one dress ain't cuttin' it."

"Leave it to us," the sisters said in unison.

With help, Elvina saw all the different options she had. She stuck with styles that were much simpler than what she had grown accustomed to. With everything she tried, people rated what they thought. Of course, Owen always gave her high scores.

Now, with proper undergarments underneath, Elvina wore a dress that laced in front of her chest. It had a rounded neckline and flowing bell sleeves. A band around her waist gave her figure definition. The skirt skimmed the ground, just hiding her boots. Best of all, it was a lovely shade of purple—her favorite color.

She pulled the curtain aside and stepped out of the small changing room, twirling around to show off the dress for the others. "I really like this one!"

Owen glanced away from Nola, momentarily forgetting their conversation. He looked her over, a smile already on his face. "I think that's my favorite one!"

"Elvina, you look quite ravishin'," Rory complimented with a wink. "As always."

Urian nodded. "Not bad, Chipmunk."

She looked back at Melva. "I think I will make this the last one." After all, this would be her third outfit of the day. Owen insisted that she get at least three, so she had met the minimum requirement.

Clasping her hands together, Melva beamed. "I hope you had fun shoppin'."

Elvina eagerly nodded. "The most fun I've had in ages."

Melva walked over to the counter where the other picks

were so she could pack them up, along with what Elvina had worn into the shop. "You better come to us for your weddin' dress, Elvina," she said warmly.

She smiled. "I will look into that when the time comes."

"When's the weddin'?" Nola inquired, looking at Elvina and Owen.

"I'm surprised there hasn't been an announcement yet," Melva commented.

"W–Weddin'?" Owen stammered.

Elvina made eye contact with him and quickly looked away. She was positive her cheeks were pink as she stood there, wringing her hands together.

"Not again," Trevor groaned, holding a hand to his face.

"They're not a thing, actually," Urian clarified, much to the disappointment of the sisters.

"She should be betrothed to me," Rory said.

Owen shot him a look. "As if!"

It dawned on Elvina that she wasn't in her kingdom. The shop owners of Arnembury knew who she was and expected payment later. "I just realized that I have no means of payment," she said rather lamely.

"Did you really think I'd suggest shoppin' and not pay for you?" Owen asked, tilting his head to the side.

"Yes," she quietly admitted.

He walked over and looked slightly down at her due to their height difference. He had a good amount of inches over her. "You're my guest while you're here in Tiramôr. I'm gonna take care of you, Elvi."

She smiled at his words.

"I had no clue you were such a poet, Freckles," Urian jested.

He turned to look at the guard with an impish grin. "Thanks for offerin' to carry Elvi's things."

"Wait, what?"

"Oi. Did you have anythin' else that needed to be done since we're in the city?" Trevor asked.

"Nope," Owen replied. "We can go home now."

After saying their goodbyes, the five left the shop and headed back to the castle. Trevor and Rory were in the lead, leaving some space behind them for Elvina and Owen, with Urian bringing up the rear.

"Did you have fun?" Owen asked.

She nodded. "I enjoyed myself immensely."

"Good!"

"Thank you."

He smiled. "Seein' you happy makes me happy."

She knew the feeling.

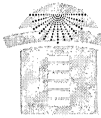

CHAPTER ELEVEN

Back at the castle, the four guys were all surprised by what Elvina had just said.

"Chipmunk, whaddya mean you've never been to the beach before?" Urian questioned.

"If you look at a map of Grenester, you'll notice it's surrounded by the three other kingdoms on this continent," Elvina commented. "There are other forms of water, but no oceans."

"Haven't you traveled outside of the kingdom before?" Rory asked.

She shook her head. "Never. Well, not until now, I suppose."

Owen's eyes lit up, and he looked at his friends. "We hafta take her."

"I don't know 'bout swimmin', but we can still go to look," Trevor remarked.

Elvina felt excitement grow inside of her.

From sitting at his spot in the lounging room, Owen jumped to his feet. "Let's go!"

"When?" Elvina asked.

Owen smiled at her. "Now!"

☙——❧

Elvina's eyes were wide as she took in the sight as they approached. She and Owen were in the lead, while the guards brought up the rear. The beach was much more than she ever imagined.

The water sparkled underneath the sunshine, light reflecting everywhere. Gentle waves rolled onto something that was tan in color, being darker when wet. That area was between the water and wild grass.

"What is that?" she asked, looking at what was unfamiliar to her.

"What's what?"

"Between the grass and water. What is that stuff?" She pointed.

"Are you talkin' 'bout the sand?"

"That's what it looks like…"

"You're actin' like you've never seen it before," he chuckled.

"Never."

He fell quiet for a moment, taking in her expression. "Just wait until you stand on it."

She finally tore her gaze away from the beach to look at him. "Is it that much different than grass and dirt?"

"Wait and see…" he said in a teasing voice.

Right before they stepped onto the sand, he held out his arm to stop her in her tracks. "Take off your boots," he instructed.

The absurd request left her confused. "Why?"

"Dontcha wanna feel the sand between your toes?"

"I can do that?" she asked in awe.

He smiled. "Of course." He bent down on his knees and started unlacing her boots.

"I'm more than capable of doing that myself," she huffed. She had grown accustomed to someone else, typically Millicent, helping her dress and undress, that it seemed natural. But a prince from another kingdom taking off her boots was utterly bizarre.

He tucked her socks into her boots before he took off his own. He moved backward, stepping down from the grass and onto the sand. He looked up at Elvina and held out a hand for her if she wanted help. "C'mon." It was clear to see that he was eager and excited to see her reaction.

Holding her breath without realizing it, she took his hand as she lowered her foot onto the sand. looking down to watch her foot make contact. The feel of it was much different than anything else she had felt before. It was soft, dry, and somewhat warm all at the same time. She could relate the texture to crushed sugar cubes, though it wasn't nearly the same.

She lowered her other foot, so now both were on the sand. She wiggled her toes around, feeling the grains between them, engulfing her feet the more she moved. With a big grin on her face, she finally looked up at Owen. "This is wonderful!"

He laughed. "Good."

"Is it like this all of the time?"

"Not when it's wet." He led them to the waves, not going too fast because of Elvina.

The sand was much different to walk on, but it was easy enough to manage. She absentmindedly forgot that she didn't need to hold Owen's hand anymore. The new sensation enthralled her.

Along the way, she inhaled deeply. The air here was something that she had never smelled before.

"That's the salt you smell," Owen said. "Brine."

"Brine?" she mused. "Is that so?"

"Helidinas. Brine City, or the City of Brine. It has its name 'cause of the smell of the sea."

She nodded. "That does make sense. Very literal that way."

She mentally braced herself before she stepped onto the wet sand. Apart from it being darker when wet, the sand was mushier and clumped together. It was also colder.

"I like it better when it's dry," she commented, trying not to make a face.

"I think it's best when you're in the water," Owen said.

"In it?"

"Swimmin' is a lotta fun, but it's also great just to stand in the water."

"Can we do that?"

He laughed. "We can do whatever you want, Elvi."

Using her free hand, she gathered the skirt of her dress so it wouldn't get wet. While she did that, Owen rolled up his pant legs. Once they were both set, she was the one who led the way closer to the water.

The little waves splashed against her ankles before riding up to the beach. She gasped at the brisk, but refreshing feel. After more steps, the water was up to the duo's lower shins.

She squealed with happiness. "This is wonderful!"

"I like comin' out here," he told her. "Even better when the sun's settin'."

"A sunset is just a sunset."

He smiled at her. "Not until you've seen it the way I have."

"Perhaps I will someday."

"I don't see why you can't later today."

"Do you mean that?"

"I've kept my promises so far, right?"

"That you have." She returned her gaze to the water.

Right now, it felt as though she and Owen were the only ones around. She glanced over her shoulder to find the guards, with their boots on, meandering their way to the water.

"Everythin' okay?" Owen asked.

"I was just wondering where they were," she replied, looking back around.

"They take their time, so I can have time alone. I guess for us to be alone this time."

The Thunder Squadron did the same for Elvina. "Alone, but not alone."

He nodded. "Pretty much."

Her eyes scanned the water again. The view was simply amazing. She couldn't get enough of it. "Where land and sea meet," she murmured, recalling what Owen had told her about Tiramôr.

He cracked a grin. "*Yn wir.*"

"An-weer?" she attempted to repeat. "What does that mean?"

"Truly."

"Then why do you not say that from the start?" She puffed out her cheeks. "You know I don't know your language."

"'Cause it's been fun teachin' you a little 'bout it," he admitted.

"Even though he's probably a terrible teacher," Urian teased, having overheard.

Owen whipped his head around since the guards were just out of reach from the waves. "Oi, what was that?"

"Elvina, how do you like it so far?" Rory inquired.

She looked back at him with a smile. "I love it. I wish there was something like this back in Grenester."

"Doesn't Grenester have a lotta trees and land?" Urian asked.

113

She nodded. "Some hills and valleys as well." After all, Grenester had its name due to all the green land in the kingdom. "There are some bodies of water, but nothing like this."

"It doesn't compare to you, Elvina," Rory said. "You're clearly the view wherever you go."

She playfully rolled her eyes at his flirtatious ways.

"Elvi didn't come here for you to fail at flirtin' with her, Flirtsalot." Having thought of something, Owen snickered. "Or should I say, Flirtsafail?"

Each of the guards had a different reaction. Trevor appeared to be unfazed, Rory looked taken aback, and Urian cracked up.

"That wasn't very nice," Elvina scolded, failing at hiding her smile with the back of a hand.

Owen pointed a finger at her. "You think it's funny!"

"When do you two think they'll stop holdin' hands?" Urian loudly stage whispered.

Both Elvina and Owen looked down at their hands that were still together. She quickly tore her hand away from his, feeling embarrassed.

"Looks like now," Trevor responded.

"Which means, Elvina can hold my hand," Rory said.

"No way," Owen immediately snapped.

Elvina ended up using her free hand to also hold the skirt of her dress. Now both were occupied, and no one could hold either one. That settled things.

Owen merely folded his arms across his chest to show his displeasure about the turn of events.

"How often do you swim here?" Elvina inquired, creating a topic to talk about.

"Whenever Freckles is up for it," Urian replied. "It's great durin' hot summer days."

"And it's a good exercise for us," Trevor added.

"Surely you have a good swimmin' spot back home," Owen said.

"The only swimming I've ever done has been inside a bathtub."

"Uh, I don't think that really counts as swimmin'," Rory commented.

Urian elbowed him. "That's the joke. Keep up!"

"You can't swim?" Trevor inquired, taking note. It was something that hadn't come up before.

Elvina shook her head. "Not at all."

"Wow, you're missing out!" Owen exclaimed.

"At least she's missin' out on the sunburns," Rory said, wincing at painful memories.

Urian slapped him on the back. "You just burn too easily."

Rory shot him a look, rolling out his shoulders. "I wonder why?"

"I bet that you all stay out here for hours," Elvina mused, imaging the fun they must have.

"We can't be out for too long," Trevor informed her. "Just a couple of hours or so. Freckles likes havin' some fun when he doesn't have his princely duties to worry about."

"And while he's havin' fun, we hafta keep him outta trouble," Urian grumbled. "We're like a group of babysitters for him."

"Just a group of babysitters..." Elvina gasped when a name came to her. "The Babysitter Brigade!"

"The what?" Trevor asked.

She laughed at the new name. "It's quite fitting." The Thunder Squadron had a name, so why couldn't the ones guarding Owen have one as well?

"If the lovely Elvina says it's fittin', then it's fittin'," Rory agreed.

Urian threw his head back laughing. "We'll be known as the Babysitter Brigade from now on."

"Don't I get a say in this?" Owen asked.

"You're not a member, so no," Urian teased.

"You're the reason we're a thing in the first place," Rory added.

"Oi!" Owen exclaimed.

"Do you think you can come up with a better name for us?" Trevor challenged.

Owen opened his mouth to speak, but nothing came out. He cleared his throat. "I mean, I dunno why it hasta be *that...*"

"Give it up," Urian said. "It's final."

"I'll accept it since Elvi came up with it." He shot her a glance and winked.

She smiled. "At least you have yielded."

That term only irked Owen. "What was that?" He took a step toward her. "Was that a challenge?"

Anticipating his actions, she stepped closer to the beach. "No," she responded, trying to hide her giddiness.

He saw right through her. "No?"

"No!" She quickly raised a foot to kick water at Owen and made her escape to the shore.

"Oi!" he laughed, going after her.

All that Elvina mentally told herself was that she needed to get out of the water. She would have a better chance when she was on proper land. However, mere steps out of the water and onto the sand, she was captured.

Owen's arms wrapped around her waist and she was lifted clear off her feet, her back against the front of his torso. "Do you yield?" he questioned, the smile evident in his voice, even though Elvina couldn't see it for herself.

"Never!" she laughed, releasing her hold on her dress and grabbing his arms with her hands. She wasn't strong enough to pry him away from her.

Moving to the dry area, Owen turned until they faced the

water and plopped down on the sandy ground. He spread his legs apart so she could sit between them, sand sticking to their damp legs. Keeping his arms around her, he leaned forward and rested his chin on her shoulder.

"Whaddya think 'bout the view?" he asked.

"It's spectacular."

It felt as though they were the only ones in the world, though she knew they weren't. She looked around and noticed that the Babysitter Brigade slowly moved away from them, walking along the beach. Trevor and Rory had their backs to Elvina and Owen, while Urian walked backward with ease. At least one of them needed to keep an eye on the duo and an eye out for possible danger.

"They won't go far," Owen assured her.

She focused on the moment she was having with him. She was truly enjoying herself and felt wonderful. "Thank you, Owen."

"For what?"

"Thank you for bringing me here."

He cracked a smile. "You're welcome, Elvi."

She appreciated this time with him, feeling as though they were a natural fit. Nobody could take away this moment from them.

"Hey, Elvi?" Owen questioned, breaking up her thoughts.

"Yes?"

"Excludin' the circumstances, I'm happy you're here."

She smiled. "As am I."

"I promise we'll come back here later so you can see the sunset."

"I'm already looking forward to it."

❧

Hours later, Elvina wore a simple blindfold to ensure she

RACHAEL ANNE

couldn't steal a peek. Trevor and Rory were in front of them with lanterns to light the way. Owen was on Elvina's left side, holding her hand to guide her along. Urian was last, holding another lantern and a bundle of blankets.

"How much longer?" Elvina inquired, anticipation rising within her. She was more than eager to see the sunset over the water.

"We're almost there," Owen assured her, giving her hand a little squeeze. "I promise."

When they came to the sand, Elvina had her boots and socks removed by Owen again. He carried them in his free hand.

Just by listening, she knew they were close to the water. She could hear the waves roll onto the shore.

"Okay, wait here, Elvi," Owen instructed, releasing her hand to walk away.

She stood in place, listening to the world around her. She heard a blanket unfurl and footsteps in the sand.

"We'll hang back there," Urian told her.

"We'll take all the lanterns, too," Trevor added.

"Better scenery that way," Rory assured.

Elvina heard someone approach her as three others moved away from behind her.

Owen took both of her hands and pulled her forward. "This way."

After a few steps, the sand beneath her feet was gone as she reached the blanket. "Sit down however you want," Owen instructed, helping her with the process. "I'm gonna take off the blindfold, but keep your eyes closed until I say when. Okay?"

She merely nodded, keeping her eyes shut once the fabric was removed.

He nestled beside her, wrapping a rather large blanket around the both of them to keep warm. It would be chillier before they both knew it since the sun was sinking in the sky. "And open up."

Her eyes opened before growing wide at the sight before her. It was beautiful and breathtaking. The sky was full of colors, like the trees during autumn. It was full of fiery reds, warm oranges, and golden yellows.

"Oh, wow…" she breathed in awe.

"Pretty lush, huh?"

She nodded, observing the gorgeous evening sky. She agreed that the scene was pretty amazing.

The two simply sat in silence before Elvina turned to face him. "Owen," she said.

"Yeah?"

"Thank you for sharing this with me."

He smiled. "You're welcome, Elvi."

CHAPTER TWELVE

Alone in her bedchamber, Elvina was ready for sleep after another eventful day. She was back in Owen's tunic, finding it more comfortable than the previous chemise she wore. She blew out the candles and crawled into bed. She pulled the blankets up around her and nestled down for the night, even though her mind raced. There still hadn't been any sign of the Thunder Squadron, which worried her. On the other hand, her letter should reach Millicent sometime tomorrow. That is, as long as the messenger hadn't encountered any issues along the three-day journey. Her days in Tiramôr would be limited once news of her whereabouts was known.

Knocking sounds interrupted her thoughts. She was surprised because it didn't come from the door to the bedchamber, but over by the double doors that led out to a balcony. When the knocking stopped, Elvina sat up. Was it even possible for someone to be on the other side of the doors?

More knocking ensued. She finally got out of bed once curiosity had gotten the better of her. She made her way over to the doors and opened one, astonished at who was on the other side.

"Owen?"

"Hey, Elvi," he greeted her with a grin as he stood outside under the night sky. He had yet to dress for bed.

"What are you doing?" she asked. "How did you even get here?"

He merely shrugged, feigning as though it was nothing. His brown eyes swept over the room from where he stood.

"Are you ensuring Urian isn't here?" she teased, thinking his actions were sweet. "Or perhaps Rory?"

Having been caught, he flinched. "No. Of course not."

She laughed and fully opened the door so he had a better view. "See? No visitors with me, except for you."

"You're my guest. I only wanted to check on you," he reasoned.

"Even though you walked me here not too long ago?"

"Hmm..." He nodded, taking her point. "And why're you wearin' my shirt?" The smile on his face showed he was pleased that she was in it again.

She briefly looked down at herself. "It's more comfortable than what I've been wearing. Besides, the chemise isn't in my possession as of now because it was taken for washing."

He didn't expect that kind of answer. "Oh."

She looked up at the sky and gasped. "Oh, wow!" It was too cloudy to see the stars last night, but now it was glistening with them. She brushed past Owen to walk out onto the balcony, ignoring the cold stone against her bare feet. "It's so pretty."

"I forgot how much you like the stars."

"I love them." She leaned against the railing using both hands. "I've always found them quite fascinating. I used to stargaze with my nannies when I was younger." Her smile faltered. "But one nanny thought I was too old for it and made sure I always went to bed before I could. It wasn't until years later that I started again." She left out the part that at least one member of the Thunder Squadron had accompanied her since that time, so she was never alone.

He stood on her left side and gingerly placed his hand over hers, giving it a little squeeze. "I'm no replacement to a nanny, but I'll stargaze with you."

"Thank you." She shivered. Perhaps she should have grabbed a blanket to swaddle herself in before she left the bed.

"I gotcha." He moved to stand directly behind her, the front of him pressed against her back. He even wrapped his arms around her waist to hold her close for good measure. "Stand on my boots."

"Your b–boots?" She was frazzled by his intimate actions, even though she was warmer.

"Your feet are probably freezin'. I don't mind if you stand on me."

She glanced down so she could see where his feet were before she did as she was told. "Before I learned how to dance, I used to do this with my father. It was fun back then."

"It can still be fun now."

Elvina thought back to the times she had danced with royals and suitors, some of which got a little too handsy to her liking. "I suppose dancing is fun."

"Turn around."

She stepped off his boots to face him, not even questioning his instruction.

"Hop back on."

She did.

Keeping his left arm in place, he used his right hand to take her left. With her on his boots, he started a slow dance.

She laughed as she slipped her right hand onto his shoulder. "I see what you mean now."

"Told you," he said with a grin.

They slowly spun in place, sometimes moving to and fro. The duo simply enjoyed one another's company without someone watching over them. Elvina felt bittersweet, torn between now and when this time would become a memory. She was happy it was happening, but at some point, she would leave. She couldn't stay in Tiramôr forever.

"What's wrong?" Owen inquired.

"There will come a time I'm to return home."

His face fell, but he continued dancing. "Why?"

She gave him an incredulous look. "Why?" she echoed. "Owen, I have my own kingdom, my own people."

"But what 'bout all the people you're leavin' behind here?"

"Perhaps I'll visit," she chuckled. "It will be a planned visit, though. Not one where you find me lost and disheveled in the forest."

"And no gettin' attacked by bandits again."

She laughed. "No more bandits."

"That'll be lush." A frown tugged at his lips. "Until that time comes, I'm sure Nye's gonna miss you."

"I'll miss him, too."

However, the two knew they weren't referring to the cat.

"Maybe I'll visit you in Arnembury someday soon," Owen surmised.

Her heart skipped. "Really?"

"I don't see why not. Although, I might hafta wear a disguise."

She chuckled at the idea. "I promise I won't give away your secret."

"We'll manage."

Questions were on the tip of her tongue. Did she want to risk ruining the moment by asking them? There was always tomorrow…

"You look zonked," he commented. "You should probably get inside to warm up."

"But I like spending time with you," she blurted.

He chuckled at her response. "There's always tomorrow."

"Tomorrow." That was her official deadline to bring up her two topics.

                              ☙━━━❧

Elvina had tossed and turned but still felt wide awake. Perhaps Trevor had been right during their ride earlier. The people who started the rumors paired her with the wrong prince. Right now, she wanted to break off her betrothment with Kennard because she believed someone else was a better match for her. She wanted to propose an idea to her father, Owen, and Mervin. All of it seemed rather ludicrous for her to do because of the first challenge. She would have to go against her father's wishes, and that task alone was a monumentous thing.

She finally roused herself out of bed and made her way over to the doors that led out to the balcony. She opened one of them and peeked outside, noticing no sign of Owen.

Sighing, she closed the door and paced around the room to exert energy. She finally stopped and glanced at the door that led out into the hallway. She tended to roam the halls of her home whenever she had trouble sleeping, and always felt better when she returned to her bedchamber, seeming able to fall asleep quickly.

She decided to leave the room and closed the door behind her. Her feet treaded quietly through the hallway. Only now did she realize that she should have brought along a candle to light her way. Torches along the walls were lit, but she would feel better with one of her own.

After inhaling and exhaling deeply, she felt better and

chuckled to herself at the very thought of how ridiculous she must look wandering the castle at this hour in her current attire.

"Who's there?" a voice demanded.

Elvina froze in her tracks.

Two guards with lanterns in hand rounded the corner and crossed her path, one being nearly a head taller than the other one.

"What're you doin'?" the shorter guard inquired.

She said the first thing that came to mind. "I wish to speak to Second Prince Owen."

The taller guard blinked in surprise. "Do you know what time it is?"

"I do."

"And you still want to see the prince?" he asked.

"I do."

The two guards exchanged a quick glance. "She *is* his guest," the taller guard reasoned.

"If we get in trouble for takin' her to him, I'm blamin' you," the other said.

They looked at her. "Come with us," the taller guard ordered.

Elvina followed after them through the different hallways until they came to a pair of doors.

"I'll go and check on Prince Owen to see if he'll have an audience with you." The taller guard disappeared into the bedchamber, closing the door behind him.

Silence fell over Elvina and the remaining guard until he broke it with a question. "Why do you want to speak with the prince?"

"I have my reasons," she replied.

His eyes swept over her body. "You know, if you're lonely tonight, I can keep you company..."

She refrained from rolling her eyes. "I have no interest in you," she deadpanned.

He looked taken aback. "What?"

"Are you possibly suggesting that we share a night together? Do you not think that's inappropriate? I'm a guest of Owen's."

"I know a thing or two compared to him—"

One of the doors was suddenly thrown open, and Owen, still wearing his clothes from earlier, stepped into the hallway. His eyes immediately landed on Elvina. "Everythin' okay?"

"Yes," she responded, lifting her eyebrows at the guard who offered the indecent proposal.

The taller guard left the bedchamber and bowed to Owen. "Is there anythin' else?"

"We'll be fine," he said. "Thanks for bringin' her to me."

"If you like, I can escort her back to—" the shorter guard began.

"Don't even think 'bout it," Owen practically growled.

He flinched and took a single step back.

Elvina could only assume his intensity came from having heard part of the conversation that happened moments ago.

With a gentle grip, Owen reached out and took hold of her hand. "Nobody disturbs us." With that, he led the way into his bedchamber and closed the door behind them.

Lit candles provided light in the room. It was another sign that he hadn't been sleeping.

"What's occurrin'?" he asked, checking her over with his eyes. "Are you sure you're okay?"

"I'm fine."

He seemed slightly confused. "Then why do you wanna talk to me now? I figured you'd be asleep."

"I couldn't sleep," she admitted.

"I couldn't either."

"Really? Why?"

"Too excited. Was thinkin' 'bout the future."

Thoughts of the future were the reason she was still awake as well. Her face fell, and it spoke volumes.

His expression softened and he squeezed her hand. "What's wrong?"

"May I ask you something?"

"Sure."

"And do let me know if I cross any line."

"Sure thing."

"Why did your father end the trading agreement with Grenester?" Her heart tightened. "And why did he never respond to any of the letters my father sent him?"

He tilted his head to the side. "Huh?"

"Honestly, it was rather abrupt, and no one foresaw it happening."

"My tad didn't end it, yours did," he said. "And your tad never responded to my tad's letters."

She was beyond confused. "What do you mean? Start from the beginning."

"In the fall, your tad sent somebody with a letter, a document to end the agreement. When he left to go back to Arnembury, my tad gave him a letter to give to your tad as a follow-up."

Her mind attempted to piece everything together. However, it felt as though a piece or two was missing. She was unable to see the whole picture. "But Father never sent a messenger."

"He did. And the guy was official, he was. From the royal court. I've seen him around your tad a bit before durin' visits. Mostly background stuff. Never did introduce himself to us."

A few faces came to mind. "Do you recall his name?"

He shook his head. "I've never gotten a name durin' our visits. When he was here, I briefly saw him havin' a goss with

Tad—" He stopped speaking and his face lit up. "I can sketch him!" He tugged her over to his bed. Releasing her, he leaned over the piece of furniture to grab his sketchbook and pencil. He moved down by the nightstand where a candle provided more than enough light and turned to a blank page, beginning his work.

As to not pressure him, she didn't hover. Instead, she glanced around the bedchamber. It was much more lavish and furnished than the room she was occupying.

There came a time curiosity got the best of her, and she stepped over to him. She froze up from head to toe when she caught a glimpse of the nearly completed sketch. Her eyes grew wide with surprise and a hand covered her gaping mouth.

Having noticed her reaction, he stopped to look up at her. "Elvi?"

She slowly lowered her hand. "Reeves."

He glanced down at the page. "Reeves?" He looked back at her. "Who's he?"

"The royal adviser to my father."

He whistled. "That's some messenger to send my tad with big news."

"But Father never sent him here to speak on his behalf," she reiterated. "And he never would have broken off the trade to begin with."

"Wait. This Reeves guy came here all on his own?"

With Owen watching her, Elvina paced the bedchamber and spoke out loud so she could string things together better. "Reeves had requested a week off so he could have time to himself, he said. He traveled here to speak with Mervin without my father's knowledge. For whatever reason, he sabotaged the trade agreement between the two kingdoms. When Reeves returned to Arnembury, he just so happened to have a letter from your father. He claimed that he ran into a messenger from Mervin on his way back, which was obviously a lie."

"Do you think that's what really happened?" he inquired after a moment, setting aside his things.

She stopped pacing and looked at him. "I'm positive."

"Okay, but what 'bout the letters? You said your tad sent some to mine. He never got any of 'em."

Something clicked for her. "Whenever Father finishes writing letters, he always gives them to Reeves."

"He musta made sure my tad never got 'em," he concluded.

"You mentioned your father also sent letters," she prompted.

"He did. I only sent two, though. Tad sent more."

"Father never received any."

"I sent mine to you," he clarified.

"There was never anything," she dejectedly said. "Nothing."

He clenched his jaw. "Why would he do somethin' like that?"

"The letters!" she gasped. The two letters her father wrote regarding Owen being a suitor for Elvina probably never left the castle.

"I think we've established Reeves meddled with 'em."

Reeves broke apart two families and separated two kingdoms. Elvina was betrothed to someone who wasn't Owen. Saying he 'meddled' was putting things lightly.

Emotions got the best of her, and she began to sob.

Owen immediately stood and wrapped his arms around her. "No need to cry."

She only sobbed harder. "He ruined so much!"

"We'll fix everythin'."

She pulled her head back to look at him with a panicked expression. "What if it's too late?"

"It won't be. Have some faith, Elvi."

Eventually, he calmed her down as they sat on the edge of his bed.

"It makes no sense, though, to sabotage what our kingdoms had," she said. "I'm not sure how Tiramôr fared, but Grenester did suffer a little at the loss. We had to find another kingdom to do trade with."

"How's that worked out?"

"It was a struggle at first, but we're fine now." She pondered for a moment. "I can't make sense of the matter…"

"We'll tell Tad and Ceron when they're back. This is big news."

She nodded in agreement.

"Hey, Elvi?"

"Yes?"

"Did you come here to ask that question?"

"No."

"No?"

She fiddled with the hem of her tunic. "If I struggle to sleep, I tend to walk in my home. I felt embarrassed when those guards questioned why I was awake when normally no one does."

He cracked a smile. "You're so weird."

"I am not."

"Yeah, you are."

⊚────⊚

Drowsiness had finally claimed Elvina, even though Owen was faring well. Currently, the two stood by the doors that led out into the hallway.

"Are you sure you don't want me to walk you back?" he inquired a second time.

"I'll be fine," she assured him. "I know the way."

"It won't be any trouble at all."

"Perhaps another time."

He grinned. "You plan on more visits, do you?"

"Perhaps you will be the one visiting me," she mused in a teasing manner.

With that, he opened one of the doors for her and gestured with a bow.

"Why, thank you," she giggled, stepping out of his bedchamber.

He couldn't stop his growing smile. "Anythin' for you, Elvi."

"I bid you a good night, Owen."

"G'night, Elvi."

As she ventured a little farther away, she heard the door shut. A loud whoop sounded from Owen's bedchamber, and she merely giggled at his reaction, feeling as though a weight had been lifted from her shoulders.

CHAPTER THIRTEEN

The next morning, Elvina had trouble looking away from her reflection in the mirror. It was an odd sight to see with her own eyes. She had worn dresses her whole life, and now for the second time since yesterday, she wore something much different. Matching the color of her black boots, the tight trousers showed off the curves of her legs for all to see. She also had on a deep blue blouse with bands above her elbows to keep the sleeves against her arms before they flared out until they stopped at her wrists. The scoop neck highlighted some cleavage, and the band around her waist gave her more definition.

Her look was complete due to the hairstyle she had done herself. Her locks were pulled back into a single, simple braid. Millicent was the one who taught her how to braid and had even let Elvina practice on her. The two certainly had bonded during those moments.

"If only Grenester could see their princess now..." she quietly mused to her herself, turning to the other side. She stepped closer to inspect her face. Freckles created a trail from one cheek to the other over the bridge of her nose. They seemed more prominent than normal.

Ready to begin her day, she walked over to the door and opened it to leave.

Owen was on the other side, a loose fist raised to knock on the door. He stared at her before looking at his hand and hiding it behind his back. "Mornin'."

"Good morning."

He quickly looked her up and down. "I've never seen you not in a dress."

"I've never worn trousers before."

"That blue suits you." It just so happened that the fitted blue tunic he wore was practically the same color. "Very becomin'."

"Do you think so?"

He nodded. "Breakfast's almost ready, and I'm here to getcha."

She peered around. "No guards?"

"They're all downstairs."

Now she was perplexed. Trevor had been with Owen yesterday. Did something happen?

"Thank you for getting me." She stepped out into the hallway, closing the door behind her.

"I told you I would, didn't I?"

"You were true to your word indeed."

As they reached the end of the stairs, a familiar face passed by with a personal guard trailing behind him.

Prince Ceron was practically the same. He was still slightly taller than his younger sibling and carried himself with poise and strength. Dark brown hair went past the nape of his neck and parted down the middle. His brown eyes had a certain calmness to them, much like his demeanor. One significant difference about him was that he had some facial hair along his jaw.

He was caught off-guard by the sight of her. "Elvina?"

She gave Owen an accusing look. "You didn't tell him?"

"Oi, I didn't know he was home."

"I arrived moments ago," Ceron said, and addressed Elvina. "When did you arrive?"

"A few days—" she began.

"Can we have a goss in private?" Owen interrupted.

"Of course," Ceron replied.

The two brothers and Elvina were in front, while Ceron's personal guard kept behind them.

"Where's Tad?" Owen asked, so they didn't walk in complete silence.

"He'll probably be home tomorrow," Ceron answered. "He wanted to further discuss the plans with Gwendolyn's family. He had me go on ahead."

"The wedding will be here before you know it," Elvina commented.

Ceron arched an eyebrow. "You're aware of it?"

"Owen talked about it when Kynan and Siriol visited."

"Much happened while I was away."

They entered a secondary dining area that had more than enough room for the three of them. Ceron had his personal guard remain stationed in front of the door so they wouldn't be disturbed.

"Thanks for that," Owen said. "Only Walla and Pipsqueak know who she is."

"You've kept your identity a secret?" Ceron questioned.

"I didn't think it would have been wise to reveal it," Elvina concluded. "It could have spelled trouble."

"Originally," Owen corrected.

A confused look came across Ceron's face. "What?"

They jumped around with the timeline, from when she first arrived to the discovery made last night, but now Ceron knew what they knew.

"When Tad returns, we'll tell him everythin'," Ceron urged. "He needs to be notified immediately."

"Those are my thoughts exactly," Elvina agreed.

"In the meantime, if you want to keep your title a secret, then so be it. I'll instruct those who could recognize you to act as though they don't know you."

"Thank you."

"Do you think that's best?" Owen asked.

"Perhaps we should wait until an official announcement is out," Elvina reasoned.

"I agree with her."

Owen nodded. "We'll wait, then."

Ceron took a moment to observe how close Elvina and Owen stood next to each other. "Is there anythin' else I should know?"

"Hmm, can't think of anythin'," Owen responded.

Ceron looked at him. "I want to have a goss with Elvina. You can leave."

Now he was the one caught off guard. "What? Why?"

"Just a little goss between the two of us is all I want," was his simple reply.

"Can't she at least eat breakfast first?"

"No."

Owen strode past his sibling and bumped into his shoulder. "No funny business," he growled under his breath.

"She'll join you for breakfast afterward."

"I'll be waitin'," he stressed before shutting the door behind him.

Now alone, Ceron eyed Elvina.

"Is something the matter?"

"Do you know what this means?" He sounded rather excited.

"I don't believe I understand."

"You and Owen. It could happen! You can't deny how

fond he is of you. He's clearly attached, he is. You should have heard him go on and on about you since the agreement ended. He drove Tad and I mad some days."

Her heart squeezed.

"Since I got betrothed, Tad has gossed 'bout settin' Owen up with a bride."

A lump formed in her throat.

"When everythin' is cleared up with our tads, the two of you—"

"There's one problem with that," she interrupted.

"I don't see one."

"I'm betrothed to a duke from my kingdom. The Thunder Squadron and I were traveling to see him when the bandits attacked."

His face fell. "That wasn't mentioned earlier."

"Owen doesn't know, only Trevor does. It had slipped out on accident when it was the two of us," she sighed. "I've been meaning to tell Owen about it."

"Break off the betrothment. You and Owen are clearly better suited for one another."

She smiled, silently agreeing with him.

"Who's the duke?"

"Kennard Endicott."

His face twisted in displeasure. "No."

"Trevor had a similar reaction," she chuckled.

"You agreed to marry him?"

"Father arranged it. He's met with Kennard, but I haven't."

"Marry Owen instead," was his solution to the problem.

The three words were entirely bold. Elvina's heartbeat became erratic. Was it loud enough for Ceron to hear?

He walked away, turning his back to her. "Perhaps you can convince your tad there's a prince from another kingdom who wants to take your hand in marriage."

She was grateful he couldn't see her red face. Now alone

with the door shut, she started to pace around in an attempt to calm her nerves. So many thoughts raced around her head. Should she run and tell Owen she was betrothed? Did he necessarily have to know if she planned on telling her father to break it off?

She felt as though the walls were closing in around her, trying to suffocate her. She wanted out so she could breathe again. She raced to the door and threw it open. Not seeing anyone in the hallway as she looked around, she bolted.

She was thankful that the way outside of the city wasn't near the main dining hall. Elvina wasn't risking Owen or the others spotting her as she raced through the castle. None of the guards she passed seemed to question her actions because none stopped her. She was in the clear.

Once outside in Helidinas, she inhaled deeply. Unbeknownst to anyone, she was out and about all by herself. For the first time since she was alone in the forest, she was truly on her own. It hit her that she had freedom. No one here knew her identity, so she was safe. With no attention on her, she was free to move about and go wherever she chose. Best of all, no one could tell her what to do or not to do.

Her head clear, she looked around at the people who were still preparing for the upcoming festival. It was easy to tell progress had been made since yesterday, but there was still more to be done from the looks of things.

Something caught her attention. She thought she saw a familiar shade of unruly black hair from up ahead. Her heart skipped as she ran forward, boots pounding against the ground. "Vallerie!" she shouted, hoping her voice carried over the sounds around her.

Unfortunately, the person didn't stop.

"Vallerie!" Elvina weaved in and out of people, trying to reach the one she believed to be a member of the Thunder Squadron. She glanced around, seeing if another one of her friends was possibly around. "Vallerie!" She bumped into someone but kept going.

"Oi, you!" a male voice barked in annoyance. A hand grabbed a hold of her left shoulder, just below her injuries, and jerked her backward.

She struggled to break free, keeping her eyes on the person with dark hair. "Unhand me at once!"

A burly man with graying dark hair tied back in a messy ponytail forced her to face him. His green eyes burned with exasperation, glaring down at her. Vexation twisted his face into an ugly look. His beard was tangled and unkempt, only adding to his appearance. "Where do you think you're goin' in such a damn hurry?"

She nearly gaped in surprise at the ferocity of his words. Never had anyone used such a coarse tone with her. "Release me."

He merely laughed. "Now why would I do that? You ran into me and caused me to drop somethin' of mine."

She glanced down at the ground, noticing a brown sack. "I apologize for the accident. I meant no harm." She momentarily looked around for the person who might be Vallerie. "But now I must be on my way."

The merchant gave her a good squeeze. "As if!"

"Excuse me?"

"I'm Lloyd Maddox, and I'm your new master! Time to put you to work!"

She was stunned. "Wh–What?"

"You've set me behind, so you're gonna be the one to fix that."

By now, people had stopped what they were doing to watch the scene take place. No one dared to step forward and stop Lloyd.

"I'll do no such thing," Elvina snarled.

His grip tightened and he jerked her around like a dog with a bone. "Pick up the sack and get to work!"

Losing her patience, she kicked him right between his legs as hard as she could.

"Why you—!" he shouted, tossing her aside to grab hold of his injury.

She landed against the stone ground and skidded to a stop. The back of her right hand stung from where it made contact with the stone, so she used her other hand to push herself up, evaluating her situation.

Lloyd sauntered over, smirking down at her. "Are you gonna get to work or—"

She swung out one of her legs, knocking his feet out from under him and sending him to the ground. She quickly stood, backing away to put distance between them while looking around, no longer able to see the person she thought might be Vallerie. Her heart sank.

With a shout, Lloyd rushed to charge her.

She avoided his punch when he took a swing at her. Knowing she didn't stand a chance against his brute force, she would only get away if she could outsmart him somehow.

Elvina looked past Lloyd with a big smile. "Prince Owen!"

Lloyd turned around but didn't see Owen anywhere in sight. "Huh?"

Before he could notice, she had already begun running in the opposite direction. Perhaps she would have speed on her side.

"Oi, get back here!" Lloyd gave chase, determined not to let her go. He needed extra help because no one wanted to work for him. Having a beautiful worker with an accent would certainly bring attention and get him more customers.

Thoughts raced through her mind. Elvina didn't know this city nearly as well as Lloyd, giving him the advantage.

Maybe she could lose him somehow, or find help before he caught her. Even though she was being chased, she was on the lookout for the person with the unruly hair.

Elvina made a sharp left and avoided a cart full of goods a woman was pushing around. Finding her footing, she kept going. Perhaps luck was on her side, and she would come across some guards Trevor mentioned that were stationed in the city.

"Thief!" Lloyd shouted. "Somebody stop that thief!"

He spouted nothing but lies, but only those who witnessed what happened knew that. If someone believed what he said, she might end up in more trouble than she thought. However, no one aided Lloyd or did anything to stop her. Maybe he had a reputation, and people decided not to believe his nonsense.

Trouble popped up when a group of playing children scampered across Elvina's path. To avoid a collision, she veered right and sprinted down a path between two buildings. She followed it, making a left and skidding to a stop. Much to her horror, it was a dead end.

She needed to backtrack before Lloyd caught up to her. As she turned around, she heard his running footsteps getting closer and she looked around. Surely there must be something she could use to fend him off. Hiding was pointless due to what was around her. She ended up with a broken broom that was missing its head when Lloyd rounded the corner.

He slowed his pace now that he saw she was trapped. A wicked grin formed on his face.

"Leave me alone or you'll regret it!" she warned.

He merely cackled, eyeing her weapon of choice. "Do you really believe you can win with that?"

She didn't budge, remaining firm where she stood.

He pulled out a long dagger that she didn't notice earlier. "I'm gonna teach you a lesson 'cause you misbehaved."

"This is your last chance!" she shouted, even though she had lost hope that he would walk away.

He slowly advanced toward her, twirling his long dagger around. "Time for your lesson."

She thought of different options. If she could somehow manage to get past him, she could run and escape this alleyway. If—

With a shout, Lloyd swung his weapon.

She held both ends of the wooden staff and watched as it was sliced in half with ease. She stumbled back and looked at the two pieces, realizing she had never been much of a dual wielder. They were much lighter than what she had used in the past to spar with.

"You're done for!" he snarled.

She thrust out her left arm, only to have the wood meet his torso. She swung her right arm and whacked him upside the head.

He shouted in pain and glared. "Damn you!"

She sidestepped the path of his weapon and struck again, but missed her target. He swung his dagger at her and knocked away the wooden piece in her left hand. It clattered to the ground, rolling away and out of reach.

It was time to put her first plan into action. She feigned to her left as if to strike with the remaining piece of the broken broom, but spun around the other way. She ducked to avoid his free hand and ran.

He caught hold of her braid and yanked her back. Seeing stars for a brief moment, she screamed and stumbled around as she clutched her hair. She tried pulling free, but it was no use. He tugged her around, kicking away the weapon from her hand. Grabbing her arm, he threw her up against the wall with force.

Her back smacked into it, causing her to gasp for air.

"Hmm, what should I start with first?" he mused, a mischievous smile on his lips.

A figure jumped down from above and landed nearby. Owen rose to his feet, sword drawn and aimed at Lloyd's chest. His gaze was intense and menacing, with no trace of mercy.

CHAPTER FOURTEEN

Dropping his long dagger with a gasp, Lloyd's face turned ashen. "P-Prince Owen!"

Trevor jumped down and landed with ease before straightening his legs. "Lloyd Maddox, you're under arrest."

"Under arrest?" he gaped. "Me? Under arrest? But why?" He pointed an accusing finger at Elvina. "This no good bitc—"

In the blink of an eye, Owen formed a fist with his free hand and punched Lloyd directly in the face.

Elvina was surprised but remained speechless as she watched the scene before her.

Lloyd fell to his knees while clutching his face. Blood seeped through his fingers. "My nose!" he wailed. "My nose!"

Running footsteps came from the entrance of the alleyway. Rory and Urian rounded the corner and observed what was happening.

"Dammit. Chipmunk looks hurt," Urian cursed.

Right now, Elvina was shaken up more than anything else and was frozen in place. Attempts had been made on her life before, but this wasn't the first time she had been threatened and attacked either.

"Guys, take him away," Trevor ordered.

"You got it," Rory growled.

The two got to work and grabbed Lloyd, being much rougher than necessary. They practically had to drag him away since he was still whining about his nose.

Owen dropped his sword and stepped toward Elvina. "Elvi," he whispered, and gingerly held her head in both of his hands. "Are you—"

She came undone from the shock and burst into tears. Her legs started trembling, threatening to give out.

Owen pulled her into a tight embrace, ensuring she was safe with him.

Burying her face into his chest, she continued to sob, clutching onto the back of his tunic with both hands. Pain stung her right hand, so she released him and held it away from his body so it only touched air.

"I'm sorry I didn't get here faster."

It was her fault. She shouldn't have left the castle by herself. She should have had someone accompany her.

"Elvina, your hand," Trevor scowled, noticing her injury.

"What's wrong?" Owen asked with worry. He didn't dare break their embrace to check on her, though.

"Scrammed," Trevor replied. "Doesn't look too serious, but it probably hurts."

With ease, Owen picked her up and held her princess style. "I'm takin' you to the castle to have Del check you over."

With closed eyes, Elvina focused on the sound of his heartbeat to calm herself down, taking shaky, deep breaths.

"That's it, Elvi," Owen encouraged. "Nice and easy. You're safe now. I've got you."

Trevor picked up the sword from the ground and carried it as he followed after Elvina and Owen.

After visiting Delyth, Owen carried Elvina and set her down on the edge of his bed so she sat upright. "Gimme a sec, okay?" He crouched down and began the task of removing her boots to make her comfortable.

She didn't resist in the slightest.

Trevor locked the door, a sign no one should disturb them. Urian and Rory had been dismissed for the moment, so Elvina didn't feel crowded. He took a seat in the lounging area, being quiet and keeping to himself.

Owen cast the boots aside and looked up at her tearstained face. "Walla and I will be here to watch over you nap, okay?"

"Stay." It was the first time she had spoken since they found her in the alleyway.

Unable to refuse her request, he kicked off his boots and hopped into bed. He ended up lying down on his back with his head resting on one of the many pillows.

Elvina crawled over to him and practically collapsed onto his torso. She shamelessly snuggled up to him and closed her eyes.

"I gotcha, Elvi," he softly said, wrapping his arms securely around her. He moved her so she was on his right side, tucked against his body.

He was warm—oh so warm. And comfortable. His scent was all around her because she was lying in his bed with him.

Without a word, Trevor walked over and laid a blanket on them.

She managed to mumble an incoherent "thank you" to him.

"You're welcome," Trevor replied before sitting back down.

"Get some rest, Elvi," Owen encouraged.

Her relaxed body felt so heavy, she didn't think she could budge an inch if she tried. She simply focused on the person next to her while she drifted off to sleep. She knew she was safe with him around.

❧

Elvina's eyes flickered open, recalling the horrible nightmare she'd had. Some man attacked her, but Owen had saved her. Coming to her senses more, she discovered that she was lying on her back while Owen was on his side, facing her. His right arm was tucked under his head, while his other hand snaked around her waist to keep her close. He snored quietly, his mouth slightly parted open, but no trace of drool.

A small smile formed on her face. This was a sight that she could easily adjust to seeing more often. Not realizing her actions, she absentmindedly raised her hand to touch his face but froze when she saw white. Her hand was bandaged. What she'd dreamt about hadn't been a nightmare. She snapped back to reality. She was in a man's bed with him. A man that she wasn't betrothed to. It was definitely time to wake him.

She prodded his cheek with a finger until he stirred.

He blearily blinked at her. "Love you," he managed to mumble.

She was utterly speechless. Love?

He pulled her closer to him, placing a somewhat sloppy kiss on the side of her cheek rather than his intended target: her lips. "Love you so much." He dipped his head down and tucked it under her chin, his left hand coming up to cup one of her breasts.

146

Her entire body was stiff with shock until she regained her senses and shouted his name while shoving him off of her.

Trevor was already on his feet, hand on the hilt of the sword at his waist. His eyes swept the room, looking for danger. He might have been napping as well, but he was alert.

"Wha's occurrin'?" Owen asked huskily, rubbing at his eyes. He looked over at her from the edge of the bed he happened not to fall over. "You 'kay?"

Elvina sat up, arms covering her chest as she glared at him. "Y–You touched me!"

Trevor made the connection to what had happened. "You're on your own." With that, he rushed over to the doors, unlocked them, and slipped outside into the hall.

Owen glanced away from the recently closed door to look at the clearly frazzled maiden sharing his bed. "What?" He reached his hand out for her, but she was quick to slap it away, leaving one arm to guard her upper torso.

Hurt flashed in his eyes, oblivious to the stinging sensation of his hand. Without a word, he dragged his arm back to rest in his lap.

She instantly regretted her actions and averted her gaze. "I apologize for what I just did to you. You did something in your sleep and surprised me is all."

He ran a hand through his hair. "I move in my sleep. I'm sorry for what I did. I'm also sorry if I said anythin'."

A blush tinted her cheeks as she recalled his words. "Oh." She took a shaky breath to calm herself. "I never did thank you properly for saving me earlier, so thank you."

"You got into somethin' pretty gompin'. Nobody likes Lloyd. He's got quite the temper."

She nodded, agreeing it was pretty nasty.

He tilted his head to the side. "What were you doin' out in the city anyway?"

"I wanted to clear my head," she replied.

"What did Ceron say to you?" He sounded more protective than worried.

"I can assure you, it was nothing."

He eyed her carefully with a dubious look. "You left without tellin' anybody."

"If there was an issue, you would have been the first person I told."

He seemed slightly smug at her response before his face lit up. "Hey, do you wanna go ridin'?"

The two royals led the way, their horses going at a cantering pace. Trevor and Rory were behind them. Elvina was still in the dark about the basket with Trevor. Owen had sworn the others to silence, but she doubted either of the two would tell her regardless.

"You still have yet to tell me where we're going and what we're doing," Elvina said.

Owen laughed. "I can't spoil the surprise. You gotta wait."

She huffed, unsure of how long it would be until she finally burst from curiosity.

It was a beautiful day to be out riding at least, with clouds offering some shade. The land of Tiramôr was simply beautiful from what she had seen.

The horses slowed to a walk as they made their way through the forest, Cari leading the group. Elvina was unfamiliar with this part since she and Trevor had taken another route.

"Are we just riding around aimlessly?" she questioned.

"Nope." He glanced back at her. "The spot's comin' up."

Sure enough, the place was lovely. The little clearing had coverage from trees and a nearby creek. Everything was lush and green. Pops of color came from wildflowers. Sunlight peeked through the leaves, adding to the scenery.

Owen was more than happy with her reaction. When he joined her on the ground, he took Gwawr's reins and tied her and Cari together. While they grazed, the two guards rode up on their horses.

Elvina finally looked away to glance at Owen. "But why are we here?"

He smiled from ear to ear. "We're havin' a picnic."

"A picnic? What is that?"

Three sets of eyes stared at her. "You don't know..." Trevor began, but his voice trailed off.

"What a picnic is?" Rory finished for him.

She shook her head.

Owen merely grinned. "I'm gonna show you what a picnic is."

Trevor and Rory were off to the side with food and drinks of their own, while Elvina and Owen sat on a blanket.

Back in Arnembury, she only ever dined inside the castle's walls. "It's strange to be eating outside," she commented.

"That's the whole point of a picnic, Elvi."

"It's still strange." She took a bite of her sandwich and swallowed it. "But I do appreciate the food. Thank you."

"You never had breakfast, so you're havin' it now."

"It's probably lunchtime by now."

"Late breakfast," he clarified, tearing off some meat from a chicken leg.

She laughed. "Late breakfast it is, then."

And the late breakfast was certainly enjoyable, even down to the last bite. When she finished her meal, she lied down and spread out her arms, staring up at the treetops above her.

"Hey, Elvi?" Owen asked.

She turned her head to look at him. "Yes?"

149

He seemed rather timid. "Can we, uh, have a goss 'bout last night?"

"Oi. There's a bush around here I want to show you," Trevor suddenly announced.

Rory gave him an incredulous look. "A bush?"

"Yeah, a bush. Did I stutter?"

"No, it's just that—"

Trevor dragged him along. "A bush."

Now that they were alone, Elvina sat up to look at Owen. "What do you want to know?"

"We know Reeves interfered and pulled us apart. Do you think we'll go back to how things were?"

"I believe so," she wholeheartedly answered.

He smiled. "I've missed havin' you in my life, I have."

"I didn't like the time we've spent apart. There's so much we've missed." She thought of Eilir. "Goodbyes that were missed."

Scooting closer to her, he took her hands in his and gently brushed a thumb against her skin. "We'll fix everythin'. I'll do whatever it takes."

"Takes for what?"

"To make you happy."

"You already make me happy," she admitted.

"Well, that was easy."

The duo simply looked at one another for a moment, sitting in silence. It only ended once he spoke. "Can I ask you somethin' else?"

"If you wish to do so."

"You already told me things are fine, but did my brother say somethin' earlier to you that you didn't like? Were you tampin' 'cause of him? It didn't seem like you to just leave the castle without tellin' anybody."

Ceron's words hadn't angered her but embarrassed her. After all, he practically said that she should marry his sibling instead of the duke. "He never crossed a line of mine," she assured him.

"But why didn't you tell anybody you wanted to leave? I woulda gone into the city with you. I'm sure Walla woulda, too. Not to mention, Pipsqueak or Flirtsalot." He paused briefly. "Forget I mentioned him. The point is, somebody woulda gone with you for sure."

"I just wanted some alone time. I thought I was fine on my own, but clearly, that wasn't the case."

"It was kinda stupid of you to do that," he lightly scolded.

"Trust me, I don't plan on venturing off alone again."

"Good." He brushed a thumb across her skin once more. "That's good."

Silence fell over the duo yet again. Her gaze remained lowered, looking at their hands that were still connected. She watched his thumb move to and fro before it stopped.

"Elvi?"

She looked up at him, her eyes growing wide at what she saw. A man stood out from behind a tree, a bow aimed at them. Seconds before the arrow was fired, Elvina lunged forward and knocked Owen onto his back. The arrow sank into the ground, just past where she was a moment ago.

Owen flipped her over to shield her. "Dammit!" he cursed, reaching for his nearby sword. "Walla! Flirtsalot!" The urgency in his voice couldn't be missed.

The man aimed again. Off to the side, an arrow grazed the skin of his right bicep. He shouted in pain, and blood stained his cut sleeve.

"That was just a warnin' shot," Trevor clarified, already having another arrow ready to fire.

Rory raced over to the intruder, sword in hand. "You'll be wise if you surrender."

The man tossed his bow aside and threw off his quiver.

Knowing Trevor had his back, Rory sheathed his sword

and roughly held the man's arms behind his back. He busied himself with binding him before shoving him forward toward the others.

It only took one good look at his face for Elvina to recognize him. He was the same bandit she kicked in the face the day of the attack. "You," she breathed.

Owen looked down at her. "You know him?"

"Yes."

As Owen got off of her and helped her to her feet, Rory forced the bandit to his knees. "Talk," he commanded.

He chuckled and made eye contact with Elvina, clearly speaking in an accent like hers. "You're lucky I missed you. I would have killed—" A boot ended up in his face, and he was knocked to the ground.

"She's your target?" Owen huffed, anger running through his veins.

"He's one of the bandits that attacked," Elvina explained, looking down at him. "Where are my friends?"

"Friends?" he scoffed. "Is that what you call 'em?"

"Where are they?" she demanded.

"Last I knew, we wounded one of 'em before we retreated to find you."

Her temper flared, even though his words worried her. "Who?"

A wicked grin spread across his lips. "The big one."

Her heart skipped and her blood ran cold.

"That brute with the scar on his chin," the man maliciously added, driving his words in deeper.

CHAPTER FIFTEEN

Garrick. The leader of the Thunder Squadron. The one Elvina was closest to of the four.

She completely lost her composure. She lunged for the bandit out of desperation, but Owen held her back.

"No, don't do it." He spun her around so she faced him, and held her against his chest. "He ain't worth it."

She clutched onto the front of his tunic. If the bandit spoke the truth, then one of her dear friends was hurt because of her. She was left in the dark about the condition of the remaining members of the Thunder Squadron, and she absolutely loathed it.

"Why did you attack Elvina earlier?" Rory questioned. "Before now."

The bandit cackled. "Do you really wanna know?"

Trevor crouched down and toyed with an arrow in a threatening manner. No words were needed to prompt him into speaking.

He gulped, eyes never leaving the glinting arrow. "Somebody put a price on her pretty little head."

Elvina's entire body stiffened at his words, while Owen held her a little tighter. Someone wanted her dead. They wanted her dead so badly, they put a bounty out on her. She changed her position so she could see what was happening.

"Boss is only one who knows the guy who gave us the job," the bandit quickly added. "Just the two of 'em had some sort of secret meeting. Boss knew where she was going, so he planned out when to attack. It was far enough away from Arnembury where the next town or city wasn't just a simple hop, skip, and jump away. Made sure they'd be wary after traveling."

It hadn't been some random attack.

But now she was left with even more questions. Who was the person his boss had met with? They clearly knew Elvina's destination, which left her to be intercepted by the bandits. What motive did they have? Why did they betray her?

"Why would someone want Elvina dead?" Rory questioned.

The bandit angled his head to glance up at him with an incredulous look on his face. "Don't you know that—"

"I say we take him to the castle for now," Trevor interrupted, changing the topic. "I'll interrogate him personally."

"C—Castle?" the bandit questioned with alarm. "Isn't that a bit much?"

"I'm Second Prince Owen Gravenor of Tiramôr," Owen informed him. "And you just tried killin' my mukka for the second time." His glare hardened. "I can promise you, you won't have a pleasant stay in my kingdom."

His eyes nearly popped out of his head. "W—What? The boss said she was on her way to meet some duke, not a prince!"

Owen and Rory were caught off guard. "Duke?" they asked in unison.

If this bandit kept speaking, surely Elvina's identity

would be exposed to Rory. Trevor could only interrupt him so many times before he said too much.

"Are you betrothed to two different men?" the bandit questioned her.

Elvina's heart twisted when she watched Owen's face fall as he tightened his grip on her. "Elvi..." he whispered.

She tore herself away from his hold and stepped aside, keeping everyone in view. "I don't want to marry him. I want to break off the betrothment to him."

The bandit cackled.

"What's your deal?" Trevor questioned.

"This is too good!" The bandit made eye contact with Elvina. "From the looks of things, I bet there's something you haven't told him. Something really big." He was having too much fun dangling it over her head.

Owen turned his attention to the bandit. "Tell me whatcha know."

"If I do, I wanna know my life will be spared," he sneered, wanting to have the upper hand.

With a cold gaze, Owen stared at him for a moment. "We'll interrogate you at the castle. I don't want us gettin' jumped by more bandits."

"Speakin' of 'em, I'm sure we could find their camp," Rory said. "Find his boss and interrogate him."

The bandit flinched, realizing he wasn't the only source of information. "I'm sure the others won't rat out the boss."

"Oh, and you'll squeal for us?" Trevor stood. "Knock him out, Flirtsalot."

"With pleasure." Rory used the hilt of his sword and delivered a blow to his head.

The bandit crumpled, unconscious, to the ground.

"It's time to head back," Owen said. "And when he wakes up, I wanna interrogate him myself."

"I want to be there as well," Elvina voiced.

"Why?" Owen questioned, sounding a little harsh.

She flinched at his tone.

Because of her reaction, his face softened. "I'm sorry. I didn't mean it like that." He stepped closer and pulled her against him, holding her in his arms while placing a gentle kiss on her head. "I just wantcha to be safe, Elvi. I'll be damned if somethin' else happens to you."

"Flirtsalot, let's pack up and ride out," Trevor instructed. "I'll take him with me since Rhys can handle the extra weight."

"You got it," he said before he got to work.

The two royals remained in place. "Do you wanna ride back on Cari with me?" Owen asked.

Elvina leaned back so she could look at his face. "I'll be able to ride Gwawr."

"Lemme know if you change your mind."

"Of course."

<hr/>

The group had congregated in the lounging room they typically stayed in. Elvina was curled up on one of the sofas, her head on Owen's lap. He was occupied with tracing circles on her left hand that rested against him, while the Babysitter Brigade loafed around, doing their thing.

Upon their return, Urian had been informed of what had happened. The room was quiet, except for the crackling of the flames in the fireplace and the sharpening of a blade.

Elvina contemplated when to tell Owen which duke she was betrothed to. She felt it would have been too much for him to handle after that bandit tried harming her. The atmosphere in the lounging room might be calm now, but Owen needed to know, so she opened her mouth to speak.

"I hafta go to the toilet," Owen said quietly, not wanting

to startle her in case she was dozing off. "I'll be right back, okay?"

She raised her head so he could stand.

He grabbed a nearby pillow and laid it under her head, having it act as a replacement during his absence. It was cooler than what she was used to.

"Owen?" Elvina asked, swallowing hard.

He turned to look down at her. "Yeah?"

"When you get back, I have something to tell you." She made brief eye contact with Trevor and noticed him subtly nod his approval.

"Sounds good." Owen leaned down to peck her forehead. "I won't be long." As he walked out the door, Trevor trailed after him.

Flipping over so she faced the sofa, Elvina forced her eyes to stay open. However, the hum of the room lulled her to sleep even more as she tried fighting it off. She needed to tell Owen the truth when he returned. She had waited far too long.

"He's really worried about Chipmunk," Urian commented as he continued sharpening one of his daggers.

Elvina closed her eyes, wanting to feign sleep if one of the two checked her. She didn't want to get caught eavesdropping.

"It's odd seein' him so quiet," Rory added. "I can't recall the last time he was this way."

The metal sounds stopped for a moment. "Huh. I'm not sure either."

Snapping his fingers, Rory offered, "Wasn't it when that duchess practically tried forcing herself on him durin' last year's spring ball?"

"That's the same girl Mervin thought would be a match for him," Urian chuckled. "Accordin' to Walla, her personality completely changed when she thought it was just the two of 'em. Freckles panicked and had no clue how to handle her."

Elvina could understand a situation like that. The last time she had been with a possible suitor, the watchful Thunder Squadron had been quick to react when they saw her in distress. Her heart sank. The Thunder Squadron. Garrick. She only hoped that the bandit had spewed nothing but lies to merely get under her skin.

"But now he's got a good match for him," Urian continued.

Rory sighed. "He's lucky. She's everythin' I've ever wanted."

"Every girl you've met is everythin' you've ever wanted," Urian teased.

"But she's different."

"Yeah. For starters, she thinks Freckles is funny."

Rory cracked up. "That's a mighty fine point."

Urian lowered his voice. "Do you think they could happen?"

"Happen?"

"You know, become a thing?"

"But she's said so herself, she's betrothed to a duke."

"Yeah, because her tad arranged it. I'm pretty sure he wouldn't mind if she married a prince instead."

Elvina agreed with him as she felt her consciousness slipping away.

"Has Owen even admitted he likes her yet?" Rory questioned.

"Not to me, at least. I dunno if he's mentioned anythin' to Walla, but I'm sure he woulda mentioned somethin' to us by now if he did."

"It's not like he needs to, though. It's pretty obvious he likes her."

"People even think they're betrothed to each other."

"Good point."

Elvina didn't even realize when she slipped away into dreamland.

⦿﹏⦾

She was awoken from her slumber because someone shook her shoulder. Eyelids blinking heavily, she flipped over to see Trevor leaning over her.

"I wouldn't wake you up unless it was important," he said, removing his hand from her shoulder.

She slowly sat up, realizing that less light came through the windows. Now she had no clue what time it was. What caught her off-guard even more was they were the only ones inside of the room. "What's the matter?" she asked.

"Owen," he said.

Her heart skipped. "What happened?" Maybe it was why he never came back. After all, she had full intentions of speaking with him.

"The bandit told him as much as he could. He hardly left out any details. Owen knows it's Kennard."

Time seemed to slow down for her. He knew, and she wasn't the one who told him.

"How is he?" Elvina managed to ask.

"I don't know. He locked himself in his room after the interrogation."

"When did the bandit even wake up?"

"While Owen and I were headin' back here. We crossed paths with the guard who was on his way to inform us. Of course, Owen wanted to have a goss with the bandit right away. That was an hour ago." He paused. "I'm sorry I couldn't do much to stop the bandit."

She bit her lip. "And now Owen knows..." Elvina should have been the one to tell him. If only she didn't panic at their picnic. She had the perfect opportunity to do so, but the bandit interrupted their moment. She also didn't tell him once they arrived at the castle because her mind was preoccupied with worrying thoughts about the Thunder Squadron. And when she finally convinced herself to tell him again, that plan failed. "Can...can I try talking to him?"

Trevor looked hopeful. "Maybe you'll have more luck than me." He jerked his head toward the door. "Come on. I'll show you the way."

"Does anyone else know?" she asked as they walked together.

He shook his head. "Urian and Rory are still out of the loop, but I'm positive they suspect somethin' is up. I won't say a word to 'em unless you tell me otherwise. I'll leave that up to you." He recalled something. "Oh, and Ceron and his personal guard know, too. They were there when Owen interrogated him. Surprisingly, Ceron didn't say a single word. He just watched, kinda like he was absorbin' everythin'."

She was surprised but fine with it. "What did you learn?"

"No real names are known as of now. Boss is what the bandit called his leader. Bags is the guy who hired 'em for the job. The bandits call him that because of the money bags he gave 'em. It was half up front to take the job to kill you. Boss never told his men why Bags wants you dead, but that doesn't matter to any of 'em. Durin' their meetin', Bags gave Boss information, like where you and your guards would be goin'. They knew the path, so they planned the best spot to get you.

"Apparently, on the day of the attack, Boss got greedy. They decided to kidnap and ransom you to your tad for even more money. After he paid off some of the ransom, the bandits planned on killin' you and collectin' the rest of the money from Bags. Your dead body woulda been proof they had completed the job."

Elvina's mind raced. "This Bags person somehow knew what Father planned for me? I don't know who all he told about my visit. I know that Milli and the Thunder Squadron knew. It's possible he told others."

"Like who?"

She stopped in her tracks when someone instantly came to mind. "Reeves."

"Who's that?" Trevor asked, stopping as well.

"The snake in the royal court," she seethed. "He's the royal adviser to my father."

He gasped. "That's serious stuff."

Things fell into place. "He's the sole reason why the trading agreement ended. Owen and I put that together the other night." She remembered the uncompleted sketch of Reeves. "Is that bandit telling the truth when he says that their leader is the only one who met Bags?"

"I believe him. It makes sense for not many people to know his identity. Might as well limit it to the leader of the bandits."

"If what you are saying is true, it might be pointless."

"What is?"

"Owen worked out a sketch of Reeves. I don't know if you want to try showing it to the bandit."

"It's worth a try."

Elvina was grateful for Trevor showing her where Owen's bedchamber was, as she wouldn't have remembered on her own. She stood alone in front of the double doors, took a deep breath, and knocked. "Owen, it's Elvina. I wish to speak with you."

The silence was the only reply from the other side.

She glanced down at the handles and grabbed them both, taking another deep breath. She tried them, only to find they were locked. Determined not to give up just yet, she settled with sitting on the ground and leaning her back against one of the doors. She splayed her feet out in front of her and tilted her head back, looking up at a fixture lit with candles. "Owen? I'm more than sure you are quite angry with me. You probably feel deceived. I don't blame you in the slightest."

She closed her eyes. "I should have told you about my betrothment sooner. I wanted to end it before you learned about it. I haven't even meant Kennard, and I don't mind keeping things that way. I've learned a thing or two about him from Trevor."

She opened her eyes and paused, hoping to hear any sign of Owen from inside. She was met with silence.

"I'll understand if you don't wish to see me during the rest of my duration here," she added. "I'm hoping that Milli received my letter at some point today. Maybe people are on their way here as I speak. I'll return home to Arnembury after that, and if you like, you'll never have to see me again if that makes you happy." She didn't want that to happen, though. She wanted Owen to finally emerge from his bedchamber and speak to her face-to-face. She wanted to see him again before she did leave for her kingdom.

However, the doors never opened.

Finally giving up, she stood and aimlessly walked away. "Goodbye, Owen."

The atmosphere was most odd and uncomfortable, and the six at the table could see that. Dinner was abnormally quiet without Owen's presence. So far, Rory and Urian hadn't questioned anything about the situation. Of course, the others were fully aware of what had taken place.

The food seemed bland to Elvina due to her lack of

appetite. For once, she slouched while seated at a table for a meal. She merely poked around at her food with her eating utensil.

"Normally dinners are rather rowdy with my brother present," Ceron commented, having observed the behavior of the group. "It's peculiar seein' everyone so quiet."

"It's because Flirtsalot and I don't have a clue about what's goin' on," Urian responded bluntly. "Even Chipmunk knows somethin'."

Elvina dropped her fork onto her plate and moved her hands to her lap while she looked down. Should she do it?

"Not that there's somethin' wrong with that," Rory assured her, noticing what she just did.

She stood and looked between Rory and Urian. "I'm Princess Elvina Helaine Norwood of Grenester. I'm currently betrothed to Duke Kennard Endicott against my wishes." She turned to Trevor. "I entrust you to tell Ceron of the possible discovery we made earlier." With that, she left the room in haste.

Trevor abruptly stood from his seat. "I'm Trevor Cadwallader." He wanted Elvina to know that things could still be fine between them. Nothing was broken now that her identity and betrothment situation were known by others.

She stopped in her tracks, knowing her ears weren't deceiving her.

"And I'm Urian Rees," he said as he rose to his feet.

Rory joined the other two in standing as well. "I don't have a fancy title, but I'm Rory Ó Dálaigh."

Ceron remained quiet, knowing the matter was between the four. He did not need to involve himself.

Starting over. It was like Elvina could start over with them. She could go forward from now on without hiding anything from them. She turned to face the Babysitter Brigade with a smile. "Thank you." And then she left.

No one dared to follow her. They all knew she wanted some space.

Mixed emotions were getting to her. A part of her wanted to stay with the people she had met and grown closer to. She wanted them by her side because of their good company. The rest of her wanted to leave everything in Tiramôr behind her and leave it all as distant memories.

CHAPTER SIXTEEN

Elvina was cooped up in her bedchamber. No one had disturbed her. Currently, she was out on the balcony to stargaze by herself. After learning how cold it had gotten from the previous night, she swaddled herself in a blanket and wore boots. She had been outside for some time now and had dwindling hope that Owen would visit her as he did before.

When a breeze blew, she shivered and tightened the blanket around her body, realizing she only had a few more evenings left until help arrived.

"And then I'll be gone..." she said under her breath. She felt slightly bitter about it because she had enjoyed her time in Helidinas, despite some events.

Perhaps it was finally time for her to retire for the night. After all, she was tired and chilly from waiting. She took one last look at the stars and moon before turning around. She gasped in surprise, suddenly feeling wide awake.

Owen was to the left of the doors, leaning against a portion of the wall.

"Owen..." she breathed.

"Whole time," he suddenly said.

She was puzzled. "Whole time?"

"Since before you came out here. I was here first, actually. I just stayed quiet when you came out."

She wasn't sure how to feel about this. He had been watching her wait for him the whole time. "Oh…" was all she could say. "Owen, I would—"

He held up a hand to silence her. "Can I go first? I've got a feelin' once I start, I won't stop."

She merely nodded.

"I'm not bein' funny." Now it was his turn to take a deep breath. "I know. The bandit practically spilled his guts with everythin' he knew 'bout you travelin' to see the duke you're s'posed to marry. Which, by the way, I'm still gonna investigate why somebody hired bandits. Anyway." He averted his gaze from her, staring down at his boots. "It's still weird knowin' you're *betrothed*." He ran a hand through his hair before continuing. "I s'pose I can be stubborn 'bout this and ignore you until you leave, avoid you at all costs just so I don't hafta see you." He paused. "But I don't want that. I wanna be around you."

His words earned him a small smile from her, and it didn't go unnoticed by him. He took that as a signal and sauntered over to her. "Can you clarify somethin' for me quick?"

"What is it?"

He stood in front of her, looking down due to their height difference. "You're betrothed to Kennard, the no-good, lyin', rotten bast—"

"Yes," she interrupted before he could go on. "But I wish to break it off."

"You don't like him?" he huffed.

"We've never even met. Besides, Trevor was kind enough

to inform me he's not the exemplary man people believe him to be."

"And you're only betrothed to him 'cause of your tad, right?"

"Yes. But I'll say it again, so you don't forget—I want to break off the betrothal."

Little by little, he perked up. "You mean…I've got a shot?"

She was surprised by his words. "What?"

"Do I have a shot with you?" He grinned from ear to ear. "I'm pretty sure you know I like you, and I strongly believe you like me. So why not?"

She was frazzled, her emotions tugging her in different directions. She was ecstatic and delighted, yet anxious and concerned.

"Didn't you notice how I said 'the duke you're s'posed to marry' in the beginnin'?" he asked, a small grin tugging his lips upward. "There ain't no way I'm gonna be able to sit back and see you with somebody else. I'll be damned if that happens."

Happiness coursed through her. "And you can positively say that?"

He snorted. "Says the one who was originally gonna marry some guy she'd never met before."

She puffed out her cheeks. "Only because there was no other match for me."

He clenched his jaw. "I clearly shoulda said somethin' sooner. You wouldn't have gone through everythin' that happened."

She wanted this. She wanted him. Without even thinking about her actions, she opened up the blanket to envelop him as she wrapped her arms around his neck.

He laughed, slipping his arms around her waist to keep her close. "Well, hello to you, too." He rubbed noses with her, lightly shaking his head from side to side as a form of affection. "You're cold."

"I'm much warmer now." It was the truth. For some reason, he was abnormally warm for someone who had been standing outside without a blanket. It was like he was his own source of heat.

"That's good..." he murmured, slowly lowering his head to hers.

She stiffened. Was he going to kiss her? Was she finally going to have her first kiss with Owen?

Just as his eyelids fluttered closed, they snapped open and he jerked his head back. "Sorry. Got carried away there, I did."

She was rather disappointed and took matters into her own hands. Literally. She gingerly took the sides of his face and stood up on her tiptoes so she could properly press her lips to his. They were soft and warm, much better than what she had expected they would feel like.

Their mouths broke apart, and a lazy grin formed on his lips. "I could get used to that."

"But not too used to it I hope," she playfully mused.

"Never." With that, he swept her off her feet to carry her inside of her bedchamber.

A fit of giggles took over. "You must stop doing this!"

"As if." He used a foot to open the cracked door and stepped inside, hooking his other foot around the wood to close it. The room was still lit due to the candles, and the two were able to see.

"Why did you hesitate to kiss me before?" she asked.

A bashful look came across his face. "Didn't wanna do somethin' to you that you didn't like, especially somethin' like a kiss." He set her down on the bed before plopping down next to her. "I don't wanna screw this up."

"What is *this* exactly?" she inquired as she removed her boots to be comfortable.

"What do you mean?"

"What are we?" One boot fell to the floor before the other. "What's next for us?"

His response was straightforward. "We get married, have seventeen kids, and live happily ever after."

She laughed. "Seventeen? That seems like an absurd number."

He shrugged. "My tad wants a lotta grandkids."

"I'm sure that Ceron and Gwendolyn can add to that number themselves."

He grinned. "But our kids are gonna be better lookin'."

She found herself thinking about what they might look like. She certainly took after her late mother, but she hoped her children would take after their father. She lied down, the blanket falling away from her and exposing the black tunic she wore.

"You're still wearin' that?" he questioned, secretly delighted this was the third time he had seen her in it.

"As I've said before, it's comfortable," was her reply.

"At least you look good in it."

"It looks better on me than it ever did on you."

He feigned insult, holding a hand over his heart. "How dare you say somethin' like that?"

She giggled before sobering up because of a question. She flipped onto her side to face him. "By the way, just how long were you outside?"

"I was only in my room for a bit before I climbed out onto your balcony. Just wanted to be alone."

"Which means, you never heard Trevor at your doors."

"Nope."

"Or me."

He tilted his head to the side. "What?"

She laughed at herself. "I feel like such a fool."

"You've got no reason for that."

"I thought you were inside of your bedchamber, so I spoke. I suppose my words were all for naught."

"Never." He lied down on his side to join her and ended up toying with a strand of her hair. "It's too bad our tads didn't try gettin' us together. They shoulda made a twist in the rumors."

"As if they would have paired a second prince with a princess before the first prince."

"But we're the winnin' combination," he said with a wink.

She couldn't help but smile. "Do you really think so?"

He looked her in the eye. "I know so, Elvi."

❦

The duo ended up talking as the candles burned down to only tiny flames. The room had grown dim. He was too tired and lazy to return to his bedchamber, so he had decided he would stay with her.

"It seems rather silly for a prince to sleep on a sofa," she admitted. "You can only share the bed if you don't go under the blankets. I'm sure there are some spare blankets on the sofas you can use."

"Have it your way." After kicking off his boots, he reached for the hem of his tunic.

"What are you doing?" she demanded in a frazzled voice, her heart erratically beating.

"Takin' my clothes off," he casually replied.

Her cheeks felt like they were on fire. "No! Clothes stay on!"

"Who sleeps with clothes on?"

"Who sleeps without clothes?"

"Oi. Sleepin' naked is one of the best things ever," he said defensively.

"I don't know what that's like." She always slept with something covering her in case someone entered her bedchamber, like Millicent.

"We should try it together sometime." He winked.

Her jaw dropped and her mind went blank for a second.

He cracked up at her reaction. "Your face! It's so funny! It was worth havin' a go with you just for your expression." He kept laughing as he walked over to one of the sofas to retrieve an extra blanket.

She busied herself with blowing out the candles, but the one by the bed remained lit for now. She slipped under the blankets and remained sitting upright. She watched him walk over to the bed. "Floor," she said.

"Floor?"

"If you wish to sleep in this room with me, you'll sleep on the floor." With that, she licked her fingers and extinguished the candle. She lied down and flipped over to face away from him.

"C'mon, Elviii," he whined.

Her lips remained closed, just so she could toy with him.

He sighed before lying down on the floor, adjusting to be comfortable.

She was surprised he actually listened to her. "Owen?"

"Yeah?" he grumbled.

"I was merely jesting. You can sleep in the bed."

Without a word, he quickly scrambled into bed and stayed on top of the blankets that covered her. He lied down on his right side as well, tucking the front of his body into the back of hers. He pulled his blanket over both of them. "G'night, Elvi."

She smiled. "Good night, Owen."

"Psst," he suddenly said.

"Yes?"

"What did you say when you went to my room?" he asked, his curiosity getting the better of him.

"A couple of things."

"Like what?"

"I wanted to apologize. I was more than sure that you were quite angry with me for not mentioning I was betrothed. Originally, I wasn't going to bring it up. Then I planned on telling you in the forest, but the bandit interrupted that. I planned on telling you in the lounging area, but you left. I fell asleep and you never came back."

He squeezed her a little. "I'm sorry 'bout that. I just needed some space," he chuckled. "But now look at us."

She giggled. "Which brings me to another topic. I thought you wouldn't want to see me again."

"'Cause that's the case now," he chuckled with sarcasm. "What else?"

She hadn't said it early, but she freely spoke now that he was here. "I think it'll be wonderful if we're able to make Grenester and Tiramôr strong again. Perhaps reestablish the trading agreement that we once had."

"I'm hopin' our tads bring it back. But sooner or later, it'll happen again. I know it."

"Things will be set right."

"And Reeves will be outta the picture." He paused for a moment. "Do you know why he's done such things?"

"I haven't the slightest clue. He's been at my father's side for seven years, and there's never been any sign of malicious intent before. I'm not sure what he's gained from meddling in our affairs," she sighed. "Perhaps he's gone mad in the head?"

"We'll hafta interrogate him."

"Oh, do you plan on being there when that happens?"

"Somebody's gotta be by your side, right?"

"And you've chosen that place for yourself?"

"You're Elvi. You're the one I wanna be with. The one I wanna spend my time with. You're absolutely incredible. Not to mention, brave and carin'. Need I go on?"

She was more than grateful that he couldn't see her pink cheeks. She hoped he didn't hear her quickened heartbeat. "Do you really think that?"

"I wouldn't have said it if I didn't think it," he replied earnestly.

Unable to stop the smile from forming, she flipped over to face him. She was able to make out his body's outline, but no facial expression. "Thank you."

"You're welcome, Elvi."

"Will I always be Elvi to you?"

"I give nicknames to people I like."

She mentally went through the nicknames he had used before. "Wait, why doesn't Ceron have a nickname? I remember you called him Cece growing up, then it stopped one time you came to visit."

"That's 'cause I couldn't say Ceron," he chuckled. "And he doesn't have a nickname because he's asked me to call him by name."

"I didn't know that."

"Now I have a question for you."

"What is it?"

"Do you remember when I first started callin' you Elvi?"

Her heart warmed. "Before the end of the first day we met."

"Really?" he asked, sounding genuinely surprised.

"Yes." She decided to remind him of something. "That was after the fact you called me ugly."

He sighed dramatically. "Will you ever let that go?"

"How could I? It clearly scarred me as a six-year-old."

"And as a five-year-old, I didn't know what I was sayin'."

"So you say."

"One of these days, you're gonna forget all 'bout that. I swear it."

"So. You. Say."

"Is that a challenge?"

She laughed. "I'm only toying with you."

"Is that how you show you care?"

She rolled her eyes. "Clearly."

"How did we even get to this point?"

"I asked you about nicknames."

"Nicknames, right. People I like have nicknames, but you're on a whole other level." From their positioning, he moved his head forward to kiss her forehead. "Trust me."

"I'll sleep better knowing that."

"You should probably get to sleepin'. It's late."

"You're one to talk."

"I'm not goin' anywhere. Sweet dreams, Elvi."

CHAPTER SEVENTEEN

The following morning, the door to the bedchamber was thrown open as Rory burst into the room. "Have you seen—" He froze in place, eyes nearly popping out of his head.

Owen held Elvina against his torso for protection because they were disturbed. His entire body was already on alert to shield her from any danger. Meanwhile, a groggy Elvina attempted to figure out why her face was being held against his chest.

"Oh..." Rory said rather lamely.

"What?" Owen asked, loosening his grip on Elvina, who was pulling away to breathe. "What's occurrin'?"

"It's the day of the festival, and you need to get ready for the event," Rory replied. "Trevor kicked down your doors since you weren't answerin' and discovered you didn't sleep in your bed."

"How could he possibly have known that?"

"Your bed was already made from last mornin'."

"Oh."

Elvina finally sat up, rubbing her eyes.

175

Rory clamped his eyes closed and even covered them with his hand. "I didn't mean to disturb you or anythin'! I just thought maybe Elvina might know where you were, so I figured I'd ask her while others looked in different places. I'll go let everyone know the search is off." With that, he hurried out of the room and shut the door behind him.

Elvina looked over at Owen. "You cause trouble without even knowing it."

He sheepishly grinned. "Must be a bangin' skill of mine."

"It must be."

"G'mornin', Elvi."

That made her smile. "Good morning, Owen."

"Did you know you snore in your sleep?"

She whacked his chest. "I do not!" She puffed out her cheeks. "At least I don't talk in my sleep and say embarrassing things."

He snorted at that. "I don't say embarrassin' things."

She arched her eyebrow. "You said you loved me when we napped together before."

Pink tinted his cheeks. "What?"

Now she was the one who had the upper hand. "You said you loved me. That you loved me so much."

He was stunned and stared at her in silence.

"I just thought it was funny that you said it in your sleep," she told him. "Perhaps you thought you were sleeping and said it any—"

He placed his hand over hers, not averting his gaze. "I love you. I love you a lot."

Her face felt like it was on fire and might melt.

Testing the waters, he slowly scooted forward, and she remained still. His head inclined toward her to kiss her. Things remained chaste between them. He leaned closer so he could angle his head better.

The door flew open once again, but this time Trevor

rushed into the bedchamber before halting. He blinked, took in the scene of the two royals jumping apart. He stepped backward before disappearing around the corner, leaving the door open.

"What just happened?" Elvina questioned, looking over at Owen.

He shrugged. "Haven't seen him do that before."

"Perhaps you broke him," she mused.

"That'd be bangin'!" He leaned over to peck her cheek. "I better get goin'. If he sends Pipsqueak in after me, things might get gompin'."

"That would be a sight to see," she giggled.

With that, he got out of bed and stretched. He moved his neck from side to side, cracking it. "If you want, get dressed so we can eat breakfast together."

"I'd enjoy that."

"See you downstairs then, Elvi." He waved goodbye before exiting the room, closing the door behind him.

Elvina fell onto her back, a smile on her face that wouldn't go away. She was happy. She was genuinely happy. When her moment of bliss was over, she got out of bed and stripped out of the tunic. She gasped at the sight of her newest, somewhat noticeable bruise on her left bicep from when Lloyd had grabbed her. She hadn't noticed it from yesterday when her mind and emotions were so disheveled.

"Perhaps it'll be best if Delyth wraps this," she mused, gently rubbing her hand across her skin. After all, she didn't want a certain prince laying his eyes on it.

Having decided to leave her hair down, she changed into the other dress she obtained from the Donnelly sisters' shop. The casual, sleeveless overdress was in a deep wine red color. Along the neckline and hem of it, there was pale gold embroidery. A metal belt around her waist helped define her figure. The skirt fell, barely exposing her boots.

Underneath the dress, she wore a flowing, plain white chemise with sleeves that stopped halfway down her biceps.

Before leaving her bedchamber, she removed the bandages from her right hand to check. It seemed like ever since she entered Tiramôr, she had been prone to injury. Perhaps that would stop happening.

Now searching for Delyth, Elvina crossed paths with a cat that had abnormally blue fur, with some of its natural orange showing through. He flopped down and meowed, demanding attention.

"Nye?" she questioned, trying to contain her laughter. "Why are you blue?"

He continued to meow until she moved closer to him. She bent down to gingerly pet his fur and looked at her fingers, finding they weren't turning blue like she thought they would. "What kind of trouble did you get into?" she mused, picking him up and holding him like a baby.

He purred with contentment as she pet his belly.

"Has Owen seen the state you've gotten yourself into?" she giggled. "I'm more than sure he'll laugh at you."

Nye continued to purr, delighted to be receiving love.

"Do you happen to know where Delyth is by chance? I'm in need of her help."

She made her way down the hallway, staying in parts she was familiar with. She didn't want to get lost in this giant castle without someone to aid her. Up ahead, two guards rounded the corner and approached her.

"Excuse me," Elvina called, quickening her pace.

The duo gasped. "You managed to catch that monstrosity!" the one with dark skin bellowed.

Monstrosity? She looked down at Nye in her arms. Was it even possible to consider him a monstrosity?

As they approached, Nye hissed and swatted a paw out at

them before leaping out of her arms and scampering away in the opposite direction.

"We can't let him escape!" the second guard shouted. "He'll keep ruinin' the decorations!"

They barreled past her, and Elvina watched them go. "But I need help," she quietly said. Straightening her shoulders, she continued on her way and ventured down the staircase, making it halfway down when there was noise from above.

"Get back here, Freckles!" Trevor shouted.

Elvina paused and looked back at the top of the stairs.

At the same moment, Owen thundered down the staircase. "You can't make me!" he shouted back, ever so defiantly. He might not be acting like one, but he looked like a true prince with his assembled attire. With black boots and trousers, he wore a detailed, deep blue doublet with sleeves that had a stiff collar and gold buttons. The black cape on his back was adorned with gold where it was held in place at the tops of his shoulders.

Trevor appeared at the top of the stairs. "Don't make me get your brother," he threatened, "'cause I will!"

Owen turned around to look at him. "I'm already wearin' this stupid getup. You can't make me wear a crown, too!"

Trevor was the first to notice Elvina and had the brilliant idea to use her as leverage. "I'm sure Elvina would appreciate it."

Owen tilted his head to the side. "Appreciate what?"

Warily, Trevor approached his charge. "Appreciate you dressin' appropriately for the festival today, and for the ball tomorrow."

He considered the suggestion for a moment. "I'll save the crown for tomorrow." With that, Owen turned and raced down the stairs, his face lighting up when he saw Elvina. "Hey, El—" His eyes suddenly grew wide with shock as he missed a step and he tumbled down the staircase.

"Owen!" Elvina shouted, rushing to help him.

"Dammit!" Trevor ran down the stairs as fast as he could.

Owen managed to stop himself and held his head as the room spun.

Elvina knelt in front of him, checking him over for injury. "Are you all right?"

"Arm," he said, trying to focus on her.

"Which one?"

"Yours."

She was puzzled. "Mine?"

Owen took hold of her left wrist to look at the latest bruise.

She sharply inhaled, wishing he hadn't seen it.

He immediately released her, believing he hurt her. "Sorry."

"You didn't harm me," Elvina explained. "I'm fine. Just surprised was all."

Trevor crouched down. "Are you good?"

"Who did that to you?" Owen questioned, ignoring the question directed to him.

"Lloyd," she replied, letting him know the truth.

His gaze hardened before growing soft. He took her wrist and brought it to his lips so he could kiss a part of the bruise. "I won't let anybody hurt you, Elvi. I promise."

She softly smiled. "Thank you, Owen."

After a quick visit to Delyth, everyone sat at the table and enjoyed breakfast. Unbeknownst to the others, Owen's right foot affectionately brushed against Elvina's left one.

"It seems like you caused quite the commotion earlier, Owen," Ceron commented. "Just where were you?"

"Elvi and I slept together in her bed last night," he casually replied.

Everyone reacted differently. Trevor spat out his drink. Urian choked on his food. Rory's jaw dropped open. Ceron only blinked, while his personal guard cleared his throat.

"Owen!" a flustered Elvina hissed, before explaining what had occurred. "He only meant that we used the same bed to sleep in. Nothing else happened at all."

"Yeah, kinda like when we slept together in my bed before," Owen added.

Trevor covered his face with his hand. "Just stop. You're only gonna make your grave deeper."

"Huh?" He connected the dots, his cheeks tinting pink. "Oh. Nope, not yet."

"Yet?" Elvina squeaked.

Urian smirked. "That's pretty bold of you to say."

"You do know that she's already betrothed to a duke, right?" Rory inquired.

Owen nodded. "Yeah, that might be true. For now, anyway. But I'm gonna marry her."

She was too embarrassed to speak.

"What do you think King Mervin will say about that?" Urian asked, looking at Ceron.

He looked at the other two royals seated at the table. "I'm sure he'll support his son's decision." He returned to eating his meal as though nothing had happened.

"Where's King Mervin, by the way?" Urian inquired. "I thought he'd be back by now since the festival begins today."

"He'll definitely be here by tomorrow," Owen responded. "No way he'd miss out on the ball."

"He's the host, after all," Trevor commented.

Elvina didn't want to be nervous about Mervin's arrival. Owen and Ceron understood the circumstances of Reeve's conniving ways, so she was confident Mervin would as well.

Noticing her silence and lack of eating, Owen took her hand that rested on her lap. "You okay?"

She looked at him and nodded.

"Are you excited for the festival?"

"I'm looking forward to it."

"Just so you know, the Babysitter Brigade is gonna be with me durin' it. I'll have a guard assigned to you as a precaution."

"I'm sure there won't be a repeat of what happened with Lloyd."

"I just wanna know there's somebody I trust lookin' out for you since I won't be around the whole time."

"As long as I don't have to dress up as a guard for a disguise," Elvina jested.

"You're tidy just the way you are." He quickly looked her up and down. "More than tidy, actually."

Ceron cleared his throat. "I'm sure there will be plenty of time for flirtin' later. Just not in the company of others while we're havin' breakfast."

He shot his sibling a look. "Oi. I'm sure you had lovey-dovey moments with Gwendolyn while you were visitin' her."

"But they're betrothed to each other," Rory pointed out.

"Elvi and I are kinda-sorta betrothed," Owen grumbled.

"Kinda-sorta?" she echoed, a bemused look on her face.

"Yeah?"

"How can one be kinda-sorta betrothed to someone?"

"Um, you're betrothed to"—he made a face—"Kennard, but we both wantcha to break that off."

A lazy grin appeared on Urian's face. "Ah, so Chipmunk's all for the takin'?"

"Exactly!" Owen replied.

"It's certainly a strange predicament," Ceron commented.

"Elvi's the one makin' it complicated," Owen huffed. "Being betrothed to some duke and all."

"We're only in each other's company again because I was on my way to meet Kennard," she pointed out.

Rory laughed. "Oh, she has you there!"

Owen smiled at Elvina. "She's had me from the start."

◈

The two princes would make their grand entrance into the city's main square for a quick announcement to commence the festival. Meanwhile, Elvina and her guard would be in the crowd to watch the whole thing. Afterward, Owen would join Elvina, and they could enjoy the festival together. That was the plan, anyway.

Right now, the group was waiting for Elvina's guard to arrive.

"Will you disguise yourself after the commencement is over?" she inquired while they passed the time.

"Probably," Owen replied. "Not sure what I'd go for. A guard again, I s'pose. That might be the safest choice to be seen with you."

"What other options do you have?"

"Wear a cloak with a hood so I could pass as a beggar or somethin'."

"I apologize for the delay," Anwen said as she approached everyone.

"Anwen?" Elvina questioned.

"Owen insisted I be your charge for the festival."

She looked at Owen. "The guard you assigned to me is the castle's head guard?"

He nodded. "Yep. I trust her." He kissed her forehead. "Go, have some fun. I'll meet up with you soon."

Not thrown off by the display of affection, Anwen led the

way into the city's square. Elvina looked all around. It was easily more crowded than yesterday, with people walking around and browsing the booths and shops.

"Is there anythin' you'd like to see before the commencement?" Anwen inquired.

Elvina shook her head. "We can wait in the square. I don't mind." She was hoping to catch sight of the person she saw yesterday while they walked around. She hoped it was Vallerie, but she had no way of knowing for sure. They had disappeared before Elvina could catch up.

The duo eventually made their way to the square and mixed in with the crowd already gathered. A wooden stage was assembled for the princes to speak at before their people. Unfortunately, Elvina saw no trace of any member from the Thunder Squadron.

A portion of the crowd grew loud with cheers and shouts. Elvina turned to look, spotting the two brothers riding their horses. They waved to the people with smiles on their faces.

"Are you able to see?" Anwen inquired.

"Yes, thank you."

Catching glimpses through the gaps of people, Elvina could spot the personal guards on foot by their charges. The small group looked so official, different than what she was accustomed to since arriving in Tiramôr.

"Anwen, why is it that Owen has more personal guards than Ceron?" Elvina inquired, only now noticing. Although, she wasn't one to talk since she had four.

"Owen causes more trouble than Ceron," she replied, lowering her voice. "And Owen has found himself in trouble because of some citizens."

"How's that possible?"

"Because he's the second prince, some believe he'll attempt to overthrow Ceron for the crown."

"As if Owen would do such a thing," Elvina scoffed.

Anwen nodded in agreement. "Owen wants to see Ceron become the king of Tiramôr. He knows that Ceron will rule just as well as Mervin."

Elvina was sure of that as well.

The princes dismounted their horses and took the stage. Ceron was the one who quieted the crowd. "My good people! My brother and I are pleased to commence the Annual Spring Eve Festival. We hope this year is the best one yet!"

The crowd applauded, growing louder with their joyful sounds. Elvina found herself caught up in the excitement, smiling and clapping like many others around her. She was already enjoying herself, even though it was just the commencement.

"And now, Second Prince Owen has some words." With that, Ceron stepped aside for his sibling.

Owen stepped forward, seeming slightly nervous. "Hey, everybody! Let's have a good time this year!"

The crowd cheered, eager to begin the festivities.

"He needs to work on his public speakin' skills," Anwen commented.

"It takes time and practice," Elvina said, speaking from years of experience. "It's easy to see that Ceron's more comfortable appearing before the people. He'll be a great ruler."

"And because Owen plans on marryin' you, he'll be the king of Grenester," she said in a hushed tone, so only Elvina could hear.

Elvina blushed, stunned that she was aware.

"Do not fear, Owen told me of your title," Anwen explained. "As for the rest, news travels quickly at the castle. I'm sure by now everyone knows about what happened this mornin' because of Rory."

"Is that so?"

"Do let me know if someone causes you trouble. I'll be quick to smite anyone who speaks ill of either you or Owen."

"I'll be sure to do that." Elvina would ensure she didn't end up on this fierce woman's bad side. She was truly a force to be reckoned with.

CHAPTER EIGHTEEN

Now wearing a disguise, Owen was free to roam the city with Elvina. He wore all black from head to toe, including a cloak. It stopped at his waist and had a hood that left his face somewhat exposed. Unless someone stopped to look at who was under the hood, he'd be fine.

"So whatcha wanna do first?"

"I'm more than fine just walking around for now," she answered, happy to spend some alone time with him. She knew the Babysitter Brigade kept their distance, though.

"Wait, c'mere." Owen grabbed her hand and pulled her over to the side.

They ended up in front of a booth that sold floral garlands and headpieces. His eyes glanced around before he gasped and pointed at one. "I'll take that one."

As the seller took it down, Owen took out the necessary payment and left the coins on the table. He stepped aside so others could get by, and held his purchase out for her to see.

It was a brown headband that consisted of flowers and pink ribbons. It was charming and finely crafted.

187

"It's time you get into the spirit of the festival," he proclaimed, placing the flowers on her head.

She laughed. "If you insist."

"There." He smiled at her, admiring his work. "Perfect."

"Thank you."

Still holding her hand, Owen led the way.

This kind of experience still felt new and surreal to Elvina. She wasn't accustomed to freely roaming without the protection of the Thunder Squadron hovering around her. Besides, when she was out and about in Arnembury, everyone who looked at her knew who she was. Here in Tiramôr, only certain people knew she was royalty. In a good way, she felt like she was invisible because no one was paying attention to her. Well, a certain second prince was...

Elvina stole a glance at him. His hood might be covering his eyes, but she could see his smile. She found herself smiling as well.

❧

While enjoying all the different sights, sounds, and smells, Elvina was still on the constant lookout for the Thunder Squadron. Unfortunately, she hadn't spotted a single member. She did have a small amount of hope that she would see a familiar face, though.

"Are you havin' fun yet?" Owen inquired, glancing at her.

"Since the start."

"Good."

A vendor with a small tray crossed their path. The young woman had green eyes and long, pale blonde hair pulled back into a ponytail. "Take and enjoy!" She held the platter of drinks out. "Take and enjoy!"

Owen grabbed two cups. "Thanks." He gave one to Elvina. "Bottoms up."

188

With a sweet smile, the vendor moved onward with the tray for other people.

Elvina inhaled the fragrance and stiffened at what she smelled. Whitley was the one who taught her to identify different poisons and drugs by their looks and aromas, and right now she smelled something familiar. It was *Nox Mortem*.

She sniffed her drink once more and she was sure of it. The bittersweet aroma was hard to miss. "Owen, don't—" Fear trickled down her spine when she saw his cup was empty.

"What's wrong, Elvi?" he asked.

She stared in horror at the cup before meeting his gaze. "Help. You need help right now." She dropped her cup and the liquid spilled onto the ground. She grabbed his hand and pulled him along.

"What's occurrin'?" he asked, sounding worried by her reaction.

"Do you know what *Nox Mortem* is?"

"Knocks mort 'em?"

"*Nox Mortem*. It's a plant. The juices from it can cause someone to fall asleep if they consume it. If they consume enough, they'll die."

"Why're you givin' me a lesson—"

"The drinks we just had were laced with it." She recalled what was taught to her. *Vita Mane*. She needed juice extractions from that plant. She could make an antidote for Owen.

He faltered and stumbled. "Whoa!"

"Are you all right?"

"I feel funny," he mumbled.

Much to her horror, it was already taking effect.

"Hehe, I feel all tingly," he said, his words beginning to slur.

Her eyes darted around as she looked for the Babysitter

Brigade. Surely one of them should be nearby. Why was it she couldn't find a single one of them now that she desperately needed help?

"Hey, why we goin' so fast?" Owen inquired, falling behind slightly.

Elvina did her best to tug him along, insuring he stayed with her. "Don't fall asleep. Do you understand me? Do not fall asleep!"

"Pfft, like I'd do dat."

She spotted a single guard patrolling around. "Guard!" she shouted, doing her best to make her way toward him. "Guard!"

The young man had very dark skin. His dark locks were slightly poofy, while his eyes were light brown. "M'lady?"

She decided that right now wasn't the time to expose that the second prince was with her. She'd do that when fewer people were around. "My friend needs aid."

"I'm fine, Elvi," Owen yawned. "Jus' zonked is all."

When the trio came together, Elvina spoke in an urgent, hushed voice. "A vendor drugged him with *Nox Mortem*. He needs a dose of *Vita Mane* immediately."

His eyes grew wide with surprise. "There's an herbalist shop nearby. The owner should have what we need." With haste, the guard supported Owen as he took most of his weight. "Follow me."

Elvina got on the other side of Owen and helped. "I'm not sure who drugged him. I don't know the woman, but I'll know her face if I see her again."

"We'll get down to the bottom of this," the guard said as they moved along through the crowd.

"I'm compl'ly fine," Owen assured them. "I jus' need sleep. I'm feelin' zonked."

"No," Elvina snapped. "No sleeping for you."

"But, Elviii," he whined.

By the time the trio reached the shop, Owen was practically dead weight.

"Get the door," the guard instructed.

Elvina left his side to hold open the door so the guard could drag Owen over the threshold. Once they were through, she followed after them.

"What can I do you all for?" a male voice asked.

"*Vita Mane*," Elvina quickly replied. "I need some juice extraction from *Vita Mane* for my friend."

The owner of the shop rounded the corner and walked into view. He had pale blond hair that came to his shoulders and green eyes. "He's been drugged with *Nox Mortem*?" he asked.

"A vendor of some sort did the deed," the guard explained.

"Bring him over here," the owner said, motioning for them. "There's a chair he can use."

The duo managed to get Owen sitting, even though he wasn't entirely upright. His head lolled around until Elvina steadied it with both of her hands. "Focus on me," she instructed, fighting back panic.

He slowly blinked, a lazy grin forming on his face. "You're preddy," he giggled. "Your flowers are preddy, too."

"Now isn't the time, Owen."

"Owen?" the guard questioned, that particular name had meaning to him.

Elvina took the opportunity to lower Owen's hood and expose his face. "Yes, Owen."

"The second prince!" the owner gasped.

Elvina stood and turned her back to the two men. "So *Vita Mane*—"

Owen tipped over and crumpled to the floor without a word.

Heart racing, Elvina spun around. "Owen!"

"That took longer than I'd originally anticipated," a familiar voice said.

Elvina's entire body stiffened and she looked over her shoulder. Sure enough, the vendor from earlier stood next to the owner. Their resemblance was undeniably uncanny. "You!"

"Regardless, a lush job, Enfys," the owner said.

She smiled at the praise. "Thank you."

"What?" Elvina whispered.

The guard kicked Owen to jar him around. "Yeah, he's out. Your sister did a tidy job with him, Tremain."

It now dawned on Elvina that she fell for their trap. The phony vendor set everything up, and the fake guard just had to wait until the drug took effect. Now she and an unconscious Owen were cornered.

"Help will be arriving," Elvina scowled, trying her best to keep her voice from wavering. "His guards will know we're missing—"

Tremain laughed. "Ah, that. We saw his guards were followin', so someone created a distraction for 'em."

"Hey, Enfys, you're pretty handy at sewin' things together," the phony guard complimented. "I look like the real deal 'cause of you, and the idiot over here didn't even recognize I wasn't really a guard."

"Of course, Broderick," Enfys sweetly said. "It's all gone accordin' to plan."

"Why?" Elvina demanded. "Why are you all doing this?"

"Why?" Tremain cackled. "Why?" He laughed some more. "We're doin' all of this for Ceron."

Elvina didn't like the situation at all. Owen was unconscious, three enemies had them trapped, and no one knew they were here. As of now, Broderick was the biggest threat since he was closest to Owen, who could do nothing to defend himself. Elvina knew that she needed to dispose of him quickly before she could worry about the other two.

"Enfys, if you—" Tremain began.

As fast as she could, Elvina shoved Broderick away as he crouched over Owen. She reached for him and quickly unsheathed the long dagger from his waist. Wanting to have the upper hand, she held it with both hands and took an abnormal stance. She wanted to appear as though she didn't know how to properly fight.

Broderick laughed at her. "Look at this! She thinks she's gonna fight to protect the stupid prince!"

"Turn yourselves in!" Elvina growled.

Enfys slyly smiled. "Do you really think you can stop us?"

"The people of Tiramôr will thank us for this deed once he's gone," Tremain advised. "We won't allow that fool to steal the crown from Prince Ceron. He's the one we deserve to rule us. He's the one who will be our king."

"Owen would never sink so low to try and steal the crown," Elvina argued.

Broderick cackled. "You don't know him."

"Clearly, you are the ones who don't know him."

"Blah, blah, blah." He stood up and pulled out his sword.

"Try not to get her blood everywhere," Tremain scoffed before looking at Enfys. "You're comin' with me since I have another job for you."

Elvina held her ground. She planned on protecting Owen since he couldn't do a thing to defend himself.

As his companions walked away, Broderick lunged with his sword, ready to land a blow. "Time to go."

Her demeanor and stance changed in the blink of an eye. Before Broderick had time to comprehend what was happening, their weapons clashed together. Minding her dress, Elvina used her right foot to firmly knee him in his stomach, causing him to gasp for air and loosen his grip on his sword. She was quick to snatch it with her free hand, disarming him.

Enfys and Tremain paused, taking in the change of scenery.

Broderick immediately held up his empty hands. "What?" He looked back at the other two. "Did you know—"

Taking the opportunity before it passed, Elvina brought down the hilt of the sword to the back of his head. He crumpled to the ground and remained motionless.

"We didn't take into account she could fight," Tremain commented.

"Is she some sort of undercover guard for him?" Enfys inquired.

"I will give you one more chance to turn yourselves in," Elvina warned.

"Enfys, prepare somethin' special for her," Tremain instructed. "I'll deal with her in the meantime."

"You got it." With that, Enfys walked away.

Elvina glanced around before grabbing a nearby vial and hurling it. All according to plan, Tremain avoided it, and it ended up smashing through a window. Elvina hoped that it caused enough of a disturbance for someone to investigate.

"You're quite the troublemaker," Tremain admonished with a narrow gaze.

"I suppose Owen's rubbing off on me."

Tremain sauntered over to the side, heading to a shelf full of vials. He selected one, uncorked it, and tried sloshing it onto Owen.

Elvina pulled out the skirt of her dress to use it as a shield for Owen, stopping every single drop from landing on him. "Leave him out of this."

"He's the reason why we're doin' this." Tremain smiled. "Now, Enfys!"

Elvina turned to look, but it was too late.

After sneaking up on her, Enfys doused the front portion of Elvina in an opaque, lukewarm liquid from a large bowl. "That should—" she began.

Elvina was quick to aim the sword at her exposed throat as she kept the siblings in her line of sight. She ignored the tingling sensation that started up along her skin. "This ends now."

The front door burst open, and guards stormed into the shop. They were quick to apprehend the trio since they recognized Elvina, even though she didn't recognize some of them.

Her left arm had finally grown so numb, the sword slipped from her fingers and clattered to the ground. The rest of her had become quite numb as well, and she struggled with keeping hold of the long dagger. She tottered around, even though she couldn't feel her legs. The liquid may be scentless, but she knew she was still inhaling it due to how fuzzy her head felt.

"Let me through!" Trevor shouted as he pushed his way toward the front of the guards. His eyes instantly fell to where his charge was lying unresponsive on the floor. "Owen!"

"Help him," Elvina managed to say as her head spun. "*Vita Mane.*"

"*Vita Mane?*" Trevor questioned as he approached her.

She stumbled away, not wanting someone to fall victim to the scentless smell from the liquid emitting from her. "Drank tea," she said, vision swimming. "Laced with *Nox Mortem.*"

"And *Vita Mane* is the cure!" he reasoned, only now becoming aware of her condition. "And whaddya need?"

No longer able to stand, she fell forward, blacking out before she hit the floor.

RACHAEL ANNE

Elvina's eyes fluttered open, and she quickly bolted into a sitting position.

From the nearby chair, Delyth jumped in surprise. "Oh, good, you're awake!"

Realizing that she was lying on the bed in her bedchamber, she looked over to her right. "What happened?" After noticing she was back in her green dress, Elvina looked down at her hands, flexing her fingers. She had proper control of her body. "I'm better. Much better."

"They used some kind of liquid concoction that numbs the skin and causes people to lose consciousness," Delyth explained. "We got you the help you needed. Clothes and all, Anwen and I dunked you inside of a tub full of water to wash away whatever was on you. Then we dressed you and let you sleep it off. You should be back to normal now."

That bath did explain why her hair was still damp. "I do have feeling once again." Elvina practically held her breath, hoping for good news. "How's Owen faring?"

"Even though the incident happened less than an hour ago, he's still unconscious. But he'll make a full recovery 'cause of you."

She sighed in relief.

"More importantly, you saved him," Delyth pointed out with a smile. "They planned on publicly executin' him in the name of Prince Ceron. You stopped that from happenin', you did."

Chills raced down Elvina's spine. "They thought Owen planned to take the crown from him. They wanted to prevent him from doing so by whatever means possible."

"There's no way he would ever do that."

"I told them that, but they did not believe me. They were blinded by their own ideas."

Unexpectedly, there was a knock on the door.

"Come in!" Elvina called.

Much to their surprise, Ceron was the one who entered the bedchamber, unaccompanied by any type of guard. He smiled when he found Elvina was sitting up and wide awake. "I'm glad you're well." He closed the door and walked over to them.

Delyth rose to her feet and curtsied. "Your Highness."

Ceron held out a hand. "There's no need for that." He turned to Elvina. "I want to express my thanks from the bottom of my heart. You saved my only brother."

"It was my fault he was in danger in the first place," Elvina explained. "I believed that man was a guard and fell for his trickery."

"You still protected Owen against the odds you faced," he reasoned. "This kingdom still has its second prince all 'cause of you. We'll be forever grateful for the actions you performed today."

Elvina smiled. "You are most welcome."

Suddenly, there was a loud commotion from outside the room, and it only grew closer, becoming even louder.

Ceron didn't even bother to unsheathe the sword at his waist. "At least he's feelin' better," he quietly said to himself.

"At least knock—" Urian began to say, his deep voice rumbling from the hallway.

The door swung open, and Owen burst into the room, the Babysitter Brigade trailing in after him. Owen was the only one not wearing boots among the four. His eyes fell on Elvina and he took long strides toward her.

"Owen!" Elvina was quick to get out of bed, and by the time she was on her feet, he stood directly in front of her with little space between them.

Without warning, he gently took her head in his hands and kissed her deep and fervently.

Her eyes grew wide with shock, having not expected this.

She did relax, and her eyelids fluttered closed, enjoying the feel of his warm mouth on hers.

Their lips broke apart, and Owen pressed his forehead against hers. "I have a proposal for you."

After a kiss like that, Elvina wasn't sure what to expect.

"Marry me."

CHAPTER NINETEEN

Elvina's heart skipped at those two words. She opened her mouth to speak, but not even a sound came out.

"You're such a poet, Freckles," Urian scoffed.

Rory nudged him. "It's the best he can do."

"Besides, we'd expect nothin' less from him," Trevor added.

"At least he chose to reveal his true feelin's for her," Ceron commented.

Owen looked over at his brother. "Wait, when did you get here?"

"I was here before you."

"Uh, I'm here as well," Delyth voiced, recovering from the surprise proposal that she didn't expect.

"Owen," Elvina softly said after collecting her thoughts.

He whipped his head back to look at her. "Yeah?"

"I'll give you a proper answer when I've ended my betrothment to Kennard." Of course, she'd say yes if she didn't already have someone she was betrothed to. Then again, she wouldn't be in this situation if it wasn't for Kennard.

Owen grinned. "Guess I'll eagerly be waitin' for it."

"I hope it will be worth it for you," she added.

"Oh, it will. I'm sure of that, I am."

With a devious smirk, Urian cupped his hands around his mouth. "Get a room."

Owen shot him a look. "Nobody asked you, Pipsqueak."

Delyth laughed. "It seems that Prince Owen's back to his normal self. My job here is done." With that, she left the room and closed the door behind her.

"Might as well announce to the whole kingdom he's found a bride as well," Rory commented.

"I'm curious to see how Tad will react once he returns home," Ceron mused. "I'm sure he'll be quite interested to hear all that's happened since Elvina arrived."

A smug look appeared on Owen's face. "At least he can't bug me 'bout findin' a wife."

"She still hasn't given you a proper answer," Trevor pointed out.

"Yet," Owen added.

"Yet," Elvina agreed.

He smiled, but his expression changed when a thought occurred to him. "You."

"Me?"

"Don't you ever risk your life like that again." He jerked his head back at the Babysitter Brigade. "They told me what happened after I blacked out."

"You shouldn't have blacked out in the first place," Trevor scolded. "You shoulda been more careful."

"By the way, how did you not recognize it?" Urian asked. "I know we've trained you to identify stuff like it. Even Chipmunk knew what it was."

Owen simply shrugged. "I was thirsty, I was. Guess I chugged it before I even thought 'bout smellin' it."

"That wasn't a good move on your part," Ceron scolded.

Owen waved the thought away. "Yeah, yeah, I've learned my lesson." He looked at his sibling. "Did they try offin' me for the regular reason?"

Ceron's face twisted in displeasure. "They thought you posed a threat to me and planned on stoppin' you from takin' the crown. They wanted to kill you before you had the chance to kill me."

"That's ridiculous!" he shouted, nostrils flaring. "I couldn't care less 'bout not bein' the king. You're more than capable, and I trust you to lead our people toward a brighter future."

"Thank you."

"And you need to tune up your skills if you plan on bein' the future king of Grenester," Urian interjected.

"Why would I be that?"

Trevor covered his face with his hand, something he does frequently because of his charge. "If you plan on marryin' Elvina, the two of you will be her kingdom's king and queen."

His eyes grew wide and he looked at Elvina. "What?"

"You should know that by now," she reasoned.

"King? Of another kingdom?" Owen ran a hand through his locks, mussing them up. "I guess I never saw that outcome for me…" He smiled a bit. "But that was before a certain woodland fairy came back into my life."

Elvina smiled as well. "I wouldn't want anyone else by my side to help me rule my people."

"Thanks, Elvi."

"So what now?" Rory questioned.

"Everyone seems fine," Trevor answered. "The festival's still goin' on—"

"Ugh, I really wanted you to enjoy the festival," Owen groaned. "Not risk your life to protect mine."

"You would have done the same for me."

"Of course."

Urian looked at Trevor. "Should we let them go back outside?"

"If they want to, but it'll be public," he replied. "No disguise or anythin' for Owen. We'll be accompanyin' him. Elvina will have Anwen, and possibly others."

"Even the lovely Elvina will have a guard or more assigned to her?" Rory questioned.

"The people saw us carry her and Owen outta that shop. I'm sure some will recognize her."

"And even if they don't make that connection, they could think more guards have been added for him," Urian mused.

"Hey, Ceron, whaddya think 'bout—" Owen stopped speaking when he looked over to discover his brother was no longer in the room.

The others looked around as well, noticing he was missing.

"When did he leave?" Elvina questioned.

"He's good at doin' that," Urian commented.

Owen looked at Elvina. "So whatcha wanna do?"

"If it won't cause trouble, I suppose we could go back."

He grinned. "Then let's go."

"First, we need to arrange guards for Elvina," Trevor pointed out. "We need to find Anwen for sure."

"And, Freckles, no drinkin' or eatin' anythin' unless we approve it," Urian warned.

He simply rolled his eyes. "Yeah, yeah…"

Now that Owen had his boots and sword that he retrieved from his bedchamber, the small group walked inside the castle looking for Anwen, and possibly another guard for Elvina.

"I'm more than sure that Anwen is quite capable of watching over me," Elvina assured the four men. "She's already proven that when she was with me earlier."

"I just want to take the necessary precautions since we're goin' back into the city," Trevor reasoned.

"We don't need anythin' else happenin' to either one of you," Urian added.

"But there'll be no need to worry," Rory commented. "I swear by my sword that—"

"Where's my youngest boy?" a voice hollered from down the hall.

Owen froze in his tracks. "He's home?" he whispered.

With a flourish of royal robes, a familiar face appeared from around the corner as he moved down the intersecting hallway from up ahead. It was Mervin. He practically looked the same since Elvina last saw him, with perhaps a few more gray hairs. Only five years older than Fitzroy, his coal black hair parted down the middle and tied back into a short, low ponytail. He had light brown eyes, and the skin around them crinkled whenever he smiled. His build was average, and his slightly tanned skin reflected his sun exposure.

Behind him were two guards, easily keeping pace. Elvina recognized them both.

Asmer Prichard stood close to a foot shorter than Mervin and had fair skin. She had russet brown eyes and curly, dirty blonde hair that was close to touching the tops of her shoulders.

The dark-skinned man was Dillan Rees. He had a daunting way about him that was hard to miss. Being slightly shorter than Mervin, he was bald, so his hair couldn't possibly get in his way. His dark eyes were sharp and ever observant.

"We'll find him," Asmer said.

"Uh, hey!" Owen called out, gaining their attention.

The trio suddenly stopped and turned to look down the hallway.

"That was easy," Dillan commented.

Mervin bolted down the hall as his guards simply walked after him.

"Uh, you guys might wanna stand back," Owen warned as he prepared himself for impact. He even slipped off his sheathed sword and tossed it to Trevor.

"Owen!" Mervin collided into his son, wrapping his arms around him in a strong grip. With arms trapped at his sides, Owen didn't have much room to try and escape. He couldn't stop his father from lifting him clear off of his feet.

"Nice to"—he wheezed—"see you, too."

Asmer made eye contact with Elvina, who smiled at her. She nudged Dillan with an elbow and nodded her head at Elvina, so he noticed her as well, rubbing his eyes to make sure he wasn't seeing things. Elvina raised her right hand to wave.

Mervin set Owen down on his feet and firmly placed his hands onto his son's shoulder. "Why have I been hearin' I almost lost you today?"

"So you do know 'bout that."

"Of course!"

"Yeah. These crazy people thought I was gonna steal the crown from Ceron." Owen shrugged. "They decided to off me before I had the chance to off him."

"I can't believe—" Mervin had to do a double take when he finally noticed her. "Elvina?"

"Hello, Merv—" she found herself engulfed in a hug. Unsure of what else to do, she just allowed it to happen.

When he released her, he looked rather excited. "Are you here 'cause of the ball? On a whim, I decided to send an invitation to Fitzroy in hopes that we could make amends. Is he here, too? We need to speak to each other!"

Until now, Elvina had been completely unaware that he did such a thing. Fitzroy never received anything from Mervin since the trading agreement ended. "My father received no such invitation from you."

His brow furrowed. "What?"

She looked at Owen. "Reeves will be finished with his tampering in our affairs."

"We'll put a stop to it," he agreed.

"What're you two havin' a goss 'bout?" Mervin inquired.

"There's a snake in the royal court of my kingdom," Elvina replied with disdain.

"There are things you need caught up on," Owen said, looking at his father. "Like, a lot."

Mervin glanced back and forth between the two royals before him. "We can go to my study."

❦

With two guards posted outside to prevent anyone from disturbing them, the others were inside Mervin's study. Their personal guards stood off to the side to listen, with Elvina and Owen on one sofa, and Ceron and Mervin on another. Someone figured that Ceron should be present, so Elvina and the Gravenor family were all on the same page.

"What do I get to learn first?" Mervin asked.

Elvina looked him in the eye. "Can you confirm for me that Reeves, the royal adviser to my father, paid you a visit last fall?"

He nodded. "That, I can."

"He tricked you," Owen said. "Fitzroy was tricked, too."

Mervin was surprised. "What?"

"For whatever reason, Reeves sabotaged the trading

agreement between our kingdoms," Elvina informed him. "He requested a week off and used that time to travel here to speak with you. You gave him a declaration ending the trading agreement, and he gave that to my father when he returned to Arnembury. However, he claimed that on his way back, he just so happened to run into a messenger from you.

"From our viewpoint, we believed you suddenly ended the trading agreement because of a rash decision. My father wrote to you multiple times, but you never replied to a single letter."

"I never received anythin' from Fitzroy," Mervin confirmed. "Not even a peep."

"Owen and I have concluded that Reeves ensured you never did. My father would have given him the letters to send out to you."

Mervin connected the dots. "That scoundrel!"

"I'm not sure of his motives," Elvina advised. "Besides, wanting me dead is much different than ruining the bond our two kingdoms had."

Owen and Mervin both appeared shocked. On the other hand, Ceron already knew because of what Trevor had shared the night her betrothment was revealed.

"Wait, what?" Owen demanded.

"Whoa, who said anythin' 'bout Reeves wantin' you dead?" Mervin questioned with alarm.

"There's no proof, but Trevor and I believe he hired the bandits. When my father gave away my hand in marriage, I'm sure he told a select few. Apart from my personal guards and my lady-in-waiting, I'm quite sure that Father would have told his royal adviser. He had been in the room when I was told about it."

Mervin thought for a moment. "If you did die 'cause of the bandits, then what?"

"There's no bloodline heir." Helaine was an only child, and her parents had no siblings. Fitzroy was the youngest of three boys growing up. His older siblings fought over who would take over after their parents passed on the ruling. One killed the other, and the remaining one was mortally wounded from their fight. He died days later, leaving Fitzroy as the rightful ruler.

"Who's next in line to rule Grenester?" Ceron inquired.

"Father has already worked out that if I'm to pass and he doesn't have another child..." Elvina let that point hang in the air as chills raced down her spine.

Owen looked at her with worry. "Elvi?"

"Then the royal adviser would take over," she numbly whispered. "Because he would have the most knowledge to rule the people."

The room fell silent.

"The bandit did say Bags knew what you'd be doin' and where you'd be goin'," Owen growled as he pieced things together. "Bags hasta be Reeves. I'm guessin' Fitzroy did tell Reeves 'bout his plans for Elvi."

Something dawned on Elvina. "Now that I think about it, Reeves probably convinced my father to have me travel so I could be away from Arnembury. I was an easier target that way." She thought for a moment. "It did always bother me that I was to visit. It made more sense for him to visit the place he'd someday call home."

"Not if I can help it," Owen assured her.

"Wait, what?" Mervin asked, feeling left out of the loop.

"Has Tad been caught up with everythin' else but *that*?" Ceron asked.

Owen ran through past events. "Days ago, Elvi and her guards were travelin' to the duke she's currently betrothed to. We're assumin' Reeves hired the bandits and told the leader everythin' they needed to know. She escaped and ran into the forest where I found her because I was there with my guards. We brought her back here and Del"—he quickly glanced at Asmer—"patched her up.

"Since then, she's written to her lady-in-waitin' to explain what happened. They should be arrivin' soon." It was clear to see he remembered something else worth mentioning. "Yesterday, a bandit tried killin' her 'cause there's a bounty out on her head. We captured him, and now he's bein' held prisoner. We've gotten some information from him, but not a whole lot. He's not toward the top of the chain."

No one said a word when he finished.

Mervin finally cleared his throat. "That's a lot—"

"One more thing." Taking Elvina's hand, he intertwined their fingers together. "I love her, and I wanna marry her."

Mervin and his two personal guards were beyond shocked.

"He even proposed to her not too long ago," Urian commented. "Before we ran into you guys."

Dillan's eyes grew wide. "What?"

"However, the lovely Elvina won't give him an answer until she's broken off her future marriage to the duke," Rory added.

Mervin laughed wholeheartedly. "You finally choose a bride and she's already betrothed to somebody else! Owen, you never cease to amaze me."

"We wouldn't expect anythin' less from him," Ceron commented.

"Just for clarification, have all matters been taken care of that happened earlier today?" Asmer inquired.

"Bad guys are bein' held prisoners," Urian responded. "Owen and Elvina are both alive."

Rory nodded in agreement. "That pretty much sums everythin' up."

"By the way, who saved you?" Dillan asked, looking at Owen. "Some guards have mentioned a guest of yours."

He grinned. "Elvi did."

Mervin immediately looked at Elvina. "You protected my son?"

She nodded. "I did."

Dillan looked at Urian. "You let a royal protect a royal?" he demanded.

"It wasn't their fault," Owen said, quick to defend the Babysitter Brigade. "All of us were set up. I was just lucky Elvi knows how to fight."

"You can fight?" Asmer questioned.

"Garrick taught me himself," Elvina proudly replied, leaving out the part that her father was unaware.

"Sword and bow," Trevor added with a grin.

Mervin glanced at his son, a sly smile on his face. "Just another reason for you to be fond of her."

Ever so inconspicuously, Owen squeezed her hand. "It's more than that."

Asmer sighed. "Why is it drama always happens when we're gone?"

"Just how these kids like it, I guess," Dillan mused.

"Where were all of you headed before we ran into each other?" Mervin inquired.

"We wanna go back out to the festival," Owen replied. "With added guards. Has anybody seen Anwen by chance?"

"You plan on lettin' him go back out?" Dillan demanded, looking at Urian.

"Relax, old man."

"Old man?" Elvina questioned, familiar with that term.

Urian nodded. "Yeah, he's my tad."

"And Amser is Delyth's mam," Trevor added.

"Is everyone connected somehow?" Elvina asked.

"Well, not to brag, but the king is my tad." Owen shrugged. "No big deal, though."

She playfully rolled her eyes. "Is that supposed to impress me?"

"Are you sayin' it doesn't?"

"Owen," Mervin suddenly said.

He looked at his father. "Yeah?"

"You need to be mindful that Elvina's betrothed to somebody."

That thought was still in the back of her mind, but she didn't want to think about the duke she didn't want to marry.

"I know that," Owen said.

Mervin glanced down at their still connected hands before looking his son in the eye. "I mean, she's off-limits."

His whole demeanor changed in an instant. "What?"

"She's still betrothed to somebody."

"But she doesn't wanna be."

"Tad, she's betrothed to Duke Kennard Endicott," Ceron calmly said to provide insight.

"Regardless, I don't want to stir up any trouble for Fitzroy —" Mervin's eyes grew wide with surprise, and he glanced back and forth between his two boys. "The *same* Duke Kennard that we know?"

They simply nodded, one much more eagerly than the other.

Mervin groaned and gave his attention to Owen. "I'm sure things will work out in the end *after* everythin' blows over, but wait until then. Please." He sighed when he saw the disappointment settle over his youngest son's face. He cleared his throat. "I wantcha to promise me this, Owen. I don't want somebody who doesn't know 'bout Elvina seein' the two of you together. It could be misleadin' and start trouble if they think you and she are together. It might cause a problem for Elvina and Kennard. Can you promise me that?"

Reluctantly, Owen released her hand, his shoulders sagging. He almost looked defeated.

Elvina couldn't remember a time that she had seen him express this kind of emotion before. Seeing him like this was an odd sight.

"Do you still want to go out into the city?" she inquired, hoping to cheer him up.

"Uh, I dunno now."

"If you would like, we can do something else."

"Lemme think..." Owen's face lit up. "The thing!" He whipped his head around to look at Trevor. "Is the thing ready?"

"The thing...?" Trevor's face registered to what Owen meant. "I'm not sure. I haven't received word that it's ready."

Elvina felt as though she was out of the loop. "The thing?" she inquired.

Owen looked at her with a big toothy grin. "Yeah, the thing."

"Should I be concerned?"

He laughed. "Nope." He grabbed her hand again and stood, pulling her along. "Let's go find Anwen and see if the thing's done."

CHAPTER TWENTY

Back in the streets of Helidinas, the group made their way amongst what was happening at the festival. They walked at a steady pace, but it was clear for all to see that Owen was rather excited and eager to move faster. Of course, Elvina was more curious than ever to learn what this thing was.

"Relax, Freckles," Trevor said.

"They've only had two days to work on it," Rory pointed out.

"Yeah, give 'em some time," Urian added. "They might even need tomorrow to work on it."

Owen gave Urian a look. "Oi, don't say that. You might jinx it."

"You're certainly eager about this thing," Anwen commented.

"And no one is saying what the thing is," Elvina pointed out.

Owen smirked at her. "Aw, feelin' left out?"

"Quite so."

He chuckled. "Good. It's a surprise for you."

She was certainly surprised having learned that fact. "A surprise? For me?"

He nodded. "That's what I said, Elvi."

She had never been one for surprises. It was always best if she knew nothing was planned. As soon as she caught wind of some sort of surprise for her, she remained anxious until the moment happened.

Elvina noticed they were approaching a familiar shop owned by two sisters. "But I don't need any more dresses."

Owen wagged his eyebrows at her. "Or so you think..."

"I'm positive."

The front door swung open to reveal Melva. She smiled when she saw everyone. "Oh, goody, you came by! I was just about to pay a visit to the castle—"

"The thing's ready?" Owen eagerly interrupted, not meaning to be rude.

Melva giggled. "Of course. Nola and I have been hard at work to prepare it for Elvina." Leaving the door open, she stepped aside. "Come on in, everyone."

Since Urian was the last one in, he closed the door behind him.

"What is this thing?" Elvina asked, more anxious than ever.

Nola chuckled. "It seems like Prince Owen left you in the dark."

Owen stood in front of Elvina, taking both of her hands in his. "You know the ball's tomorrow night, right?"

"I'm well aware," she giggled. "Apparently, Nye was causing trouble for people preparing for it."

"Didn't you ever think you'd need somethin' to wear for it?"

Her mind went blank. She never thought about it. It was only suggested yesterday by Trevor that she attend to meet Kennard herself. "It never occurred to me, no," she admitted.

"While you were tryin' stuff on a couple days ago, I was havin' a goss with Nola," Owen explained. "We were tryin' to think of whatcha were gonna wear to the ball. Brainstormin', really."

"Melva and I worked out some ideas together, and got to work on somethin'," Nola said. "We had a base and added to it."

"We need you to try it on so we can make the final adjustments to it," Melva added. "We had a general idea of your size since you got some clothes from us before."

"You men are to remain down here to guard the perimeter while Elvina's tryin' on the gown," Anwen instructed.

"Wait, what?" Trevor questioned.

"Elvina won't be disturbed durin' the fittin'." She eyed each one of the men. "None of you will see her until she's at the ball."

"What's it matter if we see—" Rory began but stopped speaking when Anwen coldly glared at him.

"Now that it's clear what's to happen..." Anwen looked at Elvina with a smile. "Come. It's time to try on the gown."

The ladies wasted no time in herding Elvina into an upstairs room to have her change in front of a mirror. While Anwen, Melva, and Nola were looking at Elvina, she looked at the reflection of herself. She was in utter awe at what was on her body. The material was a deep blue color that reminded her of Tiramôr's flag. The bodice wasn't uncomfortably tight and displayed partial cleavage. It had a dramatic, full skirt, while the sleeves were tight around the shoulders and loose everywhere else.

Elvina turned her body so she could see the sides and back, keeping her eyes on the mirror. "Oh, wow..." she breathed.

"I absolutely adore the color," Anwen commented.

"As do I," Elvina agreed.

"Prince Owen was the one who chose the color," Nola informed her. "He requested that whatever you wore, it had to be blue."

Elvina smiled. "He did a very good job."

Melva clapped her hands together. "I'm so happy the gown looks so perfect on you."

"As am I." Elvina looked at the two sisters. "Thank you both so much."

They smiled at her. "Anythin' for a friend of Prince Owen's."

Suddenly, Anwen gasped.

"Is everythin' all right?" Melva asked.

"Shoes," she replied. "Elvina needs shoes to wear with it."

Elvina lifted the gown to reveal her boots. "I'm sure these will do."

Anwen was quick to wag her finger. "We'll have you lookin' proper for this ball."

"We can promise you that," the two sisters said in unison.

After a pair of flats was chosen for Elvina, she changed back into her green dress. The fabulous blue gown was left upstairs before the small group returned downstairs.

Owen jumped to his feet. "Finally."

"That took way longer than I thought," Trevor commented.

"Wait, so where's this dress?" Urian questioned.

"Oh, we can have it delivered to the castle later," Melva assured them.

"There's no need for you guys to carry it around durin' the festival," Nola added.

"I bet you were a lovely sight to see in that gown, Elvina," Rory said dreamily.

Anwen nodded her head. "Incredible. Absolutely incredible. Blue's a wonderful color for her."

At that, Owen perked up. "So it is blue?"

Nola chuckled. "Of course. You did request it."

Elvina looked at Owen. "It's really beautiful."

"Oh, I'm sure you're the one who makes it beautiful, Elvi."

She couldn't stop her cheeks from turning pink.

Melva slapped a hand over her mouth, her face turning red. "That was so bold of Prince Owen to say!"

"But it's true," he defended himself.

Trevor put a hand on his shoulder. "Calm down."

"Easy does it, lover boy," Urian added.

"Lover boy?" Melva squeaked. She was a big softy for lovebirds.

"It's quite easy to see just how the lovely Elvina has stolen away the hearts of all those who simply gaze upon her beauty," Rory professed.

"It's because she's a woodland fairy. Right, Freckles?" Urian questioned.

Owen grinned from ear to ear. "Woodland fairy."

Having regained her composure, Melva looked at Owen. "Feel free to enjoy the rest of the festival. We'll have the gown and shoes delivered to the castle later."

Looking at Elvina, Owen grinned. "Wanna go have some fun?"

◉━━━◉

From where she stood, Elvina could tell that Owen looked positively miserable. The Gravenor family sat up on the stage from this morning, watching their people as they danced. Mervin and Ceron seemed to be enjoying themselves, while Owen probably wished that he could be anywhere else.

The sun had since set, so the open area was lit with torches. The scenery was pretty from the decorations, and music drifted across the air from the nearby band. They had drums and stringed instruments, creating lovely music Elvina enjoyed. When the current song ended, a couple's dance started. People cleared the dancing area, while others were eager for the dance to begin.

So far, Elvina had been perfectly content watching everyone enjoy themselves and listen to the music. During the balls and events she had attended, she had danced with different suitors, and rarely did she ever dance with the same man twice. And never a third time. At least, not yet she hadn't.

Anwen acted like a guard on duty, standing off to the side to watch the people. In reality, she stood away from what was happening, because Elvina remained along the side to watch. "Elvina, you're sure you're enjoyin' yourself?" Anwen inquired.

She nodded. "Positive. It's different watching others dance than being the one to dance myself. It's a nice change."

There was a slight twinkle in her eye. "I have an inklin' that you'll be dancin' at some point tonight."

A certain individual came to her mind. She could only be hopeful. "Is that so?"

"Care to dance, fair maiden?" a stranger asked, holding his hand out for her.

"Unfortunately, I must decline your offer," she replied.

He took a step closer. "Are you sure?"

"She's waitin' on someone to arrive," Anwen interjected, a small smile on her face. "Her first dance will be with him."

"I made a promise," Elvina agreed, going along with her idea. She hoped he would go away if he believed she was already taken.

The stranger's mood deflated a little. "Oh, is that so?"

"It is so," Owen said as he approached the trio, carrying himself upright and with purpose.

"P–Prince Owen!" The stranger stepped back a little bit and bowed before him.

Owen waved a hand. "Hey, it's okay." He held out his hand to Elvina, a grin on his lips. "Dance with me?"

"Is it because you need practice for tomorrow's ball?" she teased.

"Very funny."

Elvina placed her hand in his. "I would love to, Owen."

Leaving the stunned stranger and Anwen, the duo made their way to where the others danced and joined. To say the least, Elvina was pleasantly surprised Owen knew the moves and steps to this particular dance.

"It's one princely thing I can do 'cause of the years of lessons," Owen commented, noticing her expression.

"Oh, lessons must have been quite torturous."

"You do understand my pain."

Elvina giggled. "Dancing can be fun."

"When it's with the right partner."

"Indeed," she agreed.

Following the part in the song, Owen twirled her around before a hand of his returned to her waist. He didn't let it stray any lower than it was. Going with the flow of things, they moved in sync with the other dancing couples. Everything was perfect.

"Hey, Elvi?" he suddenly said.

"Yes?"

"Things are always more fun when you're around."

She beamed. "I feel the same way about you."

"I'm glad we're together."

Her heart melted. "As am I."

<hr />

From sitting on the edge of the bed, Elvina hummed to

herself while she brushed her wet hair. When she and the others returned to the castle after the festival had ended, a hot bath had awaited her. Now she was squeaky clean and wore a proper nightgown for a lady. Not that she'd admit it out loud, but she did miss Owen's tunic. She had practically stolen it from him.

The hot water had done her good. Her fingers and toes were still pruny. Her body was relaxed, but also quite rejuvenated. She originally had assumed that she should be somewhat tired after winding down, but that wasn't the case. Rather, on the opposite side of the coin, she was wide awake.

Her mind kept drifting back to the new fond memories she had with Owen. She enjoyed their time together as they danced and laughed. Even when they stood around and chatted about whatever crossed their minds had been memorable. She felt warm and fuzzy recalling her latest favorite memories that were already quite dear to her.

"And to think I thought that someone could never make me feel like this," Elvina mused, setting the brush down on the nearby nightstand.

Before she had a chance to stand up and blow out the candles, there was a knock on one of the doors that led out to the balcony.

Elvina's heart skipped as she practically jumped out of bed and raced over, bare feet against the floor. She quickly opened one of the doors and smiled when she found Owen on the other side.

With still damp hair from his bath, he leaned against the frame in a casual manner. "Hey, Elvi."

She used both hands to pull him inside without a word.

Chuckling at her reaction, he expertly used a foot to close the door behind him.

She was in such a giddy mood and was well aware she

was exuding how she felt. "I had such a marvelous time tonight."

"I can tell." He twirled her around, much like he did earlier while at the festival. A hand of his ended up at her waist, and they slowly danced in a circle. "I'm happy that you're happy."

Bliss bloomed inside of her. She couldn't stop the smile from forming on her lips. "My happiness right now wouldn't be possible if it weren't for you."

"Is that a fact?" he teased.

"Indeed. I had such a wonderful time at the festival."

He grinned. "That might be the fourth time you've told me that."

"I'm being serious. It's the most fun I've had in years."

"Honestly?"

She enthusiastically nodded as a response to his question. "I tend to become bored at the festivities and balls I've attended in the past. Some guests have made them not so enjoyable."

He smiled. "Just wait for the ball tomorrow. I know you'll love it."

"I'm sure I will."

Without a word, he leaned forward, but stopped himself, his brow furrowing in frustration.

"What's the matter?"

Instead of bestowing a kiss upon her lips as he had originally planned, he simply pressed his forehead against hers. He remained like this for a moment before he pulled his head back to look at her. "I made a promise to Tad. Don't think I wouldn't otherwise."

She found it enheartening he planned on keeping his promise. "You're a good man."

"More like a crazy one," he chuckled. "Leave it to me to

fall for somebody who's already betrothed to some other guy."

"Leave it to me to fall for someone I'm not betrothed to."

Silence fell over the two. It wasn't awkward or uncomfortable in the slightest. Instead, it was pleasant and nice.

"I just came by to say g'night," Owen said after a moment.

Elvina pulled her head back so she could look at him. "What a way to say good night."

He flashed her a toothy grin. "I'll getcha in the mornin'."

Hand in hand, they walked over to the balcony's doors. He opened one of them, released her hand, and stepped outside. She leaned against the frame.

"Sleep tight, and have sweet dreams."

"You do the same."

Stepping forward, he took both of her hands in his. He leaned forward to press his forehead against hers, taking a moment to enjoy the moment. "G'night, Elvi."

Her heart flooded with warmth. "Good night, Owen."

CHAPTER TWENTY-ONE

The following morning, Owen was true to his word. He knocked before barging into her bedchamber, a certain skip to his step. "Elviii!" he shouted. "Wake up! Wake up, Elvi!"

She jolted awake, blinking sleep away. "What?"

With a devious grin and a glint in his eyes, he hopped onto the bed, avoiding her limbs. "Time to start the day."

"It's much too early," she groaned, remaining on her back. "Can I sleep more?"

He plopped down onto his rear. "No way."

She finally sat up, and the blankets pooled around her waist. "Where did all of that energy come from?"

"It's an excitin' day."

"All because of the ball?"

"And then some."

A bundle of blue fur jumped onto the bed and padded its way over to Elvina. He meowed.

"Nye?" Owen snickered, clearly surprised to see the state of his cat. "What happened to you, buddy?" He reached out to pet him but missed when Nye walked past him and comfortably nestled himself into Elvina's lap.

She giggled and pet Nye behind his ears. "He was quite the troublemaker yesterday. The guards considered him to be a monstrosity because he was ruining decorations. Can you believe that?"

Nye was already purring up a storm, even before he closed his eyes in contentment.

Owen snorted and looked at the cat. "He wouldn't be Nye if he didn't cause trouble for people every now and then."

"I wonder where he learned that from," Elvina jested.

"Obviously from the best."

Trevor knocked on the open door before stepping into the room. "Mornin', Elvina."

"Good morning, Trevor," she greeted.

"I'd suggest dressin' in somethin' casual before you get into the dress you're gonna wear this evenin'," he advised, and nodded his head at Owen. "You can probably tell that from the way he's dressed now."

"Are you going to wear your crown tonight?" Elvina teased.

"Maybe."

Trevor appeared floored by the one word. "Maybe? Did you just say maybe?"

"What's wrong with maybe?" Owen questioned, giving him a look.

"You didn't even try rejectin' it!" Trevor reasoned, waving his arms around in wild gestures. "You put up a fight with me yesterday!"

Owen simply shrugged. "Guess I'm in a better mood today."

Rory and Urian appeared in the doorway, seeming out of breath.

"The party Anwen led is comin' back," Urian said, urgency thick in his voice.

Owen became interested in the matter. "Do things look good?"

"We can't tell," Rory replied.

"What's going on?" Elvina inquired, feeling left out.

"You might wanna get dressed now," Owen suggested.

◉━━━◉

Now wearing the purple dress, Elvina stepped outside of her bedchamber to discover all the guys had been waiting on her.

"Ready to go?" Owen asked, standing upright from leaning against a wall.

She nodded. "I'm not entirely sure what's in store for us."

"Just hope it's good news," he replied.

The small group made their way through the castle. As they walked down the staircase, Anwen came into view from the lower floor. Along with her normal uniform, she wore some light armor.

"Anwen!" Owen shouted to gain her attention.

She looked up and stopped in place. "Hello."

The five met her at the bottom of the staircase. "What news you got?" Owen asked.

"The raid was successful," she replied.

Elvina was alarmed by the word. "Raid? What raid?"

Anwen arched an eyebrow at Owen. "Did you purposely leave her in the dark?"

"Of course, he did," Rory huffed.

"Safe to guess you found what you were lookin' for?" Urian asked.

"My team and I successfully found the bandits campin' in the forest," Anwen reported, looking at Owen. "The ones bein' detained will be further questioned. We're hopin' to learn the truth."

Elvina was simply stunned but kept listening.

"What 'bout the leader?" Trevor questioned.

"Yeah!" Owen agreed. "I have a thing or two to say to that dirty bast—"

"Prince Owen," Anwen interrupted, not meaning to be rude.

"Did you get him?"

"Not in the sense that we would have preferred." She proceeded to sigh. "He's dead."

"Dead?" Elvina whispered. The hopes to question him for confirmation about Reeves were now gone. However, the belief that Reeves was the culprit was still strong.

"How?" Rory inquired.

"The coward took his own life," Anwen replied.

Urian folded his arms across his chest. "He was too afraid to face us."

"I do have good news, though," Anwen stated.

"Like what?" Trevor asked.

Anwen looked at Elvina, a gentle smile on her lips. "Two people were bein' held captive and have been rescued. They claimed to be friends of yours. Their names are Vallerie and Quenby."

Elvina nearly choked on air. "Where are they? I wish to see them now!"

"Delyth is givin' 'em a once-over before they see you."

"Where are they?" Elvina pleaded. "I don't mind going to them at all. They've already been through so much because of me."

Anwen took her words into consideration. "The infirmary."

Owen grabbed Elvina's hand and pulled her along. "Let's go."

"Oi, wait for us!" Urian hollered.

As the small group quickly approached the infirmary, Elvina's heart threatened to break free from her chest. She was almost positive it would just pop out at its current rate.

Owen threw open the door, and Elvina was the first to enter. Sure enough, three sets of eyes turned to look at the group.

"Elvina!" Vallerie shouted in relief before rushing over to her side.

Quenby scrambled behind her, hot on her trail. "You're okay!"

Soon enough, Elvina found herself enveloped in loving embraces from two members of the Thunder Squadron. "I've missed the both of you so much," she sobbed, bursting into happy tears. "So very much."

"We've been so worried about you," Vallerie said.

"Vallerie's been a wreck this entire time," Quenby teased to lighten the mood.

She shot him a cold glare for outing her so quickly. "Says the one who balled his eyes out every night since we were separated."

"Hey, you promised you wouldn't tell anybody about that."

Elvina couldn't stop the laughter from rising up. "I've missed this. I've missed you both."

The trio finally broke apart, and Vallerie gasped when she noticed Elvina's bandaged left arm. "What happened to you?"

"All is well. It's merely covering a bruise." She quickly changed the subject. "Where are Garrick and Whitley? A bandit said that Garrick was injured."

"He was injured, but nothing life-threatening," Vallerie assured her.

A wave of relief washed over Elvina. A weight had been lifted from her shoulders. Now she would be able to breathe easily until she was reunited with Garrick as well as Whitley. "What happened after I escaped?"

"Garrick got hurt, and the remaining bandits left to go after you," Quenby said. "We split up. Of course, we didn't plan much since we had to act quickly before the ambush."

"Whitley went with Garrick to accompany him and make sure he got treatment," Vallerie continued. "Quenby and I went after you."

"I'm the best tracker of the team, after all," Quenby added. "And Vallerie was in full mama bear mode to get you back. We were up to the task of finding you."

"And somehow you were captured by the bandits in the process," Elvina reasoned, having pieced things together.

Vallerie nodded. "They kept us hostage rather than killing us. They were hoping to use us to get to you."

"Like, lure you to their camp somehow," Quenby added.

"Which I would have done."

"That would have been a reckless thing to do since we risked our lives to make sure you could escape," Vallerie scolded.

Elvina smiled. "So be it."

Vallerie's eyes teared up slightly, and she hugged Elvina tightly. "You can be so stubborn at times."

She returned the hug. "I wouldn't be me if I wasn't like that."

"Damn right," Quenby agreed as the two broke apart.

"When Garrick and Whitley left, did they say where they were going?"

"What do you mean?" Quenby asked.

"Were they going back to Arnembury to say what happened, or did they continue on their way to the duke?" Elvina clarified.

"We aren't sure," Vallerie replied. "Like Quenby said, we had to act quickly. We left that up to them to decide."

"Why do you ask?" Quenby inquired.

"I sent a letter to Milli," Elvina said. "I requested aid and an extra horse for me."

"Do you want to wait here for them, or do you want us to take you to see the duke?" Vallerie asked.

"I have no desire to see him at all," Elvina said rather stubbornly. "To be clear, I plan on breaking my betrothment to him."

Quenby blinked. "Say what now?"

Vallerie's expression softened. "Elvina, we've talked about this. Your father wants you to marry—"

"Oh, she'll still marry," Rory interrupted. "Elvina has somebody else in mind, though."

For the first time, Vallerie and Quenby acknowledged the existence of those who came into the infirmary with their charge. They only recognized two faces.

"Looks like you've made some friends while you've been here," Quenby commented.

"They're great friends," Elvina confirmed.

Owen spoke up. "I wish we were meetin' under better circumstances. You both already know Trevor. My other guards are Urian and Rory."

"They're also known as the Babysitter Brigade," Elvina jested.

"Ain't that the truth," Urian chuckled.

Owen shot him a look for agreeing, even though Elvina was the one who made the comment.

"Wait, back up a minute, Elvina," Vallerie implored. "There *is* someone you want to marry?"

With a smile on her face, Elvina nodded. "Yes. He's the only one I wish to marry."

Owen stepped forward and slipped his hand into Elvina's with ease. "Hey."

Vallerie gaped with wide eyes, while Quenby cracked up. "W–What?" she stuttered while he laughed some more.

"And he's determined to make it happen," Trevor commented.

"I'll fight for her hand if I hafta," Owen said in all seriousness.

Elvina rolled her eyes. "You probably won't have to."

"Hey, if things come down to it, I'll do it," he said.

"Wait until Garrick and Whitley get a load of this," Quenby wheezed as he caught his breath.

"Just wait until her father and the duke hear about it," Vallerie added, regaining her composure. She looked at Owen. "Does King Mervin know about it?"

He nodded. "Yep. But Elvi's off-limits until she breaks off her betrothment."

"Then he can propose," Trevor commented. "Again."

"Again?" Vallerie and Quenby asked in unison. She looked like she was going to faint, while he reacted like it was the best news he had ever received.

"Of course, Elvina will give him a proper answer when that happens," Rory said.

Vallerie held her head before she looked at Elvina. "Just how much has happened since you arrived here?"

"I'm sure we can take the time to talk, and I'll explain some things."

"Over breakfast," Owen added. "I dunno 'bout you guys, but I'm hungry, I am."

There was a change of seating at the table because of the latest additions. Quenby sat to Elvina's left, while Vallerie sat on her right. Across from the trio were Trevor, Owen, Rory, and

Urian. Owen insisted that he sit across from Elvina when they chose their places. While they ate, Vallerie and Quenby were filled in on the events that had occurred since Elvina had been found. Matters only turned serious toward the end when they discussed the bandits that were currently being held.

"They're bein' questioned now, but I doubt we'll get anythin' from 'em," Urian said. "They'll probably be like the first bandit we captured and not know a thing."

"But why question them when we already believe Reeves is the one behind everythin'?" Rory asked. "Everythin' makes sense if it is him. Which is probably the case."

"It's still crazy to think Reeves could have done all of those things," Quenby commented.

Vallerie nodded in agreement. "But we have the upper hand since you've pieced things together."

"He'll be in for a big surprise when Elvi goes home," Owen said.

"He's already going to be locked away for ending the truce with our kingdoms," Elvina mentioned.

Urian nodded in agreement. "Attempted murder of Grenester's princess is a hefty crime."

"Elvina, we won't let anybody harm you," Quenby told her matter-of-factly. "We haven't let you down before."

"As if there's any doubt," Elvina said with a smile.

"And you have a part of Tiramôr backin' you up," Owen commented.

Urian grinned. "The second prince and his personal guards, no less."

"King Mervin and Prince Ceron are right alongside us, too," Rory advised.

"Speaking of them, where are they?" Quenby inquired.

"They're probably gettin' the final touches done for tonight's ball," Owen replied. "They like that kinda stuff, so they probably had an early start to the day."

"And we all know Freckles isn't into that kinda stuff at all," Urian jested.

Leaning forward to look past Rory, Owen pointed his fork at him. "Oi, watch it."

"Or what?" Urian challenged.

"No fighting at the table," Elvina scolded. Of course, this wasn't the first time she had said such a thing while they had been at the table.

Owen immediately ceased his actions and continued eating.

Trevor looked back and forth between Vallerie and Quenby while he spoke. "Elvina's the only one he listens to."

"He's like a trained dog," Quenby goaded.

"I like cats more," Owen remarked, the insult going right over his head.

"Wait, so what's the plan after eatin'? We do have the ball later, but what do we do before the ball?" Rory questioned the group.

Owen made a face. "Who says we hafta do anythin'? I wanna be lazy."

"I'm sure we could find somethin' for you to do," Trevor mused.

Mischievousness sparked in Urian's eyes. "Like dance lessons."

Rory looked at Elvina. "Don't let him dance with you, or he'll step on your feet."

"Oi!" Owen protested.

"He didn't do so dancing last night," Elvina replied. "He did rather well."

"And he can do better," Trevor said.

"I'd rather spar than dance," Owen muttered.

Truth be told, so would Elvina.

Trevor shook his head. "Sparrin' won't come in handy for the ball. Brushin' up on your dancin' skills will be better."

"I can help instruct him if you want," Vallerie offered.

"She's done wonders with Elvina," Quenby commented. "A proper lady."

"Yet Vallerie's the one who helps me with shooting a bow when Garrick can't," Elvina pointed out.

After considering Vallerie's words, Owen looked at her. "If you teach me, I want Elvi to be my partner."

She smiled brightly. "I'm sure that can be arranged."

CHAPTER TWENTY-TWO

Vallerie put the final touches to Elvina's elegant updo. "There we are. Finished."

Opening her eyes, Elvina smiled at her reflection. She loved her hair. The two braids along the sides of her head led back to a low bun. It was full of volume and elegantly done. She was grateful there wasn't a single trace of anything shiny or sparkling pinned in her locks for a change. "I love it, Vallerie. Thank you so much."

Just as Elvina stood up and turned, there was a knock on the door.

"Come in!" Vallerie called out.

The door opened, and Quenby poked his head inside of the room, his eyes clamped shut. "Is it safe?"

"I wouldn't have said to come inside if it wasn't," Vallerie huffed.

His eyes opened, landing on Elvina. "Wow, you clean up good."

"Only because I had Vallerie to help me."

"The ball already started, and Owen sure is getting antsy waiting for you to come down."

Elvina found it amusing. "He can be impatient."

"When it comes to you," Vallerie and Quenby said in unison.

Elvina couldn't argue that at all. "Shall we go?"

Vallerie and Quenby escorted Elvina down to the ballroom. She insisted that she didn't need a grand entrance, so she wasn't getting one. She and her personal guards simply walked into the grand room and made their way around.

A band provided live music and entertainment. The decorations were fitting in the castle of Tiramôr, and everything had been thought of. There was an area for eating later, as well as a cleared space for dancing. Things went off without a hitch.

Elvina looked around for familiar faces. Unfortunately, she didn't see any of them.

"Do you see him?" Quenby asked.

"Not yet," Vallerie replied.

"Perhaps we should wait for him," Elvina suggested before smiling. "He does have a knack for finding me."

"You pick the spot."

"And we'll wait with you," Quenby added.

A young man stopped in front of Elvina and bowed in front of her. "How are you this fine evenin', my lady?"

Doing what she had done for years, she gathered the skirt of her gown and curtseyed. "I'm well. Thank you for asking."

He stood upright. "That accent of yours is lovely." He held out a hand. "Would you care to dance?"

Under normal circumstances, Elvina would accept. However, she wasn't in search of a future husband. "Actually, I'm waiting for someone. I will have to turn down the request."

"Has a lucky lad already stolen away your heart?" he inquired.

"I'm already betrothed," she said to make it clear she wasn't interested in him.

"What he doesn't know won't hurt him," the stranger pressed.

Vallerie and Quenby didn't react to his persistence. After all, they knew their charge could handle herself rather well.

Just as Elvina opened her mouth, Owen slid in close to her. He took her hand in his and laced their fingers together. He looked as dashing as ever, and even wore his crown, really playing his role as the second prince of his kingdom. "Are you enjoyin' yourself?" he asked her, completely ignoring the existence of the one failing at flirting with her.

Elvina smiled. "Quite so, Owen."

The stranger looked at their joined hands before up at their faces. "You're betrothed to the second prince?"

A grin formed on Owen's face. "What if she is?"

Panic flashed in the stranger's eyes, and he quickly bowed. "Excuse me."

Elvina playfully whacked Owen's chest with her free hand.

"What was that for?" he asked, even though he certainly knew what he did.

"I don't need someone spreading a false rumor that we're betrothed to one another."

"But it did scare him off."

"That, it did," she agreed.

"Now, then." Owen looked Elvina up and down, drinking in her appearance. "You look..." His words trailed off before he found his voice again, clearing his throat. "I can't even describe it."

"You have such a way with words," she giggled in a teasing manner. "Although, I suppose I have you to thank. I do have this lovely gown because of you."

"It's fittin' for you." He raised their arms and pressed his lips to the back of her hand. "Shall we?"

Without a word, she allowed him to lead her over to where the others danced, fitting right into the part of the song that was playing.

"Where's the Babysitter Brigade?"

"They're watchin' over me, no worries. They're lettin' me have some space tonight," he smirked. "I could ask you the same thing 'bout your guards."

"Point taken."

At the start of a new song, he pulled her over to the side to avoid others. Slipping a hand to her waist, he took hold of her hand with his right one. "I like this kinda dancin' with you a lot more."

Slipping her left hand over his shoulder, she smiled. "As do I."

They slowly spun in place, simply getting lost in one another, paying no attention to what was happening around them. They didn't even notice the Babysitter Brigade exchanging some coins because of a bet they placed on how soon their charge would try dancing with Elvina.

"Do most of these people hail from Tiramôr?"

"Pretty much."

"Are Kynan and Siriol here?"

"I haven't seen 'em around. They might still be visitin' family."

"But you're family to them."

"But I saw 'em recently."

"They didn't see your father and brother," she pointed out.

"True," he agreed. He opened his mouth to speak more, but words didn't come out.

"Is everything all right?" she questioned.

He ended up smiling. "I got lost in your eyes there for a bit."

She giggled.

Owen found himself slowly leaning forward. "They just suck me right in—"

A bread roll made contact with the side of Owen's head and he jerked back, eyes looking around for the perpetrator.

The Babysitter Brigade all looked rather innocent and avoided any possible eye contact with their charge. Surprisingly, no one ratted out who threw the bread.

"They're trying their best to keep you in line is all," Elvina said to justify their actions.

"They didn't hafta throw some bap at me," Owen grumbled.

"At least it wasn't something harder. And we both know it's called a roll, not a bap."

Ceron strolled over to the duo and held out his hand for Elvina. "May I cut in?"

"Sure thing." Owen stepped over to his older brother and made him his new dancing partner.

Elvina had an absolute fit of giggles as she watched Ceron struggle to break free from his brother. It was a sight she never imagined she would ever see.

"Owen, release me this instant!" he chided.

"But I wanna dance with my bangin' big brother," he said as they spun around.

A few others noticed the spectacle and laughed at their antics.

Elvina wiped away a tear from her cheek.

Vallerie and Quenby approached their charge so she wasn't alone. "He's a real character," he commented.

"And he's the one you want to marry?" Vallerie asked, even though she knew the answer.

"Yes," Elvina replied without hesitation, a smile on her lips.

"Did you put him up to that?" Trevor inquired as he and the other members of the Babysitter Brigade approached the small group.

"Why would I suggest such a thing to Owen?"

Urian nodded. "Chipmunk does have a point."

"No one really has to put him up to anythin'," Rory commented. "He'll think of it all on his own."

"Kinda makes you wonder what goes on inside that brain of his," Urian said, crossing his arms over his chest. "Scary place, probably."

"Dearest Elvina, would you care to dance?" Rory flirtatiously asked.

"I wonder how Owen would react to seeing that," Quenby mused.

Vallerie chuckled. "I bet he would throw something much worse than a bread roll at you."

Rory looked over at her. "Perhaps you would like to dance with me instead?"

"In your dreams," she scoffed, turning her nose up at him. "I like tall men."

His mood slightly deflated. "Another time maybe."

Elvina laughed at the rejection but thought of Vallerie's response. A certain tall man came to mind, one who had different colored eyes. One who happened to be standing next to her.

"Hello, boys!" a newcomer greeted as he approached the Babysitter Brigade. He had the same accent as Elvina and her guards.

In his mid-twenties, he was practically the opposite of Owen in his appearance. Blond hair was slicked back perfectly, no hair out of place. His eyes were a bright shade of green, and he carried himself with an arrogant attitude, believing he was better than everyone else around him.

He stopped near them, but his eyes were on Elvina. "Who's your beautiful companion?"

"Oh, it's you, Kennard," Trevor greeted, wanting Elvina to pick up on the name.

She was interested. "Kennard? Are you the very same Duke Kennard from Grenester?"

"That, I am," he replied with a smile. "And I can tell from your accent that you're from the same kingdom."

"Is it true that you're betrothed to the princess?" she asked without hesitation.

He seemed utterly confused. "What kind of rumor is that?"

Now Kennard wasn't the only one confused. Vallerie and Quenby exchanged a glance with one another. The Babysitter Brigade looked back and forth between Elvina and Kennard. Lastly, Elvina was dumbfounded.

A thought crossed Elvina's mind. "Did King Fitzroy ever send you letters about your betrothment to his daughter?" Perhaps Reeves did more tampering with the mail than they knew of. He might have faked responses, pretending to be Kennard.

Kennard merely chuckled. "Oh, now that would be something, being betrothed to Princess Elvina. I've never met her, but I've heard her beauty is unmatched." He sent a smile her way. "Much like yours."

Elvina's eyes grew wide as she processed the first part he told her. Her father had been very clear their betrothment was official and final, and now Kennard wasn't taking their betrothment seriously. "Just to make it clear, you aren't betrothed to the princess?"

"I'm not betrothed to anybody," he clarified. "Well, unless you're offering."

Completely ignoring him, Elvina spun around to face Vallerie and Quenby. "I believe Reeves wrote back to Father, which means my betrothment has been a farce from the very start." Excitement blossomed within her. She wasn't betrothed to anyone, and never had been.

Vallerie nodded in agreement. "I think so as well."

"Reeves is clearly not right in the head," Quenby commented.

Kennard didn't miss a single word. "Wait, excuse me?" He looked around at the Babysitter Brigade. "What's going on?"

Urian folded his arms across his chest, satisfied at how things had turned out. "Nothin' you need to worry 'bout."

Rory looked at Trevor and Urian. "Who's goin' to tell Owen the good news?"

Kennard had no chance at grasping what was happening. "Can somebody please explain what's going on?"

Elvina faced him, deciding to leave out who she was since it wasn't necessary. "It was believed that you were betrothed to Princess Elvina. However, it appears that the two of you were never betrothed to each other in the first place. Along with others, the royal family was tricked by a snake." A snake that would certainly pay for his deceiving acts and lies.

"And how do you know about the matters with the Norwood family, hmm?" Kennard questioned.

She looked him straight in the eye. "I shouldn't have to explain myself to the likes of you."

He stood a little taller. "You should watch your tone when speaking with me."

She didn't back down. "I can say the same for you."

Neither Vallerie nor Quenby reacted. They would only do something if Kennard decided to be physical with her. Likewise, the Babysitter Brigade stood down as well.

"Do you know who I am?" Kennard challenged, believing

he had the upper hand. "Duke Kennard Endicott, from your kingdom."

Elvina tilted her chin up to show that his words weren't affecting her. "My kingdom indeed..."

"Kennard, you miiight wanna back down," Urian stage whispered to him.

He didn't look away from Elvina. "As if. She needs to know her place." Kennard smirked. "Preferably underneath me."

Elvina didn't appreciate the double meaning of his words. Perhaps she should reveal her true identity to a thorn prick like him. "I am Princess Elvina Norwood of Grenester, and you will watch how you speak to your princess."

He seemed rather dubious. After all, he wasn't entirely sure what the princess of Grenester even looked like. He only knew her by name. Kennard's facial expression showed that he believed she was bluffing. "Yeah, right," he bitterly said. "As if—"

"Elvina, are you enjoyin' yourself?" Ceron asked as he walked toward the group.

Kennard had to do a double take. "W—Wait...Is s—she truly Princess Elvina?"

"She is," Ceron confirmed. "Why do you ask? Do you doubt who she says she is?"

He clearly wanted to dig himself out of the hole he'd put himself in. "I–I guess I just wasn't expecting her to be here. Grenester and Tiramôr aren't on the best terms."

"Oh, they will be in due time," Ceron chirped. "It appears that somebody had interfered and caused confusion for King Fitzroy and my tad. Things will be better in the near future."

"Oh," was all Kennard could muster to say.

"The bond between the two kingdoms will be reinforced even more so when my younger brother and Princess Elvina marry each other," Ceron continued, without missing a beat.

Kennard's mouth dropped open, but words didn't come out.

"Speaking of Owen, where is he?" Elvina inquired, ignoring the state of the duke.

"I suggested he get you a drink," Ceron replied. "I'm sure he'll return any moment now."

Urian clapped Kennard on the back. "Isn't it great that he found someone like her to love?"

"T–Terrific," he practically squeaked.

Owen squeezed past Kennard to stand by Elvina's side. "For you," he said, offering her the drink in his hand.

"Thank you."

"Kennard," Owen bluntly said.

"O–Owen," he responded.

"Is everythin' okay? You look a little pale."

"I think I should go sit down…"

"Do you need Pipsqueak to go with you? You know, make sure you don't fall or anythin'?"

"I'm fine." Kennard was quick to get away, not even saying a proper goodbye to anyone.

"That was a little mean," Elvina chuckled.

"He's had it comin'," Rory commented.

"I think it's even better that Owen was able to steal his thunder," Trevor added.

Owen grinned. "Now that he's outta the way, who's ready to party?"

CHAPTER TWENTY-THREE

By now, Owen was blissfully content from the alcohol he had consumed. It was well into the night, and many other guests shared a similar state of being. Although, Mervin was probably the merriest of all drunkards at the ball. Elvina was perfectly content being mostly sober as she watched others around her.

Owen plopped down next to her, not minding that their thighs were touching. "Hey, Elvi," he greeted.

She giggled at him. "Are you enjoying yourself?"

"The real ques'ion is"—he playfully booped her nose with his finger—"are you?"

She couldn't stop the laughter that bubbled out of her. "I am."

He grinned from ear to ear. "Good."

"Great," she corrected.

His smile softened as he looked at her. "Great."

"Would the lady care for a dance?" a stranger asked as he approached the duo, his eyes on Elvina.

Owen took matters into his own hands and replied for her. "Nope, 'cause she's all mine."

A quizzical look came across the stranger's face. "Yours?"

With ease, Owen moved Elvina onto his lap, wrapping his arms around her. He looked the stranger in the eye as if posing a challenge that he dares to try and take her from him. "Mine," he practically growled, his chest rumbling against Elvina's back.

She merely laughed. "Not yet," she corrected.

His lips moved to her right ear, ghosting over it. "Then lemme take you away and make you mine," he breathed in her ear, so she was the only one who heard him.

Her face immediately heated up. "Owen!"

He cracked up and hugged her tightly, resting his face where her right shoulder met her neck. "You're sooo easy to tease."

She puffed out her cheeks in a defiant manner. "I am not."

"Are tooooo."

The duo was utterly oblivious to when the stranger did walk away, giving them their space.

"Hey, Elvi?" Owen asked.

"Yes?"

"Wanna take a stroll with me?"

"A stroll?" she mused. "To where?"

"We could go outside."

She thought for a moment. "It might be a little chilly out."

"I'll keep you warm."

"If you have someone fetch me a blanket, I'll consider it."

His face lit up. "Done."

❦

So what if their personal guards watched them take a stroll under the starry sky up above? As of now, neither of the two royals had a care in the world. They walked in a lovely garden, feeling as though they were the only two existing at the moment.

Elvina tightened her hold of the blanket around her, blocking out the chill. "I'm glad you suggested this."

"I'm just full of bright ideas," Owen chuckled.

With a smile on her face, she twirled around to face him. She waited on him until he stood directly in front of her.

"Hey."

"Hello." She noticed his intent stare. "Is everything all right?"

"I really wanna..." he admitted, looking at her lips before returning his gaze to her eyes. "So don't think that I don't wanna..."

A somewhat devious thought occurred to her, one that allowed her to toy with him. "Your father did say that I'm off-limits to you, and you did make a promise to him."

"Don't remind me," he grumbled.

"He never did say that you are off-limits to me," she pointed out. "And I never promised him anything."

Something sparked in his eyes. "Jus' what're you suggestin', Elvi?"

"Oh, nothing," she coyly said, batting her eyes just to tease him. "Nothing at all."

"Nothin' at all, huh?"

To return the favor from what he did inside, she stood on her tiptoes to whisper in his ear. "Nothing at all." She strolled away as if nothing happened.

"What?" He blinked, coming back to his senses. "Elvi!"

In a teasing manner, she merely glanced back over her shoulder, giggling as she faced forward, only adding more distance between them.

"Elvi!" he yelled, jogging after her.

She knew he would catch her. She couldn't move all that quickly in her gown.

"Gotcha!" he triumphantly shouted, having captured her in his arms from behind.

She couldn't do much to escape since her arms were trapped to her sides. The blanket worked in his favor because it ensured she stayed in place. Getting a sturdy grip on her, he lifted her off her feet and began walking.

"Put me down," she laughed.

"Never." He carried her over to a large boulder and sat down, resting her on his lap so her right shoulder was to his chest. He nuzzled his face up to her, his breath warm on her exposed skin. "I don't wantcha to go away."

She was surprised he brought the subject up. "Go away?"

He didn't look her in the eye as he spoke. "You'll be leavin' soon."

"That can't be helped. I'll have to return to my kingdom." She nudged him with her shoulder. "I need to inform Father that I won't marry Ken—" She cut herself off by gasping. What was she talking about? She wasn't betrothed to Kennard. She hadn't even been betrothed to him in the first place. There was no need for her to discuss with her father about who she wouldn't marry.

He noted her silence. "Elvi?"

However, she did need to discuss with her father about who she would marry. A man of her choice, not one picked for her by Fitzroy.

"Hey, Elvi?" Owen said, trying to gain her attention.

She shook her head, snapping herself back to reality. She smiled from ear to ear at him. "I have news."

He relaxed now that she seemed normal. "Oh, yeah?"

"Great news that I believe you will like." The excitement was starting to bubble over in her.

"Well, what is it?"

She took a shaky breath to calm herself down. "I was never betrothed to Kennard in the first place."

He tilted his head in confusion. "Huh?"

"When I was talking with Kennard earlier, he didn't know about my betrothment to him. He was completely oblivious to the matter."

"I don't get it."

"Kennard never received letters from my father."

"How's that even possible?"

"I believe that Reeves replied to my father, pretending to be Kennard. I'm not entirely sure how he went about doing so, but he must have figured out something. It was clearly enough to dupe Father."

He pieced things together. "It was a way to getcha away from the castle."

"Exactly."

"He's more devious than I thought."

"I feel the same way."

He sent an assuring smile her way. "Don't worry, Elvi. I'll protect you."

She knew that he meant it. "I know you will."

"I mean—*Wait!*" His eyes lit up with joy. "You're not betrothed!"

"I thought I clarified that for you only a moment ago," she jested, doing her best not to laugh at his sudden outburst.

From their position, he hugged her tightly, bringing her closer to him. As to not be awkward, she rested her head against the side of his neck.

"What has gotten into you?" she giggled.

"This changes everythin'," he breathed. He was so excited, he could only speak above a whisper.

"Everything?" she mused.

"*Everything*," he echoed, giving her an extra squeeze.

Since she physically couldn't do much else, she gladly snuggled up to him, thoroughly enjoying the moment.

"Just think, all I hafta do is talk to your tad." After all,

Mervin taught Owen that he needed to speak with the parents of the one he wants to marry. In this case, he needed to speak to Fitzroy about asking for Elvina's hand. He would ask her to marry him for a second time, but do it properly.

"And then what?"

"Then we get our happily ever after."

She pulled her head back so she could look at his face. "After all, there is someone I would much rather marry than Kennard."

"Is that so?"

"He's far better for me than Kennard." Her lips curved up into a smile. "I already care about him. He's funny and caring, endearing and thoughtful—"

"Dashin' and handsome I bet," he added.

"I believe he'll help me rule my people, and be a wonderful king. I have a feeling he'll help me raise our children and be a wonderful father to them. I'm more than sure he'll love me with his whole heart."

He was all sorts of choked up by the time she finished. He swallowed hard before speaking. "He adores you. He absolutely adores you. You're the sunshine in his day and light of his life. You're everythin' he's been lookin' for."

Happiness bloomed in her chest at the words spilling from his mouth. The very mouth she was trying her hardest to resist kissing. For now, at least.

"You're gentle, but you have a certain streak to you that even he doesn't wanna mess with," he continued. "Sometimes, you're too stubborn for your own good, but he likes that 'bout you. Shows off your personality." He smiled at her. "You're still his woodland fairy, after all—"

"Just kiss already!" a voice that suspiciously sounded like Quenby shouted from out of view.

The duo jumped, slightly flabbergasted that they had an audience watching them so closely.

Owen bounced back first with a chuckle. "Can't leave 'em hangin'."

As the blanket fell off her shoulders, Elvina cupped his cheeks in her hands and firmly pressed her lips against his. The last time they kissed like this was the previous night, and another kiss was long overdue.

He instantly fell silent, eyes fluttering shut. He secured the blanket around her so she remained warm, and they could continue kissing. He worked their warm mouths together, their lips moving in sync.

They remained like that until she pulled back, filling her lungs with air.

"Wow," he breathed, relishing in the moment.

She giggled at his reaction. "Wow, indeed."

"You've gotten bolder."

"Perhaps I've learned a thing or two from someone," she noted.

"Huh, wonder who that could be."

She took a deep breath to calm her nerves for what she was about to say. "Owen?"

"Yeah?"

"I…" She inhaled through her nose, trying to get over her nerves.

He smiled, adoration in his eyes. "I love you, too, Elvi."

Now back inside to enjoy the ball once more, Owen had gone off to request a specific song from the band. However, his actions had since been interrupted by a person. Probably similar in age, her skin was a few shades lighter than Urian's. Dark hair was in the form of a pretty updo, her dark russet eyes focused on the one in front of her. She showed an obscene amount of cleavage. It was more than enough to attract a suitor. The light blue gown she wore certainly looked amazing on her, though.

"Who is that?" Elvina inquired, doing her best to not appear jealous.

"Duchess Iorwen," Trevor replied in a lackluster tone.

"At last year's ball, she forced herself on Owen," Rory added.

At those words, Elvina recalled the conversation that he and Urian had had.

"She's, uh"—Urian scratched his chin—"what's the best way to describe her?"

"Obnoxious?" Trevor suggested. "Unbearable? Intolerable?"

"She's good on the eyes at least," Rory commented. He might be a flirt, but he dared not to flirt with her. In fact, he showed no interest in her when she was around. He knew that he didn't stand a single chance in handling a woman like her, and he had no plans to do so.

"There's more to a person than just their looks," Elvina commented. She had met a few people whose looks were ruined by their wretched personalities.

"She's plenty determined to make Freckles hers," Urian commented.

"He doesn't belong to her," Elvina muttered.

"So do somethin' 'bout it," Trevor said.

She looked at him. "What can I possibly do about the situation?"

"Just go on up there and start talking," Quenby suggested.

"She might as well say that Owen is with her at that rate," Vallerie huffed.

Elvina went back to looking at Owen and Iorwen so that she didn't miss anything happening between them. "If she continues to bat her eyes the way she's been doing, Owen might believe she has some form of eye infection."

"Are you jealous that he's receivin' attention from her and not you?" Trevor teased.

"No," she denied all too quickly.

Urian chuckled. "Green's a good color on you, Chipmunk."

True to her nickname, Elvina puffed out her cheeks in dismay. "I prefer purple." She did like the green dress she owned because of Owen. However, she refused to bring that up now.

Mischievousness sparked in Rory's eyes. "I have an idea..."

"Do tell," Elvina said.

"Follow my lead." He took her hand and led her to where others danced.

A funny thought occurred to Elvina. "Do you intend for me to literally follow your lead?"

"You're already catchin' on to my genius plan," he chuckled. He put his right hand on her waist, being mindful of its placement so he didn't cross any boundaries, before taking her right hand with his left. They started dancing, keeping pace with the music.

"You dance well," she complimented, adjusting where her left hand was on his shoulder to be comfortable.

"I'm typically Owen's dancin' partner," he informed her. "We don't particularly like speakin' about it."

She giggled to herself, picturing the two dancing. "That must be a sight to see."

"A better one than him and Urian dancin'," he jested, giving her a little twirl.

"But perhaps this is your way of dancing with me," she teased.

"Oh, no. The brilliant Elvina has seen through my evil plan. Whatever will I do?"

She rolled her eyes, slightly curious about what he did have in store for her.

"Okay, now laugh," he instructed.

She was puzzled. "Laugh?"

He nodded. "Owen will hear you. He'll recognize your laugh."

She saw where he was going with this.

"It'll be more effective if I'm the one who catches him lookin' at us rather than you," he reasoned.

She trusted his judgment. "All right. Here goes." She laughed, ensuring that her voice would reach him.

Not being inconspicuous about it at all, Rory blatantly stared at Owen to gauge his reaction.

He immediately looked in their direction, paying no attention to Iorwen, who was in the middle of speaking. His eyes narrowed in on where Rory was touching Elvina with his hands before he made eye contact with the bespectacled guard.

"Well?" Elvina inquired since she couldn't see behind her.

"Oh, he noticed," Rory replied. "I'm not sure what he'll do next, though."

"Then we better keep dancing."

"Of course." He did a little spin solely so Owen could see Elvina's smiling face as she focused on Rory. He knew exactly how to get to his charge when Elvina was involved.

"This is fun," she mentioned.

"I mean, as long as you're havin' fun."

She smiled a little. "That sounds like something Owen would say."

"We tend to rub off on each other."

"Only in the best way, though, right?"

"Definitely," he chuckled, and twirled her around once more.

They were interrupted when a hand grabbed Rory by his

shoulder. It belonged to a particularly disgruntled second prince.

"Oh, hello, Owen," Elvina greeted.

"How did you escape Iorwen?" Rory asked.

"I told her I had a matter to attend to," Owen replied.

"A matter, huh?"

"An important one." He eyed Rory carefully. "Perhaps you should comfort her durin' my time of absence."

He stiffened up at the very idea. "I'll pass."

"So trade me places."

Smiling at a job well done, Rory released his hold on Elvina and bowed at his waist.

Owen was quick to stand in place to keep Elvina close to him. He intended to not let her dance with another unless she wanted to do so. "Ask the band to play *'Wraig Deg y Môr',*" he requested.

Elvina understood only the last word because of what Owen had explained about Tiramôr's origin of the name. At least she believed that he used the word for sea.

"Will do," Rory said as he walked away.

"What did you just request?" Elvina inquired.

"'Fair Lady of the Sea,'" he replied.

She became a little excited. "So you did say that word?"

He seemed slightly confused. "Wait, which word?"

"*Môr.*"

He lit up with a smile.

"I thought that's what you said, but I was not entirely sure," she explained.

"It makes me happy you picked up on it." He assumed the position to slow dance with her. "Just like you make me happy."

She smiled. "How do you say happy in your language?"

"*Hapus.*"

"That's simple enough."

Just then, the current song changed to another one. It was lovely and whimsical. A harp and other string instruments were used, along with a whistle and flute. It flowed together and just worked as a piece.

Due to the practice from before, it was as if Elvina and Owen had been dancing together for years. They knew each other's cues so well. Some people took notice that the second prince of their kingdom was dancing with a beautiful girl they had never seen before. Right now, their faces were ever so close together.

"They can't throw any baps at me now," he jested.

"That's what you think now, but just wait…"

"I'll just catch it and throw it back at 'em."

"Which means, you must let go of me."

He squeezed her a little tighter. "We can't have that, now." He slowly twirled her in place before bringing her back to him.

"How do you say I love you?" she inquired.

"Rwy'n dy garu di."

It seemed vaguely familiar like it was on the tip of her tongue. "Have you said that before?"

"Yeah."

"When?"

"Our first time in the stable, when you asked if there was a phrase I liked."

"Even then?"

A quirky grin appeared on his lips. "We both know it was before then."

"You never told me before then," she pointed out.

"I shoulda said it sooner."

"Now you can say it as much as you like."

His grin grew. "My woodland fairy. My Elvi." He dipped his head closer to hers for a chaste kiss.

It was over before they both knew it.

"What if Iorwen saw that?" she questioned.

"Then she'll know that you're mine and I'm yours, *cariad aur.*"

"What does that mean?"

"It's a term of endearment."

"Is that so?"

"Yn wir."

CHAPTER TWENTY-FOUR

Elvina felt graced with luck since Vallerie and Quenby had given her alone time now that the ball had ended. Otherwise, they would know about Owen sneaking into her bedchamber for a little visit. The two currently lounged on the bed, her body snuggled up to him in his warm and comforting embrace. Candles provided lighting in the spacious room, and everything felt right in the world at this moment.

"Did you have fun at the ball, Elvi?" he inquired, making small talk as he toyed with a strand of her hair.

"I did indeed," she replied, glancing up at him with a smile. "Did you?"

He nuzzled the top of her head with his chin in an affectionate manner. "Of course. I got to spend it with you."

"Because that's the best way to spend one's time," she jested, rolling her eyes.

"Oi, you're worth it. You're always worth it. Don't ever think that you're not." His lips barely ghosted her forehead and he dropped his voice to an endearing whisper. "You're worth my time, Elvi. Always. I wouldn't wanna spend another minute any other way."

She moved her head forward just so she could peck the tip of his nose. "Thank you."

"You're welcome."

A comfortable silence fell over the two, which was interrupted when the door to the bedchamber burst open. Reacting instantly, Owen held Elvina as if to protect her from whatever was happening.

"Have you seen"—Trevor's eyes landed on his charge —"Freckles?" he finished lamely.

"Nope," Owen quickly denied with the shake of his head. "Not here." He shooed Trevor away with a free hand. "Go look somewhere else, Walla. *Tara 'wan!*"

Elvina knew that his last words were way of saying goodbye.

After shutting the door behind him with a foot, Trevor firmly crossed his arms over his chest, his eyes never leaving his charge. "How exactly did you manage to get in here? You were last seen in your room. I dropped you off there myself, I did, and there's no way you could have left because no one saw you in the hallway."

"But here I am," Owen laughed, proud of himself.

"How?" Trevor pressed. "How could you possibly have snuck out?"

"'Cause I'm bangin', of course."

Elvina playfully smacked his chest. "There's no need to be so cocky now."

"Don't make me get Vallerie," Trevor threatened. "Or Anwen."

Owen's face turned ashen. He knew that Vallerie would be protective of Elvina and hurt him if he ever laid an unwanted hand on her. On the other hand, Anwen would surely have his head for being caught with her, even if they weren't doing anything wrong.

"You have to the count of three," Trevor warned, narrowing his gaze.

Words rushed out of his mouth. "My balcony. Scaled the wall. Her balcony. The end."

Trevor's eyes nearly popped out of his head. "You scaled the wall?"

"It wasn't the first time!" Owen said to defend himself. "I've gotten good at it, I have!"

Trevor's jaw dropped open. "What?"

"Surprise!" Elvina added to take away the stress of the situation.

Inhaling deeply to calm his nerves, Trevor attempted to relax. "You—"

"I've done it since before Elvi came here," Owen informed him. "It gives me a chance to have alone time, and not just stay in my room. Don't worry, I've always taken precautions and wore a hood or somethin' to disguise myself, even at night."

Trevor thought for a moment and opened his mouth, but closed it before he managed to say a single word.

"Wait, why did you check on me in the first place?" Owen inquired.

"I had a question."

"Are you gonna ask it?"

Trevor's eyes flickered between the two relaxing in the bed before he shook his head. "I guess it can wait until mornin'." He looked at Elvina and gave her a short nod. "Sleep tight."

"Good night," she told him.

Spinning on his heels, Trevor turned around and opened the door before looking over his shoulder at Owen. "You better be in your room when I come to wake you up, or I'll mention to Anwen *and* Vallerie that you're probably in here."

"You got it," Owen promised, hoping there was no fear in his voice.

With that, Trevor shut the door and left the two alone.

"Just make sure you don't get too tired to scale that wall," Elvina teased.

"Trust me, I'm wide awake now."

"I bet you are."

"Just lemme know when you start gettin' sleepy and I'll head back to my room."

"Is that so?" She snuggled up to him, pleased that he was naturally warm in body temperature. He did make an excellent person to cuddle with when it was cold out. On the other hand, he might not be as pleasant when it was hot.

Realizing what she was reasoning, she blushed. She wasn't even betrothed to him yet, and she was already thinking about sharing a bed with him.

"Oi, what's occurin'?" Owen inquired, noticing her expression.

"Nothing," she quickly said.

He poked her cheek with a finger. "Are you sure you don't wanna mention it?"

"I'm positive."

"Really?"

"Yes."

"In that case..." A hand of his found its way to her stomach and he tickled her.

"O–Owen!" she giggled. "Stop it!"

"I will if you tell me!"

She kicked her legs and squirmed, but to no avail. "I y–yield!"

Now that she was red in the face, he let up. "Are you gonna talk for real?"

Wheezing to catch her breath, she held up a finger to signal she needed a moment. When she returned to normal, she closed her eyes while she spoke to help with her embarrassment. "I have strong feelings for you, I really do. I care for you, and I can't wait for the day when we can truly be together."

"Argh, why'd I agree that I'd leave you?" he groaned. "Now that you said that, I don't wanna leave you."

"You'll see me tomorrow," she pointed out, opening her eyes. "You have the morning to look forward to."

He frowned. "Yeah, but that means I'll sleep alone tonight, and so will you."

She giggled at his childish behavior. "I've slept alone many nights before. I'm more than sure I'll survive another, and I'm sure you will as well."

"But I don't like it anymore," he whined.

"Should we have a future together—"

"*When* we have one," he corrected without a second thought.

She smiled before she continued speaking. "When we have a future together, we will no longer have to worry about being alone at night."

"Or asleep," he chuckled.

Her face heated up in an instant. "Owen, that wasn't funny."

Despite her words, he was laughing. "Oh, c'mon. It kinda was."

With a huff, Elvina flipped onto her side so her back was to him. A bit of silent treatment would do him good.

"Aw, Elvi."

As punishment, she didn't acknowledge him. She didn't even harrumph in response.

"Elvi?"

She continued to show no sign that she heard him.

"Elvina?"

She finally glanced over her shoulder. It was the first time he had called her by her real name in years. Now able to see his face, she could see he was genuinely worried.

"I was only jokin'," he said. "I didn't mean to step on a boundary of yours. I'm still learnin' those as we go."

Resuming her old position, she was once again on her back. "I suppose there's much time to learn more about one another."

He cracked a grin. "Your head's probably gonna hurt after all you learn 'bout me."

"Then it's a good thing I'm always up for a challenge."

Time passed and soon enough, she was drowsy with sleep. Her eyelids were heavy, but she was determined to stay awake for as long as she could before Owen went on his way.

"I think it's time I get goin'," he softly said.

"I'll walk you to the door. That's the least I can do."

He booped her nose with a finger. "Nope, you're stayin' in bed. You look pretty comfortable. And I'll blow out the candles while I'm at it."

She smiled at his thoughtfulness. "Thank you."

With that, he got out of the bed and tucked her under the blankets. He caressed a cheek with his fingers in a gentle manner. "Sweet dreams, Elvi."

"Until morning, Owen."

Elvina woke up to someone poking her cheek. Lying on her side, she peeked through one eye to find Owen resting his upper torso on the bed, keeping his distance for his safety in case she was grumpy.

He smiled at her. "G'mornin', Elvi."

"Good morning," she mumbled, still in the process of waking up.

"I was thinkin', we could have breakfast and go ridin'. Whaddya say?"

She sat up, the blankets pooling around her waist. "I like the sound of that very much."

"Great." With much energy, he jumped to his feet. "Okay. Get dressed and we can get started."

"Are the others awake already?" she inquired, rubbing her eyes.

He nodded. "The guys are makin' sure breakfast will be ready by the time you're downstairs."

"I won't take long," she assured him as she got out of bed, placing her bare feet onto the floor.

"Good." With that, he walked over to the lounging area and plopped down on a sofa to face her. He remained upright and only took up a single space, hands resting on his lap. It seemed as though he didn't have a single care in the world.

Making sure she was seeing what she thought she saw, she blinked a couple of times. "Owen?"

"Yeah?"

"What are you doing?"

"Waitin' on you. What's it look like I'm doin', hmm?"

"But I have to change." She motioned down to herself. "And you're here…"

"Oh, right." He closed his eyes to give her privacy.

Frowning, she grabbed a pillow from the bed and threw it at him as hard as she could.

It hit him right in the face and fell onto his lap. He looked at her with surprise, shocked she did that to him. "Did you just throw that at me?"

She planted her hands firmly on her hips. "Of course! Do you expect me to change with you in here?"

A devious glint appeared in his eyes. "You just declared war with this prince. Prepare yourself."

Her eyes grew wide as he raced for her, pillow in hand. She grabbed another pillow to defend herself before he could strike her down. She hopped onto the bed and stood on it to gain a height advantage. "Stop it!" she cried, unable to hide the amusement in her voice. "I have to get ready!"

"After I destroy you." He swung the pillow around but missed her shins as she stepped back. "Then I'll leave."

She moved back even more as he hopped onto the bed to join her, not minding his boots on the blankets. "You don't stand a chance against me," she taunted. "Your skills are no match for—Eep!" Not realizing how close she was to the edge of the bed, she stepped back too far and fell off.

Fear flashed in his eyes. "Elvi!"

Her feet crumpled beneath her and she was down on the floor, not moving at all.

As quickly as he could, he abandoned the pillow he had and scrambled over to her. He cradled her in his lap, checking her over. "Elvina, answer me."

She wearily looked up at him. "Owen, I"—she bopped his face with the pillow still in her hand—"win."

He blinked once. Twice. His lips slightly parted open, but not a single sound came out.

She giggled at his reaction. "And the victory goes to—" Her words were cut off when she started laughing up a storm due to the fingers tickling her sides. "Ssstop it!"

"Never!" he cackled, not relenting in the slightest. He showed her no mercy for the little stunt she had just pulled on him.

"P–Please!" she sputtered.

He eased up a little bit. "What was that?"

"Please," she huffed. "No more."

"Hmm, I don't think so." He continued to tickle her. "Not

after what you made me go through." He only stopped when her face was bright red.

Her chest heaved as she tried catching her breath. For good measure, she grabbed the pillow she let go of during the tickle attack and attempted to whack him upside the head with it.

However, his reflexes were too good and he caught it before it hit him. He tossed it onto the bed, making sure it was out of reach so she couldn't use it against him a third time. He leaned down to kiss her forehead. "I'll wait for you outside of the room while you change. See you soon, Elvi."

After breakfast, Elvina, Owen, Vallerie, and Trevor were the ones outside riding. The three other personal guards opted out to remain at the castle until the others returned.

"Wow, it's a lot different now that Rory isn't here!" Owen commented as they trotted through a field toward the forest.

"Is that because he isn't constantly talking to me?" Elvina giggled.

"We can actually hear ourselves think for once," Trevor teased.

"He really is horrible," Vallerie groaned. "All he ever does is flirt with any female in sight."

"Vallerie, one of these days, he'll realize that he has no chance with you," Elvina commented.

Trevor chuckled. "We don't call him Flirtsalot for nothin'."

"You got that right," Owen agreed.

"I don't think there's anyone like him back in Arnembury," Vallerie mused. "Or even all of Grenester for that matter."

Elvina nodded. "Agreed."

The horses slowed to a walk, and Owen steered his horse close to Trevor. "Wanna race?" he asked.

"We both know Cari's faster than Rhys," Trevor huffed. "You just wanna show off in front of Elvina."

"No way."

Elvina hid her grin with her hand.

"Why impress her when you already have her?" Vallerie asked.

"Can't have her lose interest, now can I?" Owen responded.

"She definitely won't be bored with you," Trevor laughed.

Owen gave him a look. "Are you makin' fun of me, Walla?"

He looked at him with a big grin. "Why would I ever do somethin' like that, Your Highness?"

Quenby laughed at his sarcasm. "You two haven't changed. It's just like old times."

A deep horn sounded off in the distance, coming in the direction of the castle. Both Owen and Trevor looked toward it.

"What's wrong?" Vallerie inquired.

"Somethin's goin' on," Owen answered.

"We have to go back to the castle," Trevor advised. "Now."

CHAPTER TWENTY-FIVE

When the group arrived at the stable, Quenby, Urian, and Rory awaited them.

"What's occurrin'?" Owen asked as he dismounted from Cari.

"We gotta get Chipmunk to the throne room," Urian replied.

"Why's that?" Vallerie inquired.

"People from Arnembury have arrived." Rory began to usher Elvina toward the castle.

She inhaled sharply. Millicent had received the letter she had written, and now they were here. It seemed surreal after all that had happened during Elvina's stay since Owen first found her in the forest.

Because Elvina wore the attire with trousers, she didn't have to worry about holding the skirt of a dress as she ran.

"Wait for us!" Trevor shouted as the others raced to catch up with her.

"There's no way she's gonna do that!" Quenby laughed.

Her mind was an absolute whirlwind. Castle guards were here in Helidinas, then she'd be off with them to return home. She'd speak with Fitzroy and tell him about all that Reeves had done. She'd then tell him she wished to marry Owen since she had never been betrothed to Kennard in the first place.

Her boots pounded against the ground, her heart pounding away in her chest. She was a complete bundle of emotions right now. From surprised to anxious, too excited and cheerful.

She ignored the looks that she and the others received as they made their way through the castle. The double doors to the throne room were already open, and no one wasted any time rushing inside. They all stopped short when they took in the scene.

Her eyes grew wide as she took everything in. At least fifteen of Arnembury's castle guards were mixed in with important people to her. Garrick, Whitley, and Millicent mingled with Ceron and Mervin, but her father and his personal guard were nowhere to be seen.

"You all..." Elvina whispered. The entire room was silent, so everyone heard her.

"El!" Millicent shouted, making her way over to her. "El!"

"Milli!" Leaving the others she had entered the room with, Elvina rushed over to meet her embrace.

Garrick and Whitley held back, wanting Millicent to be reunited with her friend. Whitley beamed with joy at the sight of her charge, while Garrick had a reserved smile on his face.

Millicent held Elvina close to her, even kissing the top of her head. "El, you're all right. I've been so worried about you since Garrick and Whitley returned without you and the others, but you're safe."

"That, I am," Elvina replied.

Millicent held her back by the shoulders to look her over. She was still her lady-in-waiting, but it was more than that.

They were friends. "We wouldn't have known better without that letter I got from you."

"And here you are." Elvina looked over at Garrick and Whitley with a smile. "Along with them."

"Okay, it's our turn," Whitley said, holding her arms out for a hug. "C'mere, you."

Millicent released Elvina so she could run to them.

Elvina was ready to hug Whitley, but Garrick intercepted her. She was lifted off her feet and held against him in a tight hug.

Not letting Garrick steal Elvina away for good, Whitley joined in on the hug.

Going with the moment, Vallerie and Quenby walked over to add to the embrace. They were all back. The Thunder Squadron and their charge were back together, the five finally reunited.

They eventually broke apart, and Elvina was set back down onto the floor.

"I expected a couple of guards to come with a horse for me," Elvina voiced.

"You got more than you expected, it seems," Garrick laughed.

"Your father would have been along as well, but he's sick," Whitley informed her.

"Sick?" Elvina whispered, her blood running cold. She had an unsettling feeling hovering over her. Perhaps her secret fears about her father had been confirmed. What if Reeves was targeting him as well?

"He became ill the next morning after Whitley and I returned," Garrick explained. "The castle doctor believed he wasn't taking the news about you well."

"How bad is he?" Quenby asked.

Whitley shrugged. "We dunno. Haven't seen him."

"Reeves insisted that your father wants to be left alone," Garrick added.

"We have to go," Elvina urged, her stomach churning. "We have to go home right now!"

Garrick couldn't ignore her distress. "What's gotten into you—"

"The sooner, the better!" she insisted, not meaning to be rude by interrupting him. "I believe that Reeves did something to Father. He might have even poisoned him for all I know."

"That's a big accusation, ain't it?" Whitley asked.

Owen strode over to the five. "Reeves hired the group of bandits to attack you that day. He gave away your path and destination. That's how the bandits knew where you'd be."

"He's also the reason why the trade agreement between Tiramôr and Grenester ended," Mervin added. "That man isn't to be trusted."

"We also learned that Elvina was never betrothed to Duke Kennard," Vallerie continued. "There was a ball last night, and he attended. Kennard confirmed that he never received a single letter from King Fitzroy."

Quenby folded his arms across his chest. "Reeves faked those letters, and he's messed with the mail. King Mervin didn't receive a single letter. Reeves also interfered with the letters King Mervin sent out, too."

Garrick nodded. "We'll leave now, then."

"Elvi, I'll come with you," Owen offered, wanting to be there for support. He quickly glanced at Mervin, who showed no sign of disapproving of the idea.

"If he goes, then we go," Trevor added.

Urian folded his arms across his chest. "We're a package deal."

"I'll help Tad get our horses ready," Rory said before taking off.

"Elvina has one to ride, so just prepare as many as you need for your people!" Whitley called after him.

Elvina's heart skipped, thinking that Luna was waiting for her to ride home.

"Help me pack what we need," Trevor told Urian.

The two quickly left, leaving their charge without any of his personal guards.

"Do you need packed, El?" Millicent inquired as she approached.

"I've gained a few outfits, but I don't want them slowing us down."

"Nonsense." Millicent linked her arm with Elvina's and led her out of the throne room. "Let's get them packed up right now."

Garrick looked at the other guards from Arnembury. "Remain here. We'll be back."

Owen walked along at Elvina's side, with Whitley, Garrick, Vallerie, and Quenby lined up in a row behind them. "Do we need to be caught up on anything?" Garrick asked.

Whitley nodded. "Yeah, what all have we missed?"

"What else is there besides Reeves being a treacherous snake?" Elvina scoffed.

"We think Reeves is also the reason why Elvina did the traveling," Quenby added. "He somehow must have convinced King Fitzroy to get Elvina to travel so she could be out in the open for the bandits to attack."

"It's mostly negative things due to what Reeves has done, and is perhaps planning," Vallerie summed up.

Whitley whistled. "Wow. That's a lot about Reeves." She looked at Elvina. "Anything else you wanna share? Something positive?"

Elvina looked back over her shoulder at her. "Not that I can think of…"

Garrick observed just how close Owen walked next to

Elvina and noticed she didn't mind his nearness. "Really? Nothing else at all?"

Elvina looked at Owen for help. "Is there anything you can think of?"

He merely smiled at her and playfully nudged her. "You're tellin' me you can't think of somethin' positive to tell 'em?"

Finally getting the hint, she lit up with a smile. She looked back over her shoulder at Garrick and Whitley. "During my time here, I did find someone I do wish to marry."

Whitley's jaw just about dropped open as she skipped in excitement.

On the other hand, Garrick stared Owen down. "Is that so?" he practically growled.

Breaking eye contact with him, Owen swallowed hard and stepped closer to Elvina for his safety.

"Getting Garrick's approval will be the hardest," Quenby stage whispered to Owen. "You haven't seen anything yet."

For intimidation, Garrick carried himself at his full height as he narrowed his gaze at the back of Owen's head. He would fully play out his role as a menacing figure.

"You've already passed with me, so that's a great start," Elvina assured Owen.

"Only three more tests to go," Whitley said, and jerked her head at Millicent. "Eh, make it four."

Millicent nodded.

"Wait, *four*?" Owen asked, being able to only account for two.

"My father," Elvina replied, just as the members of the Thunder Squadron said, "King Fitzroy."

Although, now that Elvina thought about it, her father might already approve of Owen if he had tried writing in the past about the two marrying each other.

"And me," Whitley added, even though she was plenty warmed up to him. "Millicent, too."

"Hey, I passed with Elvi," Owen said as he tried to be confident. "That's gotta count for somethin.'"

Garrick smirked as though he had the upper hand. "Think again."

Owen lost some confidence—some.

"He isn't like past suitors," Elvina assured Garrick. "You know that."

"I mean, it's saying *something* you wanna marry him," Whitley pointed out.

"Exactly." She suddenly recalled that Garrick had been injured. She gasped, abruptly stopping and turning in place to face him.

"What's wrong?" multiple voices asked.

She looked at Garrick. "How are you faring? I heard that you were injured when the bandits attacked."

"It's nothing to be worried about," he assured her. "I'm much better now."

Whitley playfully punched Garrick. "I wouldn't have let him come along if he wasn't in good shape."

"Knowing Garrick, he would have found a way," Quenby offered.

Vallerie silently nodded in agreement.

Garrick used both hands to turn Elvina around by her shoulders and prompted her to walk forward. "No wasting time. We'll leave once everything is set."

"He's got a soft spot for Elvina," Quenby whispered to Owen.

"All of us do," Whitley said wholeheartedly.

Owen smiled at her, taking her hand. "Yeah, we all do."

The action didn't go unnoticed by Garrick.

"At some point, Garrick and I need to be filled in on what happened after we all got separated," Whitley advised, attempting to redirect Garrick's attention away from their joined hands.

"I'm sure we can swap notes later," Quenby said.

"Everything has been rather crazy this past week," Garrick commented.

Owen decided to keep quiet about the matter in case he said the wrong thing in front of Garrick.

"At least we are all back together now," Elvina said, a small smile on her lips.

☙———☙

Halfway there. The group was halfway to reaching Arnembury. Elvina was more than eager to return home as soon as possible. Concerned for her father's safety was at an all-time high. She also wanted to put an end to Reeves' malicious and clandestine intentions once and for all. However, it was time for the horses to have a break. They needed their rest, after all.

Elvina had since busied herself with pacing in the grass that was shaded by a tree. Her mind was not at ease. What if she arrived too late to save her father? What if she never had the chance to speak with him again?

No one had yet to approach her. The guards minded their own business, knowing that one of her friends could comfort her better than they could. Each member of the Thunder Squadron was waiting for one of them to go to her, or for her to come to one of them. Millicent figured that she just needed to blow off steam alone. The Babysitter Brigade waited for Owen to step up while he was waiting for Elvina to reach out a hand.

Finally, Owen was the first to crack. "You're gonna drive yourself mad if you keep overthinkin'," he said as he approached her. "Or make a trench with all the pacin' you're doin'."

"I can't help it," she said, still pacing.

He moved his head back and forth as he watched her. "We'll be in Arnembury before you know it."

"That can't come soon enough."

"Elvi."

She finally stopped and looked at him. "Yes?"

He walked over to her and gently held her arms. "Take a deep breath," he instructed.

She did so, filling her lungs.

"And exhale."

She let out the air she had been holding.

"Feel better?" he inquired. "Any better?"

"A little." She smiled at him. "Thank you."

He returned the smile. "You're welcome, Elvi." He pressed his lips against her forehead. "Do you wanna sit down?"

She nodded. "I believe I'd like that."

"Stay here. I'll be right back." He took off without another word, only to return with a blanket from his pack. He figured that staying away from where the majority of the others were would be good for her. After spreading the blanket on the grass, he held out a hand.

"Thank you," she said, taking his hand and easing herself down into a sitting position.

He sat down next to her, leaving some space between them.

She was the first to notice Garrick approaching in a casual manner. "Hello, Garrick," she greeted.

"What's occurin'?" Owen asked.

"Just looking for a place to sit," he nonchalantly replied.

Owen arched an eyebrow, catching onto things. "But way over here—"

Without a word, Garrick readied himself to sit down in the little space between the duo.

To avoid getting squished, Owen quickly scooted away from Elvina. Now he was nearly off of the blanket.

Elvina puffed out her cheeks in dismay, knowing exactly why Garrick did what he did.

He merely sighed in contentment. "Ah, this is a great spot."

"Garrick," Elvina huffed, a warning tone in her voice.

"Don't mind me." He lied down, hands clasped behind his head with his eyes closed. "Feel free to carry on with whatever you were talking about."

"We were pickin' out names for all the kids we're gonna have," Owen teased.

Garrick's eyes remained closed. "That time will happen *after* marriage because Elvina shouldn't be expecting any children until *after* marriage." He cracked open an eye to look at Owen. "And *if* she is—"

"No, nothing of the sort like that," Elvina quickly assured him, wanting to take the pressure off of Owen. She needed him alive to marry and build a family with him. Not to mention, rule her kingdom alongside her.

"Yet," Owen added with a chuckle.

"*Yet*," Garrick echoed before closing his eye.

Owen looked at Elvina with a pout on his face. Sure, they were riding next to each other on their horses, but it wasn't the same as sitting next to the other. Especially without Garrick in the way.

"What kind of accent do you think our children will have?" Elvina mused, sticking to the topic.

He seemed a little confused. "Whatcha mean?"

"They'll be surrounded by people with my native accent. Assuming the Babysitter Brigade joins us, only four others will have a different accent."

"Not to mention, slang."

"Exactly."

"I think they'll take after you in that sense. Like you said, they'll be around people with your accent."

"But I like your accent."

He smiled a little. "Doesn't mean I won't teach 'em my language. I'm doin' it with you, so why can't I do the same for 'em?"

"Remind me what your favorite saying is again." She just wanted to hear him say it.

"Rwy'n dy garu di," he sweetly responded, the sincerity in his voice hard to miss.

CHAPTER TWENTY-SIX

Since the sun would be low in the sky, the group prepared to set up camp for the night. At least tomorrow they would be able to stay at a town's inn before arriving in Arnembury early the next day. A storm had taken out a bridge that would add to the journey. At least the group still had provisions they brought from Helidinas that would last them until then.

"Owen, your tent will be clear on the other side of camp, so you're away from Elvina," Garrick instructed, so he and the Babysitter Brigade knew where to pitch their tents.

He wasn't pleased with the idea. He found it absurd. "Why's that?"

Garrick narrowed his gaze at him.

Owen gulped. "Er, I guess that's a valid point."

Wanting to get hands-on, Elvina planned to distract herself from worrying. "Can I help set up my tent?" she asked, looking at Whitley.

"It's not the most exciting thing to do," she replied.

"It's better than nothing."

"Do you want me to help, too?" Millicent offered.

277

Elvina turned her attention to her. "You already do so much for me."

She smiled. "What are friends for?"

⁂

Along with many others, Elvina's tent was ready to go. Her unmarked wedge tent was flat in the back and front and furnished with some blankets and pillows for comfort. Four people could fit inside if they slept horizontally, but Elvina wouldn't have company.

As of now, Elvina, the Thunder Squadron, and Millicent had been caught up on what happened after the bandit attack for the most part. Elvina and the Thunder Squadron all shared their sides to the story. However, Garrick, Whitley, and Millicent were completely unaware that Elvina put her life on the line to protect Owen. They did know that Owen had saved Elvina on more than one occasion since he saved her in the forest.

The six sat around a fire together, not being disturbed by any others.

Whitley whistled. "Sounds like you had a lotta fun at least."

"It was different each day," Elvina said with a nod. The front half of her was warm enough from the dancing flames. She'd like a blanket around her to keep her backside from the chill, but other than that, she had no complaints. She shifted in place on the log she was sitting on, trying to be casual about things.

"I'm still impressed they were fine with Elvina," Quenby admitted. "You know, considering the relationship Grenester and Tiramôr have."

"Had," Millicent corrected. She was pleased that the relationship would be great for the two kingdoms once again. She was also more than eager to see the relationship bloom between two particular royals hailing from those kingdoms.

"I never denied being a princess," Elvina stated. "Likewise, I never openly admitted that I was one."

"She gave just enough information for them to know if they already didn't know her," Vallerie said. "That was smart on her part."

Garrick merely nodded in approval, still proud of his charge for her thinking and actions.

"As if she could deny being from Grenester," Whitley commented. "The accent's a dead giveaway."

"At least she didn't try saying that she was from somewhere else," Millicent added.

Vallerie looked past Elvina. "Owen?"

Elvina looked behind her just as Owen put a blanket around her shoulders.

"Don't mind me." Owen made direct eye contact with Garrick. "Feel free to carry on with whatever you were talkin' 'bout."

A grin twitched along Garrick's lips. It was faint, and Owen was the only one who noticed.

Elvina and Garrick were the only ones who were aware that Owen just quoted Garrick.

With that, Owen strolled away without looking back at the group.

"Now that kid has some guts," Quenby commented.

"Or he's just crazy," Vallerie said.

"Crazy in love," Millicent gleefully added.

Whitley laughed. "I agree with Millicent."

"Perhaps it's a mixture of all three..." Garrick mused, as though it was an afterthought.

Elvina smiled, believing that he was onto something about Owen.

Whitley looked at Elvina. "Okay, I gotta know something."

"What?"

"Who liked who first between you and Owen?"

The other members of the Thunder Squadron and Millicent were interested in knowing as well. Garrick attempted to seem the least bit interested. However, anything important to Elvina was important to him.

Elvina thought about things for a moment. "I had feelings for him before we were reunited. I can't tell you when they started exactly." She recalled her conversation with Owen from nights ago. "Owen had mentioned that he should have spoken up sooner."

"Aw," Millicent cooed.

"But the *real* question is, who admitted it first?" Quenby inquired.

"Owen did."

"When were his feelings confirmed?" Vallerie questioned.

"There were some little hints along the way."

Whitley started laughing. "Because proposing to you was a doozy."

Elvina fondly recalled that moment, smiling a little. "That was unforeseen."

"The next time he proposes, he better do it right," Garrick commented.

Quenby nudged him with an elbow. "Are you saying you approve of him?"

"As a suitor, no," he grumbled.

"No, not yet," Whitley corrected. "Give it time, though."

"What about you, Whitley, Millicent?" Vallerie questioned.

"I definitely like him," Millicent answered. "And I think he's cute for El." She sent her a little wink. "Brown eyes and all."

Elvina recalled when she had been with Millicent the night before she and the Thunder Squadron had left Arnembury. Back then, she had told Millicent that she loved brown eyes.

"I think I'm getting there," Whitley responded. "He scored points with the blanket."

"Yeah, how did none of us notice that you wanted one?" Quenby asked. "We're your personal guards."

"He had time to get to know me while I was staying with him," Elvina reasoned. "We spent time together. Days at a time."

Suddenly, Urian hastily approached the group of six. "We got company comin' down the road," he announced. "Arnembury guards on lookout spotted 'em."

"Where's Owen?" Elvina asked, immediately thinking of his safety.

"With Walla. Flirtsalot went to tell them while I came here."

Garrick rose to his feet. "How many?"

"Hard to tell in the dark," Urian replied, looking at him. "We can make out a carriage. Some on foot. They've got torches for light."

Elvina didn't doubt that their torches could be used as weapons, especially if it came down to using them.

"Hopefully, they'll just pass us by," Whitley said. "We don't want trouble."

Millicent nodded. "We don't need any more trouble."

Elvina agreed with both of them. Trouble had been finding her, and she wanted to be left alone.

Owen rushed up to the group with Trevor and Rory on his tail. He seemed relieved when he saw that Elvina wasn't too shook up about the news.

Everyone was standing now.

"What're the odds of 'em ignorin' us camped here?" Trevor questioned.

"If we're a bigger group than them, and they mean us no trouble, they should overlook us," Garrick replied.

Quenby grinned with confidence. "If they don't, they'll be in for a surprise since all of us can fight."

"Uh, I can't," Millicent voiced.

Rory shot her a wink. "Don't worry, I'll protect you."

"Oh, you have no chance with her," Elvina said.

Urian cracked up. "Shot down again."

"Oi, one of these times I'll get it right," Rory argued, shooting Urian a look.

"But tonight isn't that time," Owen chuckled.

Rory rolled his eyes. "I still can't believe that someone like you got someone like Elvina."

Owen smiled. "Me neither."

She smiled a little, securing the blanket around her a little more as if to bury herself and hide.

"Is he always this sappy?" Quenby asked.

"Ever since he got closer with Elvina," Trevor replied.

Rory nodded in agreement.

"Nuh-uh," Owen denied all too quickly.

Urian arched an eyebrow and held up two fingers at him. "Two words: woodland fairy."

Only Elvina, Owen, and the other members of the Babysitter Brigade were aware of the meaning of that.

"You came up with Chipmunk not much later," Owen pointed out.

"But which one sounds more affectionate?"

"Woodland fairy," Whitley coughed out.

Quenby patted her on the back. "Better watch that cough of yours."

"I'm allergic to sap," she replied in a teasing tone.

"You'll go up in hives if you're around Owen any longer," Rory jested.

Some others laughed, including Elvina. Owen merely accepted the laughter with a slight pout on his face.

Moving light caught Elvina's attention. She could see the torches from her position. "I wonder why they're traveling at this hour," she mused aloud.

The others looked toward where she was looking and watched.

"Everyone has their reasons," Garrick told her.

Not much later, the torches were out of sight. The group never stopped. Everything seemed fine.

Garrick looked at the other members of the Thunder Squadron. "Have guards check the perimeter and the forest for intruders. That could have been a distraction to divert our attention from the forest behind us."

Elvina could understand him taking precautions.

"Wait, really?" Millicent asked, sounding surprised that there could be more possible danger.

"I'm not taking any chances with two royals here," he responded with reason. "Especially if they're to be the future rulers of my kingdom."

"Wait, does that mean—" Owen started.

"I said *if*," Garrick clarified, not letting him off so easy.

Taking their weapons with them, Vallerie, Whitley, and Quenby walked away to do as they were instructed.

"What if something happens?" Millicent inquired.

"It's nothing we can't handle," Urian assured her.

"Stick with Elvi at that rate," Owen said. "She can protect you."

"What do you know about her fighting skills?" Garrick questioned.

A confused expression came across his face. He looked at

Elvina. "Didn't you tell him what happened durin' the festival?"

"He already knows about us sparring," Elvina replied, wanting to sweep the topic under a rug.

"What does that have to do with the festival?" Millicent asked, slightly eager to be in the loop.

"It does not matter," Elvina simply replied.

"What are you talkin' about?" Rory scoffed. "He's *alive* because of you."

Garrick narrowed his gaze at Elvina. "What happened at the festival?"

"The both of us are fine, and that's what matters," she groaned.

"I want details."

Millicent nodded in agreement. "Me, too."

Elvina tried thinking of ideas to put it off, hoping that Garrick and Millicent would forget about it. "If I tell it now, I'll have to repeat it when Vallerie and Quenby are back."

"Fine, then. I won't have you repeat it." Garrick looked at Owen. "Talk."

He immediately stiffened. "What?"

Garrick shifted his gaze to the members of the Babysitter Brigade. "Or one of you can talk."

The trio exchanged glances with one another.

"Er, Freckles is a great storyteller—" Urian began.

"Owen was targeted by three people solely 'cause they thought he was gonna steal the crown from Ceron," Trevor informed them. "Attempts have been made on his life in the past 'cause of that reason. This time, Elvina got caught up in it."

Millicent gasped.

"One of 'em posed as a vendor and gave Owen and Elvina drinks drugged with *Nox Mortem*," he continued, explaining the turn of events.

Garrick silently considered his words while Millicent asked a question. "How did you know they needed help?"

"We"—Trevor motioned to himself, Rory, and Urian —"were followin' 'em. A fourth person had caused a diversion. When it was handled, we noticed Owen and Elvina were gone. I was with a group of guards when we heard noise comin' from the shop. There was a broken window."

Elvina never knew that breaking the window trick worked until now, and mentally patted herself on the back for it.

"Elvina mentioned that you taught her how to fight," Rory commented, looking at Garrick. "She's alive 'cause of you."

"She's alive because of what Whitley and I have taught her," Garrick corrected, and turned his attention to Elvina. "And she's alive because of her own quick thinking."

She smiled a little.

Elvina was restless. Sleep evaded her. All the tossing and turning she had done was fruitless. Perhaps a nightly stroll would do her good. People were still awake, judging by the quiet noises and low voices that she could just barely make out.

Without warning, the flap of the tent opened. They poked their head inside, keeping the lantern outside as to not blind her. "Are you doing okay in here?" Whitley inquired.

"I think I need to stretch my legs," Elvina admitted as she sat up, facing Whitley.

"Another night you're having trouble sleeping, huh?"

"Not a wink."

Whitley sighed in defeat. "Whelp, it's time to bring out the secret weapon."

Elvina made a face. "Secret weapon?"

"Sit tight. I'll be back." Whitley slipped out of the tent.

Now looking at the closed flaps, Elvina was left puzzled. Secret weapon? She wasn't entirely sure what Whitley was referring to, and she could only wait and see.

Soon enough, footsteps approached her tent. Once again, the flap opened up, but this time someone slipped inside.

"Whitley?" Elvina asked. She couldn't make out who it was in the darkness.

"Guess again," a male voice softly chuckled.

Oh, it certainly wasn't Whitley. "Owen, what are you doing here?" she inquired, remembering to keep her eager voice down.

"Whitley said you needed me," he replied, sitting on his rear to take off his boots.

A secret weapon indeed.

"She said you're havin' trouble sleepin," he continued. "You're not zonked at all."

She didn't admit it out loud. "What if Garrick finds out?"

"Whitley already assured me of my safety. She'll have a goss with Garrick. Somethin' 'bout your best interests in mind."

"Have you come to talk with me until I fall asleep?" she teased.

"I plan on that exactly. Now, move over." He scooted himself closer to her to lie down next to her.

She was too surprised to budge. "Why?"

"I'm sleepin' here for the night to keep you company. We can talk until you fall asleep."

Her cheeks heated up. "Garrick will have your head."

"Like I said, Whitley assured me of my safety. As long as 'no funny business happens' or else."

"I'm more than sure that Whitley was assuring you safety from *her*. You should be afraid of her, too."

"Might as well be afraid of the Thunder Squadron altogether."

"That, too."

They got comfortable under her blankets, snuggling close. Things felt right between them, like a natural fit.

"If I'm gonna be your husband, I hafta know you better than I do now," Owen said, hoping to distract her from thinking about Fitzroy and Reeves.

"You've known me for years," she pointed out.

"Yeah, but I missed out on eleven months. Now, what're things you like doin'?"

"I enjoy riding Luna and playing the harp. Training with the Thunder Squadron is fun as well."

"Is purple still your favorite color?"

"Yes."

"You do have that one purple dress from the Donnelly sisters."

"And you'll see more purple dresses when I'm back to wearing my clothes. Some are a little extravagant for my taste, but there are some that I do like."

"I bet you make 'em look great."

"You think everything I wear looks great."

"Exactly."

"Now, what's your favorite color?"

"Hmm, hard to say. Brown and green are startin' to grow on me on."

It completely went over her head that browns and greens made up her hazel eyes. "What's your favorite type of animal?"

"Chipmunks," he answered without hesitation.

Only now did she catch onto him. "Why?" she pried with a smile.

"They're cute and adorable." The smile in his voice was hard to miss.

"Is that so?"

"Quite so. And what 'bout you?"

She was a little confused. "What about me?"

He chuckled. "What's your favorite animal?"

"Oh." She smiled when a particular mare came to mind. "Horses."

"I coulda guessed that."

"Yet you still asked."

"Oi, I was returnin' the question."

"So you claim."

He changed his position slightly to get more comfortable. Snuggling even closer to her, he sighed in contentment. "I like this. I like us like this. Together. I'm sure things would be more comfortable in an actual bed, but it's kinda like campin' this way."

For a change, she missed her bed. "I think camping like this can be fun, but I prefer my bed."

"You haven't experienced real campin' yet. The Babysitter Brigade and I do it for fun on our guys' nights. Bein' in the forest with the stars above us is great."

"Even better than the sun setting over a beach?"

"Okay, now that's a toss-up."

The rest of their conversation varied from topic to topic. In the end, they fell asleep when tiredness overcame them. Nightmares didn't haunt her dreams this night.

Unbeknownst to the duo, Garrick sat just outside of the rear of the tent with his back to it. Not that he doubted her, but Whitley had been right. There was nothing for him to worry about.

He quietly stood and walked away with the folded blanket he had sat on in hand.

CHAPTER TWENTY-SEVEN

rnembury was within their sights. Elvina resisted the urge to have Luna gallop so she could reach the castle faster. She was bursting at the seams right now. Her home and father were practically within her grasp.

To make their grand entrance into the capital, all the guards donned their uniforms. Some carried green flags that had the Norwood crest on them, a clear indicator that someone of the royal family was within their company. Elvina wore the dress that she first received from Owen. It was one of the nicer ones she had with her.

Owen smiled. "Nothin's changed."

"Not at all," Trevor agreed.

"It's better than you described, Elvina," Rory told her.

She smiled, sitting up a little straighter, filled with pride.

"Has anythin' changed since the last time Freckles was here?" Urian asked.

"It's all the same, really. Although the garden has grown lovelier I think."

Owen perked up. "The one by the gazebo?"

"The very same."

"I've missed that spot."

"I haven't missed trackin' you down there," Trevor quipped.

"And now you have two more guards," Elvina mused.

"Speaking of guards, who was assigned to you first, Chipmunk?" Urian inquired out of curiosity.

"Vallerie and Quenby were the first two. Whitley came along soon after, so there could be a third." She thought of another member of her personal team. "As for my lady-in-waiting, Millicent was before Whitley."

Because Owen and Trevor had witnessed the additions with their visits, Rory and Urian were surprised. "Wait, Garrick wasn't a part of the original Thunder Squadron?" Rory questioned.

"He might be our leader now, but he was the last to join," Vallerie responded.

"Wait, so what's the backstory?" Urian asked, intrigued.

"It was my fifteenth birthday," Elvina said, easily recalling the time. "Whitley was sick and resting back at the castle. Vallerie and Quenby were with me, and two other guards as well. I was with those four in the city when it all happened."

"I still can't believe I wasn't there to help when it all went down," Whitley muttered to herself.

"A group of men and women decided to kidnap Elvina for ransom," Vallerie continued. "There were six to outnumber us. Four to take on the guards, and two to apprehend Elvina."

"They started getting away with her," Quenby added. "The four of them were keeping the four of us plenty busy. Things were chaotic. The group had thoroughly planned things out. We couldn't get to Elvina fast enough, and they were getting away with her by the forge..."

"Cue Garrick!" Whitley cheered.

Millicent giggled.

"I wasn't going to stand around and do nothing while the

princess of my kingdom was in trouble." He motioned to the scar along his chin. "I got hurt for my efforts, but that didn't matter." He grinned. "She knocked out one of them all on her own while I was handling the other."

"If he hadn't intervened, I probably wouldn't be here now," Elvina commented. "There had been talk about killing me just to get rid of me after they got the ransom money from Father."

Urian whistled. "Wow."

"Wow is right," Rory agreed.

"You were a blacksmith before?" Urian asked for clarification.

Garrick nodded. "Having a background in weapons and fighting worked out."

"And now you're the leader of the guards for your princess," Owen commented.

"And this princess can handle herself," Elvina voiced.

Owen smiled. "You're more than a princess that way."

❦

Elvina properly dismounted from Luna and strode up the stairs that led into the main entrance of the castle. People from Garrick to Owen followed after her. Her head was held high. She was more than ready to finally face Reeves and rid the castle of his presence.

Two guards stood at their post to open one of the doors for her.

"Where is my father?" Elvina firmly inquired, stopping before the threshold.

"Resting in his bedchamber," the female replied. "He fell ill while you were gone."

Elvina believed he was ill, but not from natural causes. "And where is Reeves?"

The male guard seemed surprised she would ask such a thing. "Reeves?"

She nodded. "Yes. Where is he?"

"He's been with your father—" the female guard began to say.

Elvina hurried away, heading for Fitzroy's bedchamber as quickly as she possibly could. The Thunder Squadron, Millicent, Owen, and the Babysitter Brigade were the only ones who chased after her, leaving behind the other guards in their wake.

When they reached his bedchamber, Elvina threw open the door without announcing her presence. The only three inside were Fitzroy, Reeves, and the personal guard of Fitzroy, Swain Kemp.

Swain bolted upright from his sitting position in a chair that was at the end of the bed. He faced the newcomers, hand on the hilt of his sword like he was going to draw it. He was a big, burly man with dark skin and light eyes.

Reeves was startled, and nearly dropped the bowl of soup in his hands. He stopped in place, standing near the bed as he watched everyone enter the bedchamber.

On the other hand, Fitzroy appeared motionless in his bed and was deathly pale. He didn't even stir at the loud commotion that was happening around him.

"Princess Elvina, you are—" Reeves began.

"Silence!" she ordered, catching her breath, a little winded.

His mouth remained open as shock settled over him. He hadn't expected such an outburst from her.

"With no sudden movements, move away from my father," Elvina firmly commanded, flexing her fists. "And keep your hands up where I can see them."

"What's going on?" Swain inquired.

"Vallerie!" Garrick barked.

She was quick, ready with an arrow aimed directly at Reeves' heart. "I won't miss."

To avoid seeing anything potentially gruesome, Millicent covered her eyes with her hands, peeking between her fingers to watch.

Ever so slowly, Reeves raised his hands and stepped away from the bed, keeping his back toward it. "Do I have the right to know what's going on?"

"You're in big trouble," Owen growled.

Reeves arched an eyebrow at him. "What are you doing—"

"You are under arrest," Elvina snapped.

He stiffened, stunned by what he had just heard. "Excuse me?" he asked, clearly taken aback.

She looked him in the eye. "For treason against the kingdom of Grenester that you committed last fall."

"What are you talking ab—"

"You're also under arrest for hiring a group of bandits to murder me, Princess Elvina of Grenester," she interrupted.

His eyes grew wide with shock. "What?"

"Lastly, you're under arrest for the attempted murder of King Fitzroy of Grenester."

The bedchamber fell silent. Everyone remained still.

"Princess, those are heavy accusations," Swain advised. "Quite heavy, really."

"I'm Second Prince Owen Gravenor of Tiramôr, and I can confirm the first charge," he said. "He's the single reason why our two kingdoms ended their trade agreement back then."

Elvina never looked away from Reeves. "I came to learn a thing or two about you after the bandits attacked and I escaped with my life. You aren't as loyal as I once thought you were. You're nothing more than a cunning snake with malicious intent. You will suffer the consequences of your actions."

Reeves' lips remained in a firm line. He knew he couldn't save himself from the deep hole he had dug for himself.

Swain turned to face Reeves, clearly looking at him in a whole new light. "Fitzroy trusted you. As his royal adviser, he trusted you."

"The sudden death of a healthy man would have raised suspicion," Elvina said. "However, if the same man was grieving over the possible death of his only child and fell ill, well, that would be more plausible. It would take time for his condition to worsen."

Reeves knew he had been completely found out. There was nothing else for him. With rage and desperation in his eyes, he lunged for Elvina. The bowl in his hand clattered to the floor and broke.

At the sound of the arrow firing, Elvina clamped her eyes closed. She didn't need to see.

Likewise, Owen was quick to turn Elvina around and held her against him. He didn't want her looking upon the scene either.

Knees fell to the floor, and Reeves wailed loudly. "Why didn't you kill me?"

Elvina flipped over to look. Reeves was still alive, only injured, gripping the arrow lodged in his left shoulder.

Fanning herself so she didn't faint, Millicent looked anywhere but where Reeves was. She was highly squeamish. Perhaps she should have kept her eyes closed from the start.

"As if I would shoot you dead," Vallerie scoffed.

"We need you alive"—Quenby leaned against Whitley —"for her."

She nodded in agreement. "You're gonna tell me what you've been poisoning the king with. I need to brew up an antidote and treat him."

"And if you don't tell her," Garrick threatened, "we have ways of making you talk."

Swain walked over to Reeves and forced him to stand, not being gentle with him at all. "Let's go," he demanded.

Elvina and Reeves had a silent staring battle. When he limped by, he spat at her face.

Owen was quick to pull her away and wiped her face with his sleeve, muttering curses under his breath.

Garrick roughly shoved Reeves in the back. "Get moving."

He merely groaned in response.

Without realizing she was holding her breath, Elvina left Owen's side and approached her father's bed. She treaded over carefully as if her footsteps might wake him. She sat on the edge of the piece of furniture, reaching for his hand.

"Hello, Father," she greeted in a gentle voice.

"Should we give them space?" Millicent whispered.

Everyone heard her, due to the silence in the bedchamber. Garrick nodded.

"I think Elvi would like that," Owen replied.

One by one, they left. Elvina was oblivious since she was solely focused on her father.

This was the worst she had ever seen Fitzroy look. He had been sick before, but this was much, much worse.

"I made it back home, safe and sound." She scooted closer, using her left hand to take his right hand that rested on top of his covers. He was cold to the touch. Facing Fitzroy, she lied down on her side and held his hand with both of hers.

"When you wake up, we'll have much to talk about," she said, not sure if he could hear her or not. "I can tell you all about the adventures I had while in Tiramôr. Yes, Tiramôr of all places. You might be surprised by the friends I made while there..."

Elvina was slightly groggy when she came to. She shifted around but discovered that something was amiss.

"Sorry," Owen said as he adjusted his hold on her. "Didn't mean to wake you."

She looked up at him, discovering that he was carrying her. "What happened?" she mumbled, still waking up.

"We let you have some time with your father," Garrick replied, his voice coming from behind her. "When we checked on you after some time, you were asleep."

Elvina craned her neck around to look at him. "What's happening now?"

"We're takin' you to your room," Owen replied.

"The both of you?"

Garrick grinned. "He wanted to take you but didn't know the way from your father's chamber. I offered to help."

"What about everyone else?"

"They are all getting situated," Garrick replied. "Millicent has already unpacked your things. Vallerie and Quenby are nearly squared away with Reeves, while Whitley's nearly done with the antidote. As for the Babysitter Brigade..." He looked at Owen, cueing him to speak.

"They're all probably crashed in the room we're borrowin' while we're here. You know, since none of us are sure 'bout how long we'll be stayin'."

"I can't keep you from your kingdom for too long."

"Hey, think of it like a royal exchange, Elvi," Owen teased. "Helidinas had you, so now Arnembury has me."

She smiled. "Is that so?"

"Definitely."

Recognizing where they were, Elvina looked at the door to her bedchamber. "What if I wish not to rest?"

Owen stopped in place. "Then you don't hafta."

"Can you put me down?"

Without a word, he did so.

She smoothed out her dress, unsure about what to do now.

"Elvina, just so you're aware, you have visiting relatives," Garrick informed her.

She was highly surprised. "Really? Who?"

"Your grandmothers and grandfather." He was referring to Fitzroy's mother and Helaine's parents.

"How long have they been here?"

"They arrived after we left for Helidinas."

"And they have been here since?"

Garrick nodded. "All three of them are currently in your lessons room."

While thinking, Elvina slightly puffed out her cheeks. "With Father being ill, was their visit planned?"

"They haven't said why. They all have voiced that they want to speak with you, though."

Noticing how tense she was, Owen slipped his hand into hers. "Relax, okay?"

She took a deep, shaky breath. "I can do this."

He gave her a reassuring squeeze. "Yeah, you can."

"Come with me?"

He blinked in surprise. "Huh?"

"My grandparents will be relatives of yours soon enough."

"I guess that's true." Owen ran a hand through his hair. "Are you sure?"

She nodded. "Positive."

"I guess I can't letcha down."

"When have you ever?"

Suddenly, Garrick put a hand on Owen's right shoulder, gripping it tight. And without a word, he turned and walked away. He didn't look back or even spare a partial glance over his shoulder.

Owen blinked. "What just happened?"

"Seal of approval," Elvina replied, watching Garrick leave.

His face lit up. "Really?"

She looked over at him and nodded. "I suppose that Garrick was—"

He picked her up and spun her around. "That's great!"

She giggled when he kissed her nose and set her down on the ground. "All I hafta do now is talk with your tad and get his approval."

She was caught off-guard. "Wait, Whitley already voiced hers?"

"Yeah, while you were nappin'. That left Garrick as the second to last one to get approval from." With his cheeks hurting from smiling so hard, he gently pressed his forehead against hers. "I'm a step closer, Elvi. I can almost taste it."

Being rather bold, she pressed her lips against his and pulled her head back to gauge his reaction. "If it means anything, I think it tastes rather good."

Pink tinted his cheeks. "Yeah?"

She giggled at his reaction.

"We should find your family before I take you away and talk 'bout how much I love you."

She smiled. "To my lessons room, then."

CHAPTER TWENTY-EIGHT

Elvina was the first to enter the room where her normal princess lessons took place. Everything from her harp and books were there. It was furnished with whatever she might need to improve herself as Grenester's future ruler.

Low and behold, three people were also inside.

Idella was the mother of Fitzroy. Looking at her, it was easy to see who her son took after. They both had the same dark, hazel eyes, hers behind oval-shaped glasses. Her graying brunette locks were held back in multiple braids, while her bangs were left down. She was tall and slender, holding herself with complete grace.

Elvina's only living grandfather was Jerrell. His somewhat wavy gray hair was kept short for easy maintenance. Both of his eyes were brown, his right one noticeable shades darker. He was missing his right hand from an accident that occurred before Elvina was born.

Lillian was married to Jerrell. Her honey brown hair, now turning silver, was pulled back into a low bun. Her eyes were soft green. Helaine bore a resemblance to her; much like Elvina bore a resemblance to her mother.

Elvina was all smiles as she approached her family.

After stepping into the room, Owen closed the door behind him. He stayed back, wanting Elvina to have a moment before she shared her family with him.

Being the most concerned about Elvina's well-being, Jerrell stepped forward to tightly hug her first. "We were so worried when we first heard the news about you."

"All is well now," Elvina assured him, truly meaning it. "I promise."

When Jerrell let go, Lillian took her turn to hug her granddaughter. She looked Elvina over. "You seem well."

"I am."

Lastly, Elvina and Idella hugged one another. "I hope that you didn't cause too much trouble while you were gone," Idella jested.

"Oh, never," Elvina teased.

When they finished hugging, Elvina faced her grandparents. "If you don't mind me asking, why are the three of you here? Did Father happen to send for you all? Did you plan a surprise visit?"

Lillian looked over at Owen. "You there, can you fetch me some tea?"

"Er, sure." He looked at Elvina. "Where would I go for that?"

However, she ignored his question by addressing Lillian. "Grandmother, Owen isn't a servant. I suppose I should have introduced him sooner."

Owen took that as his cue and walked over to the others. "I'm Second Prince Owen Gravenor of Tiramôr."

Elvina's relatives all showed their own levels of surprise.

"What would a member of the royal family from Tiramôr possibly be doing here?" Jerrell questioned.

"That's a long story," Elvina said. "But I can promise you, Owen means no harm. He's a guest here."

"Was his visit planned?" Idella inquired.

"He and his guards traveled with us from Helidinas," Elvina replied. "And by others, I mean my personal guards and some other castle guards."

"We have only heard that you arrived home not too long ago," Idella told her.

"When we came to visit Fitzroy, we learned that you were in Tiramôr," Jerrell added. "Two of your guards and others left to bring you back here."

"A lot has happened since the last time I was here," Elvina admitted.

Idella solemnly nodded. "Which is why we"—she motioned to herself and her in-laws—"are here. Fitzroy asked for us to come."

"Why?" Owen asked.

Lillian looked at him. "I asked you for something to drink earlier since we need to speak to Elvina alone." Although, she did mistake him as a castle attendant due to his plain clothes. He wasn't dressed like a royal.

"Whatever you need to say to me can be said in front of Owen," Elvina assured her. "He's to be my husband, Grenester's king."

Idella's brow knit together in confusion. "What about Duke Kennard? Fitzroy had mentioned you were to see him."

"That was all Reeves," Owen interjected. "He was the one writin' back to King Fitzroy. A single letter from him never made it to Kennard."

"Kennard was oblivious to the betrothal when I addressed him about it," Elvina added. "All of it was a trap to get me away from the castle. It made the bandits' job of killing me much easier."

Silence fell over the room.

RACHAEL ANNE

"K–Kill you?" Jerrell stuttered.

"Everything was set up by Reeves," Elvina advised. "He hired bandits to kill me. He tricked Father into thinking that Kennard accepted my hand in marriage so I would leave the castle. I was out in the open that way."

"Reeves didn't count on Elvi escapin' and gettin' found by me," Owen added. "He also didn't count on us uncoverin' the truth 'bout him."

"He's the sole reason my father and Owen's father ended their trading agreement. Both kingdoms suffered because of him, and a tear was created. We also came to learn that Reeves hired bandits to kill me. He took it upon himself to poison Father. With both of us dead, that would leave Reeves to take over the throne."

The grandparents all exchanged glances with one another. Lillian was the first to speak up. "Perhaps we should sit down."

"Why?" Elvina questioned.

A solemn expression crossed Jerrell's face. "There's something you need to know about your father."

For support, Owen took Elvina's hand, squeezing it before leading her over to the sofa.

Elvina sat down in the middle with Owen on her left and Idella on her right. Jerrell and Lillian sat before them in chairs that he had fetched from the nearby table.

Lillian took a deep breath before speaking, looking at Elvina while she did so. "You never met my husband because of an illness. He died, and Fitzroy took the throne when he married Helaine." Her voice became a little bit unsteady. "That illness probably robbed him of half his life. The doctors could never figure it out. No cure was ever found."

Elvina was unsure why his history was being shared. How was it possibly relevant?

"It seems as though history is repeating itself," Lillian continued.

Elvina's heart seized up. Gasping, she took hold of Lillian's hands with both of hers. "No, I'm sure there is hope for you. There has to be."

A weak smile formed on Lillian's face. "I am...not referring to myself."

Elvina slowly glanced over at Jerrell and Lillian.

Neither of the two said a word.

"So...like father, like son?" Owen asked, clenching his jaw.

Time seemed to slow down for Elvina. She finally connected the dots due to Owen's words. Her blood ran cold. "B–But he's ill because of Reeves." She dragged her hands into her lap and balled up the skirt of her dress in her fists. "Reeves poisoned him."

"He was showing signs before that happened," Jerrell voiced.

"Reeves' actions only made things worse for Fitzroy," Lillian grimly added.

Idella sighed heavily. "Fitzroy started writing to us before he first wrote to Kennard, informing us of his situation. He knew about the early signs that he was showing because he saw his father go through them." She grew a little misty-eyed. "It's the same illness my husband had. There's no doubt about it. Fitzroy will die in due time."

Elvina felt numb to her core. She didn't want to believe what she was hearing. Her eyes glassed over. A tight ball formed in her throat. She must be in some sort of twisted nightmare.

Owen bit back tears. He could cry for Fitzroy when Elvina wasn't around, because he needed to be strong for her now. If she saw him cry, she would probably start balling.

Wiping away tears, Idella continued speaking. "He only

pushed for you to marry so suddenly because he wanted to see you on your wedding day."

Silent tears streamed down Elvina's face. "What?" she whispered, her voice cracking.

"Fitzroy wanted the assurance that his only daughter would have a bright future ahead of her, even if he wasn't there," Jerrell explained.

"He wanted someone else to love you in his absence." Lillian spared a glance Owen's way. "But it seems that you found love all on your own."

Elvina sniffled rather loudly, trying to keep what little composure she had left. "Why would he k–keep something like this f–from me?"

Idella gently stroked her right cheek with the back of a hand. "Oh, Elvina, he didn't want to worry you. He also wanted the attention on you, not him. The focus on him was to come later."

"Unfortunately, it came sooner than expected," Jerrell said.

"H–How much?" Elvina questioned.

"How much what, dear?" Lillian asked.

"How much time"—Elvina sniffled—"does Father have?"

"He'll be lucky to see the first snowfall," Idella replied honestly, before averting her gaze to her clasped hands. "But because of Reeves' actions, it might be sooner."

It was early spring now. The winter season wasn't that far away when one thought about it. Although, the illness could claim Fitzroy before then.

To give Elvina strength, Owen placed his hand over hers.

She jumped in surprise at the sudden touch before looking over at him. "Owen…" She burst into tears, imagining a world without her father in it. She knew that the day would come, but perhaps when he was a grandfather or great-grandfather.

"Elvi." Owen quickly wrapped his arms around her and hugged her against his chest. There wasn't much that he could do for her except let her cry in his arms.

With eyes clamped shut, she shook from crying so hard. The tears showed no sign of stopping anytime soon. Her heart ached. She felt weak. There was nothing that she could do for her father.

❦

Elvina's eyes were red and puffy from the crying she had done. Her haggard expression didn't help anything. There was no denying what she had been doing.

She blankly stared at the half-empty glass of water in her hands. Lillian fetched it for her, and what Elvina had consumed had done her some good. She felt a little better, but at the same time, she felt lost. She wasn't entirely sure what to do now. All she could do was wait for Fitzroy to awaken.

"How 'bout you take a hot bath and eat?" Owen suggested. "Or do whichever you wanna do first?"

She merely nodded without saying a word. Perhaps a hot bath would thaw away the numbness that she felt from head to toe.

"Elvina, I can take that from you," Jerrell said, reaching out for the glass with his hand.

She raised her head to look at her relatives. "Even though the circumstances aren't pleasant, I'm happy to see you all again."

Lillian sent a small smile her way. "We're always happy to see you, Elvina."

She slowly rose to her feet, doing her best to keep her head held high.

Owen was quick to stand as well. He didn't plan on letting her out of his sight anytime soon.

After hugging each of her grandparents, Elvina left the room with Owen at her side, using her sleeve to dab away her tears. "I apologize that you had to see me like this."

"Don't be sorry. I'm serious, okay?"

"All right."

The duo made their way to her bedchamber.

"Where do you reckon the others are?" he asked to create small talk.

"I'm not entirely sure," she replied. "They can be up to anything right about now."

"Probably trouble knowin' the Babysitter Brigade," he jested.

"Don't confuse yourself with them," she teased, a small smile tugging at her lips.

It didn't go unnoticed by Owen. He believed it was a start. A tiny one, but it still counted.

Upon entering her bedchamber, Elvina and Owen discovered that the Thunder Squadron was inside, seated around the table.

From one look at her, the four knew their charge had dealt with some emotional distress. They were all ready to jump to her aid and literally jumped to their feet without hesitation.

"Do any of you know about my father?" Elvina questioned out of curiosity.

All of them exchanged a glance with one another. "We don't know what you mean," Garrick stated.

"My father—" She stopped mid-sentence before she lost her already cracked composure. She cleared her throat and started again. "My father's ill, and he was ill before being poisoned by Reeves. He has the same illness that claimed his father."

The bedchamber fell silent.

"No one told us," Vallerie said after a moment.

"Can anything be done for him?" Whitley asked.

Elvina shook her head. "No."

"All we can do is wait?" Quenby questioned.

"Yes," Elvina replied, her voice cracking.

Owen decided to speak up so Elvina wouldn't have much talking to do. "Her grandfolks are here 'cause Fitzroy wrote to 'em. He told 'em 'bout his illness. He also told 'em how he wanted Elvi to get married soon, so he could see her on her weddin' day. Just in case his time ran out sooner than expected."

That summed things up rather nicely for now. More details could be given later to fill in any possible blanks.

"You're still going to get married," Quenby voiced, trying to be positive given the atmosphere. "It's not to Kennard, as Fitzroy had planned out, but to somebody else. Apparently, this Owen guy isn't too bad."

Elvina appreciated his humor. "I've heard the same about him."

"I mean, we've all approved of him, so he can't be all that bad," Whitley jested, and nudged Garrick with an elbow. "Right?"

He cracked a grin. "Right."

"Should I be worried if they're sayin' nice things 'bout me?" Owen whispered to Elvina.

"There's nothing for you to worry about," she assured him.

Smiling, he kissed the top of her head. "Good." He booped the tip of her nose. "I think it's time for your hot bath."

"You sound like Milli. Oh, speaking of her, where is she?"

"She was with the Babysitter Brigade the last I knew," Vallerie replied.

"Something about giving them a tour of the castle," Quenby added.

Whitley jerked a thumb at herself and the other Thunder Squadron members. "Don't worry. We can get a hot bath going for you since she isn't here. I won't mind helping you out in there either."

Elvina smiled at them. "Thank you."

"Is there anything particular you want to eat?" Vallerie inquired.

"Soup seems nice."

Vallerie nodded. "I'll stop by the kitchen and see what the cook can prepare for you."

Elvina looked at Owen. "Do you want anything?"

He shook his head. "I'm good for now, I am."

She arched her eyebrows at him.

"Promise," he assured her.

"What if I don't want to eat alone?"

"I'll eat with you. Easy as that."

Suddenly, Elvina's stomach rumbled. Pink tinted her cheeks. She hoped no one had heard her.

Owen grinned. "The sooner you bathe, the sooner we eat. I'll have somebody come get me when you're done. How's that sound?"

"Wonderful."

CHAPTER TWENTY-NINE

The next afternoon, Elvina was alone with Fitzroy in his bedchamber. He was conscious, and they were having a conversation, with Elvina doing most of the talking. Her throat had grown rather raw from all the speaking that she had done. Sipping water could only help so much. She had been telling Fitzroy about her adventures in Helidinas.

"The ball was most wonderful," Elvina continued. "Confronting Kennard about the betrothment sham was most satisfying now that I think about it. He was oblivious to it all, which only confirmed that Reeves was meddling again. He wasn't sending out the letters you wrote, and he was responding as Kennard. Anyway, the ball. I had fun. The music was different than what I'm accustomed to, but I still liked it."

While his daughter spoke, Fitzroy listened intently. He was propped up against the headboard with a plethora of pillows. This was the best he had felt in what seemed like days. He was slowly but surely getting some strength back.

"And the next morning was when help arrived for me.

Events had changed since I'd written to Millicent, which they came to learn." She sobered up a bit. "After hearing you had fallen ill, we rushed here. I figured that Reeves had something to do with it since he tried having me killed. That was only partially the case."

Fitzroy weakly smiled at her. "But we're together now. That's what matters."

She returned the smile. "Indeed." She took a drink from her nearly empty glass.

"When do I get to see Owen?" Fitzroy inquired with interest.

"Do you want me to have someone fetch him?"

"I would like that."

Taking that as her cue, Elvina stood and walked over to the door. She opened it and poked her head outside, finding Garrick and Swain both standing by. "Owen's presence is requested by Father," she informed them.

With a nod, Garrick left to fetch him.

"When he arrives, shall I have him knock and enter?" Swain asked her.

"Yes, thank you." She went back into the room and shut the door behind her.

"Owen's the one for you." Fitzroy wasn't asking a question but making a factual statement.

"We should have realized that sooner."

"We need to have the rest of the Gravenor family visit," Fitzroy mused.

She nodded in agreement. "Perhaps we can have a word with Owen before he returns home with his guards." Her heart stung at the thought of his family. Fitzroy was completely unaware that Eilir had passed away. Was now the time to tell him? It didn't seem like it.

"And to think, the rumors circulated around you and

Ceron." Fitzroy grinned. "Now you and Owen wish to marry."

"Life can be funny at times."

There was a knock on the door, and when it opened, Owen was revealed.

Elvina was slightly curious about how Garrick found him so quickly. Casting that thought aside, she beckoned him over with a hand. "Hello, Owen."

After closing the door behind him, Owen, somewhat stiffly, approached Elvina and Fitzroy. He was trying to hide how nervous he was.

"You certainly have grown since the last time I saw you," Fitzroy commented. "You look much like Mervin and Ceron."

"Yeah, I get that a lot." Owen awkwardly stood by Elvina for safety. His father and brother hadn't prepared him for what he believed might happen with this conversation.

"Elvina, do you mind if we have a moment alone?" Fitzroy inquired.

Owen stiffened even more, pleading with his eyes for Elvina not to leave him alone with her father.

However, Elvina couldn't deny Fitzroy's request. "Of course." She looked at Owen. "I'll be waiting at the gazebo." She leaned over her father and placed a gentle kiss on his forehead. "And you know where I'll be if you need me."

"I'll send for you if that happens," Fitzroy told her.

With a final look at Owen, Elvina smiled before turning her back to the two. She made her way over to the door before closing it behind her. Without a word, she moved to lean against the wall across from the door, taking a deep breath to calm her nerves.

"He'll be fine," Garrick assured her in a low voice, as to not be overheard by someone inside of the bedchamber.

"It's still a little nerve-racking."

"More so for him than you," Swain pointed out, a small grin on his lips.

"Indeed," Elvina agreed. She straightened up and adjusted the skirt of her purple dress. "I'll be at the gazebo."

"I'll escort you there," Garrick said.

The two made their way to the garden, leaving Swain behind.

"How did you find Owen so quickly?" Elvina inquired.

"He was nearby. He figured your father would want to speak with him."

"Did he imagine that he'd be alone with Father?"

"He was hoping that wouldn't be the case. He wanted you to be there, too."

"I would have stayed, but Father wanted it to be the two of them."

"Even if that is the case, Owen's a big boy. He can handle himself."

"Think of it as a small test for the future king of Grenester?" she jested.

He cracked a grin. "I like the word 'trial' for him."

Rather than sitting, Elvina paced inside the gazebo. She was unsure about how much time had passed since she left Owen and Fitzroy alone together. Likewise, she had been left alone since Garrick escorted her to the garden. No one had checked on her.

Elvina puffed out her cheeks. Half of her wanted to check on Owen and Fitzroy, while the other half wanted to remain at the gazebo until someone, anyone, came for her.

Upon hearing someone whistle a familiar tune, she immediately stopped in her tracks to look over. Her eyes lit up when she spotted him. "Owen!" she called.

"Hey, Elvi," he endearingly said. As he made his way over to her, he kept both hands in his pockets.

"How are you faring?"

"I'm a lot better now, believe me."

"Really?"

"Really, I am." He stepped into the gazebo and jerked his head to the side. "Wanna sit down?"

She merely nodded.

He waited for her to sit down first and joined her on her left side. For once, they shared the same section of the bench. He looked around the garden, taking in the scenery. "I've missed this view."

"I've missed sharing it with you."

He turned his head to face her. "We'll be able to make heaps more memories at this spot. You know, more than a few times a year."

The very thought of that excited her. "I'm looking forward to it."

He scooted a little closer to her. "So…"

"So?" she questioned.

"So my life's changed since I met you," he said out of nowhere. "And when I think 'bout it, this moment wouldn't be happenin' right now if it weren't for Reeves. Don't get me wrong, I'm not thankin' him or anythin', but we were reunited 'cause of those bandits he hired. And 'cause he gotcha to leave Arnembury. Life can be funny, I guess."

He was rambling somewhat, but she paid close attention to him.

"Your family already told us why your tad wanted you to marry Kennard, but he told me everythin'. He still wants to see you on your weddin' day. I'm sure you want that, and I want it, too. Given the timeline of things"—he looked at her with an earnest expression—"let's get married this summer. Late summer if we need more time. Early fall?"

She was slightly surprised by his idea. "Do you honestly believe we can put together a royal wedding in that short amount of time?"

"Won't know if we don't try."

She pondered the idea.

"Which means, we better get started now," he added, due to her silence. "The sooner, the better."

"Is that the plan for us, then?"

He smiled. "The plan for us is to get married, have seventeen babies, and live happily ever after."

The familiar words echoed through her mind. "I still say that seventeen is an absurd number."

"And like I said, Tad wants a lotta grandkids."

Would her children be like her and only know one of their grandfathers? Or was there a possibility both Fitzroy and Mervin would be around to see their grandchildren? Elvina wasn't sure about her mother, but Eilir had talked about wanting grandchildren. She shook her head to clear her mind. She wanted to focus on the present moment.

"Are you okay?" Owen asked, noticing her strange behavior.

"I'm all right."

He arched an eyebrow.

"I am," she insisted.

He studied her face for a moment. "Look, if I'm bein' a little, er, forward—"

"I think that you're being quite considerate," she admitted, not meaning to be rude by interrupting him. "You're taking my father's wants into consideration. Not to mention, what I want." She smiled at him. "I thank you for that."

He returned the smile. "Anythin' for you, Elvi."

"And what of you? How do you feel about a possible late summer wedding? What do you think your family will think of it?"

"They'll be happy I'm happy." He let out a chuckle. "And I'll be gettin' married before my brother who's been betrothed. What're the odds of that?"

"They seem likely since you're involved."

"Oi, you're involved, too."

"That's the point of the two of us marrying one another."

"When I go back to Helidinas, I'll make sure to tell Dad and Ceron 'bout the weddin'." He leaned over and bumped her right shoulder. "It probably won't hurt to mention it to the Donnelly sisters. They'll have to crack down on makin' your dress. Well, that's if you still wanna have 'em make it for you."

"Would it be better for me to go to them? They already have everything they need at their shop." She started to think things through. "I don't even know what kind of dress I want. I haven't ever pictured what I want my wedding dress to look like."

"Whatever it looks like, you'll make it look beautiful. That's a given."

She smiled. "You're sweet."

"Look who's talkin'."

"You're the one saying sweet things," she pointed out.

"You're still pretty sweet. And pretty. And bangin'. Not to mention, you're...Elvi. You're my Elvi. My woodland fairy. *Cariad aur.* And I love you."

"Owen, I love you, too." She decided to tease him. "If you refer to me as those names, I need names to call you."

"The love of your life is a great start."

"Brilliant."

"I'm not bein' funny. I do love you, a lot. You're precious to me."

"I feel the same way about you."

Taking his left hand out of his pocket, he ran it along her right cheek. His palm was sweaty, but at least his fingers were fine. "I never thought you'd mean this much to me when we first met, and now...now I wanna marry you. I wantcha to be the mam of my kids. I wanna grow old with you." He smiled. "But before all that, I need to do somethin' first."

She was slightly confused. "And what might that be?"

He kept eye contact with her, his brown eyes never leaving her hazel ones. He slid off of the stone bench to kneel before her.

If Millicent's sappy love stories were true, then Elvina believed she knew what was about to happen. She sharply inhaled.

"Elvina Helaine Norwood," he firmly said.

"Yes?" she whispered, trying not to hold her breath.

"Before your tad and I finished havin' a goss, he insisted I give this to you..." He raised his right hand and opened his palm.

Only now did she break eye contact with him to see the object in his hand. The ring had an intricate band with a shiny jewel at the center.

It was a ring that Elvina recognized all too well. It was the very ring Fitzroy had given Helaine when he proposed to her. Since her passing, he had kept it inside his bedchamber. He had let Elvina try it on, and they both knew she could wear it on a particular finger of her left hand.

She gasped, covering her open mouth with her hands. She blinked and blinked again. Her eyes weren't deceiving her.

"Elvi, will you—" Owen began.

He was cut off when she flung herself at him. He ensured he didn't lose the ring while he steadied himself to support them.

"Yes!" she happily responded. "Of course!"

"But I didn't even ask you the question," he chuckled.

She held the sides of his head. "If I have learned *anything* from you, it's that actions speak louder than words." She pressed her lips against his, butterflies zooming around in her stomach.

He was quick to fall for the kiss, completely getting lost in her. When their lips broke apart, he was quick to bring them back together. He couldn't get enough of her.

Because they needed air, they finally did pull away to catch their breath. He stared at her like a lovestruck idiot. "Hey."

"Hello," she giggled.

"I love you."

"I love you, too."

Something sparked in his eyes. "Oh, yeah!" Using his free hand, he took her left hand and slid the ring in place. He looked at her, smiling from ear to ear smile. "Perfect fit." He scooped her up and spun her around a good bit before gently setting her down on her feet.

"Can we tell the others?" she squealed, excited to spread the news.

"I mean, they all knew it was comin'. Only now, we're officially betrothed to each other." He kissed her forehead. "But whatever makes you happy."

"That will make me very happy. Just like you make me happy."

He gingerly pressed his forehead against hers and closed his eyes. "You make me really happy, too."

"Owen?"

His eyes remained shut. "Hmm?"

She took a deep breath before speaking with a slightly different accent. "*Rwy'n dy garu di.*"

Eyes flying open, he pulled back his head to stare at her with a mix of bewilderment and amazement. "Did you... just...?" But his voice trailed off.

"Did I say it right? I've had help practicing with an accent—"

His lips were suddenly on hers. "It's perfect," he gushed in between kisses. "You're perfect, Elvi." In his excited state, he slipped into his native tongue.

She laughed. "I can't understand you."

Realizing what he had done, he smiled and spoke normally. "Can you say it again?"

"Rwy'n dy garu di."

"Again?"

"I can only say it so much before it loses its effect."

"That won't ever happen with me. I can promise you that, Elvi."

She smiled sweetly at her future husband. *"Rwy'n dy garu di."*

ACKNOWLEDGMENTS

Alex Hook, thank you for being the best husband and personal cheerleader. More often than not, you listen when I want to talk out scenes to someone in person. You hear me go on and on about my characters like I'm talking about real people. Your support has meant the world to me and I cherish it deeply.

Mom, Dad, remember when I was fourteen and sent an email saying I wanted to be a published author? Ten years later, I'm a self-published author of my first book! Thank you both for nurturing my love of reading and writing.

I feel like I'm doing roll call here, but a special shout out to my siblings: Andrew, Noah, Emily, and Megan. *Arnembury* wouldn't exist without the five of us. Thank you all so much for providing inspiration in my life.

Twin, can you believe the friendship we have today stemmed

from all the times you ignored my messages? Look at us now! I couldn't have asked for a better twin. You constantly push and encourage me to do my best and get out there. Thank you for sticking around for the ride in getting this book self-published. Always and forever yours, F.S.

Last but not least, you amazing ladies helped me polish and prepare this book! I want to thank you all from the bottom of my heart for all the work that was put into *Elvina*. Dana Hook, it means so much to me that you could partake in this process. You deserve much more chocolate for the late nights you put into editing. Thank you so much, Freya Barker, for designing the lovely cover art for me. I smile every time I look at it. Amy Donnelly, I appreciate you diving into the first official edit. Your insight truly opened my eyes.

ABOUT THE AUTHOR

Rachael Anne grew up in Ohio, where she spent her youth writing short stories, despite her dyslexia. She married her best friend in 2018 and there are plans to make their family bigger, starting with a puppy. When she isn't writing, she's an avid reader and works as an undercover mermaid.

Elvina is her debut novel!

Stay in touch

rachaelannehook.com
Facebook.com/RachaelAnneHook
@rachaelannehook

Made in the USA
Middletown, DE
02 September 2020